A Wrinkle in Thyme

Books by Sarah Fox

The Literary Pub Mystery Series
Wine and Punishment
An Ale of Two Cities
The Malt in Our Stars
Claret and Present Danger

The Pancake House Mystery Series
The Crêpes of Wrath
For Whom the Bread Rolls
Of Spice and Men
Yeast of Eden
Crêpe Expectations
Much Ado About Nutmeg
A Room with a Roux
A Wrinkle in Thyme

The Music Lover's Mystery Series
Dead Ringer
Death in A Major
Deadly Overtures

A Wrinkle in Thyme

Sarah Fox

LYRICAL UNDERGROUND
Kensington Publishing Corp.
www.kensingtonbooks.com

LYRICAL UNDERGROUND BOOKS are published by

Kensington Publishing Corp.
119 West 40th Street
New York, NY 10018

All Kensington titles, imprints, and distributed lines are available at special quantity discounts for bulk purchases for sales promotion, premiums, fundraising, educational, or institutional use.

Special book excerpts or customized printings can also be created to fit specific needs. For details, write or phone the office of the Kensington Sales Manager: Kensington Publishing Corp., 119 West 40th Street, New York, NY 10018. Attn. Sales Department. Phone: 1-800-221-2647.

Lyrical Underground and Lyrical Underground logo Reg. US Pat. & TM Off.

First Electronic Edition: August 2021
ISBN-13: 978-1-5161-1087-2 (ebook)
ISBN-10: 1-5161-1087-0 (ebook)

First Print Edition: August 2021
ISBN-13: 978-1-5161-1089-6
ISBN-10: 1-5161-1089-7

Printed in the United States of America

Chapter One

The new home of the Wildwood Cove Museum bustled with activity. As I entered through the back door, I heard voices murmuring off in the distance, muffled by the drone of the floor sander in use up on the second story. A hammer thudded out on the back porch, and something clattered to the floor down the hall. I took a quick step to the right when a teenaged volunteer ran past me, her blond ponytail swinging.

Readjusting my grip on the heavy box in my arms, I entered a room to my left, nearly colliding with an empty dolly pushed by a man with dark hair. Like me, Frankie Zhou was volunteering his time to help move all of the museum's artifacts, archives, and furniture from the small bungalow where it had been housed for years to its new location in this beautiful Victorian.

Frankie mumbled his apologies as he scooted past me with the dolly. With the way ahead of me now clear, I crossed the room without further problems and set the box down next to several others lined up against the wall. I dusted off my hands and stretched my back as I surveyed the room. The dark color of the refinished wood floors contrasted nicely with the new coat of white paint on the walls. Deep shelving units had been installed the day before, waiting to hold the many boxes of archives currently sitting piled on the floor.

A pleasant breeze drifted in through the open window, helping to dispel the smell of fresh paint that lingered in the house. A long-time resident of Wildwood Cove, Gwyneth McIvor, had bequeathed her home to the museum. Located in the heart of town, the house was a white, two-story Victorian with front and back porches and lots of character. A crew of volunteers, which included my husband, had spent many hours fixing up the place to ready it for its new life as a museum. Those volunteers were still adding some of the final touches, but the bulk of the work on the main floor had already been done. The second story, which would serve as meeting and storage space, was still a work in progress.

This building was older than the bungalow that previously housed the museum, but the Victorian offered more space and more charm. The bungalow was cute, but the McIvor house practically oozed elegance and character from every nook and cranny. It had needed some TLC after Mrs. McIvor's death, but the volunteers had restored its stately beauty.

I paused for a moment by the window, drawing in a deep breath of fresh air. My stomach rumbled with hunger, reminding me that I shouldn't dawdle if I wanted to get home and have dinner anytime soon. I headed for the door, stopping just in the nick of time as the dolly reappeared, its wheels missing my toes by mere inches. Frankie appeared next, pushing the dolly, which now had four file boxes stacked on it. Jane Fassbender followed right on his heels. She had a clipboard tucked under one arm, and her long, light brown hair was tied back in a loose braid. I didn't know her exact age, but I guessed she was probably in her mid-thirties, like me.

Jane was currently in charge of the Wildwood Cove Museum while its curator, Nancy Welch, was on an extended vacation, traveling for a year. It was a volunteer position for Jane, but she took it very seriously and had spent hours upon hours over the past weeks preparing for the move and coordinating the teams of volunteers.

"Just stack those boxes next to the others," she said to Frankie as he unloaded the dolly. "That's the last of them."

My back and arms could have sighed with relief. I'd lost count of how many boxes I'd hauled from Frankie's truck into the Victorian over the past couple of hours.

Jane smiled at me. "Thanks so much for your help, Marley. You too, Frankie."

"My pleasure." Frankie pushed his dark hair off his forehead and flashed a shy smile at Jane before heading out of the room with the dolly.

"I'm glad I was able to help," I said as Jane and I trailed after Frankie.

He turned right, heading out the open back door, while we made our way toward the front of the old house, where two large rooms would soon display the museum's artifacts. At the moment, everything was still boxed up.

We paused in the foyer when a woman's voice called out from behind us. "Hello? Jane?"

We both turned at the sound.

An elderly woman with perfectly coiffed silver hair stood framed in the back doorway. She wore a navy blue dress and held a silver-handled cane in one hand, though she didn't appear to be leaning much weight on it.

"Winnifred," Jane greeted. "Come on in."

The woman entered the hallway and stopped to peek into the room where Frankie and I had stacked the last of the boxes.

"I don't want to get in the way," Winnifred said after she'd turned her attention back to us, "but I couldn't help myself. I had to come by to get a look at the transformation."

"You're not in the way," Jane assured her. "As you can see, it's still a work in progress, but things are going well so far."

"I'll say." Winnifred came farther along the hall to join us in the spacious foyer. "The floors are beautiful."

"Dean's done a good job."

Dean Vaccarino was the man Jane had hired to refinish the floors. He was working upstairs as we spoke. He wasn't my favorite person, but he really had done a good job with the floors.

"Marley," Jane said to me, "have you met Mrs. Winnifred Woodcombe?"

"I haven't." I offered my hand to the elderly woman. "Marley Collins. It's nice to meet you, Mrs. Woodcombe."

Keeping a loose grip on her cane, Winnifred reached out with her free hand to clasp mine. "Likewise, my dear. Please, call me Winnifred. No need to stand on formality." She eyed me more closely. "You're the young woman who moved here from Seattle after you inherited the pancake house from Jimmy Coulson."

I smiled. "That's right."

"Winnifred has lived here in Wildwood Cove her entire life," Jane said. "She knows everyone and everything about this place."

Winnifred chuckled. "I've certainly had enough years to learn it all."

"I suppose sixty-five years is quite a long time," Jane said with a smile.

With another laugh, Winnifred patted Jane's arm. "That's so kind of you, dear. We both know my eightieth birthday isn't all that far off."

"Still two years to go," Jane said. She glanced around us. "Hopefully the museum will be in order long before then."

Winnifred patted her arm again. "I'm sure it will be. Do you mind if I wander around?"

"Please, be my guest. Just watch your step. We've got boxes piled everywhere."

"I'll be careful," Winnifred assured her before venturing into the room to the left of the front entrance.

Jane picked up a stack of files from the top of a pile of boxes. "I'd better put these in my office before I forget."

She started back down the hall, and I fell into step with her.

"Winnifred donated money to cover the cost of the move," Jane told me in a low voice.

"That was good of her."

"She's a good woman. Wild West Days was her idea. She's a real champion of our local history, and she wants to find ways to get more people interested in it."

"I'm looking forward to the event, and I know lots of other people are too," I said.

Wild West Days would take place in four weeks. It was the first time Wildwood Cove was having the four-day festival, and it sounded like it would be a lot of fun. I'd heard there would be activities like gold panning, mechanical bull riding, and line dancing, as well as country music concerts and a stagecoach robbery re-enactment. The hope was that Wild West Days would kick off the summer season and draw in some early tourists. Judging by the buzz already around town, the event would have a good turnout.

"Of course," Jane said, a hint of annoyance creeping into her voice, "not everyone involved in planning Wild West Days understands the importance of historical accuracy, but my hope is that Winnifred will have a good influence on the committee."

I wasn't sure what to say to that. Fortunately, Jane didn't seem to expect a response.

As for Winnifred having an influence on the committee, I didn't think that was far-fetched. Although I hadn't met Winnifred before, I'd heard of her. The Woodcombe family had lived in Wildwood Cove since the town was founded. Winnifred was currently the oldest Woodcombe in the area, and I knew she was highly respected. She was involved in several local organizations and regularly donated to charities and other worthy causes.

Jane dropped the files off in her office, and then we stepped out onto the back porch, where bright sunshine greeted us along with the scent of freshly cut grass and the hum of a motor. I smiled at the sight of my husband, Brett, guiding a lawnmower around the yard that was enclosed by a freshly painted white picket fence. When he spotted me, he sent a grin my way. After eight months of marriage, the sight of him could still take my breath away. I hoped that would never change.

"Winnifred's from one of the richest and oldest local families, but she never flaunts her wealth," Jane continued, tugging my attention away from my husband. Her eyes narrowed. "Unlike some people."

I followed her unwelcoming gaze and spotted a man in an expensive suit climbing out of a red Ferrari convertible parked in the back lane. He hurried around the car and opened the back gate, holding it for a woman in a red dress and matching stilettos, with what looked like a designer handbag in the crook of her arm. As she headed our way, she pushed oversized sunglasses up to sit on top of her bleached blond hair. Sunlight glinted off her gold jewelry.

I recognized the couple. I'd seen them around town once or twice, but I didn't know much about them other than the fact that they owned Oldershaw Confections, a candy company that had made millions for the Oldershaw family. The company had started out locally over a hundred years ago and had since become a nation-wide success.

"Jane, darling," the woman trilled as she approached the back steps. "I've come to talk to you about the party."

"Heaven help me," Jane said under her breath, the words barely loud enough for me to hear. Then she pasted on a smile that bore some resemblance to a pained grimace. "Evangeline, you don't need to worry about the party. I've got everything under control."

Evangeline carefully navigated the steps and joined us on the porch. Her husband stayed down on the concrete walkway, his hands in his pockets as he casually surveyed the yard.

"Nonsense." Evangeline's red painted lips stretched into a smile no more sincere than Jane's. "Of course I'm going to worry about the party. It's my money that's paying for it, after all." She crossed the porch to a wrought-iron patio set, running a finger along the arm of one chair to check for cleanliness. "Come," she said, pulling the chair out from beneath the table. "Let's get down to business."

With her face angled away from Evangeline, Jane rolled her eyes, but she obeyed the command and joined her at the table. Evangeline hadn't even acknowledged my existence, and I didn't expect that to change, so I gave Jane a discreet wave and descended the porch steps.

Brett shut off the lawnmower, the grass all trimmed now. With the motor no longer rumbling, the yard would have been peaceful if not for Evangeline's constant stream of chatter up on the porch.

Her husband gave me a half-hearted smile when I reached the bottom of the steps.

"Marley Collins." I offered him my hand, determined to be more polite than his wife. "Are you Mr. Oldershaw?"

He gave my hand a weak shake. "Hobbs, actually. Richard Hobbs. My wife is an Oldershaw. Well, Oldershaw-Hobbs now."

We both glanced up at the porch where his wife sat with Jane. While Evangeline talked nonstop, Jane sat stiffly, her mouth in a firm line as she nodded every so often.

"You should see the dress I got for the party," Evangeline was saying. "I bought it last week in New York. A Valentino, of course. My sister was with me at the fitting. She said I looked just like Grace Kelly."

"I thought you were here to organize the party, Ev," Richard called, interrupting her chatter.

"Yes, Richard," his wife said with more than a hint of annoyance. "That's exactly what we're doing."

She resumed her chatter.

Richard gave a barely perceptible shake of his head. "We'll be here all day," he muttered.

"There's coffee in the kitchen," I told him. I hadn't particularly warmed to him, but I figured he was probably right—he was going to be waiting a long time for his wife. "Just inside to the right."

Richard made a sound of acknowledgment and took the porch steps two at a time.

Brett had already loaded the lawnmower into the back of the cube van he used for his lawn and garden business. Now he came along the path toward me, removing his work gloves and running a hand through his curly blond hair.

"I'm all done here for the day," he said. "Are you ready to get going?"

I kissed him and tucked my arm through his, leading him toward the back gate. "Very, very much so." I gave a subtle nod over my shoulder. "Do you know Evangeline and Richard?"

"I know *of* them, but I've never officially met them." Brett held the gate open for me. "They don't spend a lot of their time here in Wildwood Cove, and they don't much like rubbing elbows with anyone with a net worth of fewer than seven digits."

"But they grew up here?" I asked as we squeezed past the red Ferrari to get to Brett's van.

"Not exactly." He unlocked the passenger door. "Evangeline's family is from here originally, but my understanding is that she was raised mostly in New York and just came here for holidays."

I climbed into the van, and Brett shut the door before jogging around to the driver's side.

"Her family has always kept a house here, one of those big Victorians on Orchard Lane," he continued as he buckled up his seatbelt. "She and her husband spend a few weeks in town each year. They've got a small office on Main Street, but the general consensus is that they like to keep one toe in Wildwood Cove not so much because they have any affection for the town, but because they like to feel like big fish in this small pond of ours."

"Let me guess," I said, thinking back over my brief encounter with Evangeline. "They like to throw their money around and act like they rule the roost."

"Exactly." Brett guided the van out of the alley and turned onto the street. "I've seen them driving that Ferrari around town. Way too fast."

"They make sure they're hard to miss. I think they'd like to believe we all envy them."

"Does anyone?" I asked, finding it hard to believe that anybody would. I hadn't found the couple the least bit enviable.

"I sure don't," Brett said. "I'll take pizza over caviar any day."

"Same here." My stomach grumbled. "Speaking of pizza..."

Brett grinned at me. "I already called in a takeout order. One vegetarian, one pepperoni. We'll pick them up on our way home."

"Forget Ferraris and Valentino gowns," I said. "You, Brett Collins, are priceless."

Chapter Two

I'd never seen Richard and Evangeline at my seaside pancake house, and that didn't surprise me. I had a sneaking suspicion that the restaurant wouldn't live up to Evangeline's standards, despite the scrumptious food whipped up by The Flip Side's chef, Ivan Kaminski, and his assistant, Tommy Park.

Even if the couple had dropped by the morning after I'd met them at the museum, there wouldn't have been room for them. We were in the middle of the breakfast rush, which was even busier than usual. I figured that was thanks to the beautiful spring weather that was already hinting at the summer to come. It had drawn people out of their houses to stroll, jog, cycle, and seek out a tasty breakfast. The morning sunshine was so bright and warm that I'd put four small tables out front of the restaurant. It was early May, and I hadn't expected to put tables outside for another couple of weeks or so, but the beautiful morning had inspired me to do it today.

It had turned out to be a good idea. Every table, inside and out, was currently occupied. The large number of early diners kept me and my staff on our toes. Ivan and Tommy kept the pancakes, crêpes, and waffles coming, while I helped to serve customers, along with Leigh Hunter, The Flip Side's full-time waitress, and Sienna Murray, a high school senior who worked at the pancake house on weekends.

Leigh paused by the front door, which I'd propped open to let in the gentle sea breeze. "I smell summer in the air," she said, drawing in a deep, appreciative breath before continuing on her way to the kitchen with a stack of dirty plates.

"It can't be summer yet!" Sienna said, sounding mildly alarmed.

Her reaction took me by surprise. She usually couldn't wait for summer to arrive. Before I had a chance to ask her about it, she made a beeline for the pass-through window where Tommy had just set three plates, two laden with stacks of pancakes and one with a generous slice of Thyme for Breakfast Frittata—a tasty new addition to the menu—and a side of fruit salad.

I spent the next several minutes rushing to and fro, taking orders, delivering meals, and cleaning tables as soon as they were vacated. No table stayed empty for more than a couple of minutes before new customers swooped in to claim it.

I loved how busy we were, especially since it wasn't even the height of tourist season yet. The Flip Side was thriving and was one of the most popular restaurants in town. That thrilled me to pieces, but it also had me thinking about the future. If we were this run off our feet in May, we might have trouble keeping up when vacationers flocked to our charming seaside town in a few weeks' time. If any one of my employees were to get sick, we'd be in a bind.

Plus, Sienna would be heading off to college at the end of August. I didn't like to think about her leaving Wildwood Cove—she was a good friend as well as an employee—but I knew I'd have to find someone to replace her. Judging by our current booming business, I might have to hire more help even before her departure.

All thoughts about staffing would have to wait, though. At the moment, I had my hands full—literally and figuratively—and had to stay focused if I wanted to keep my customers happy.

"Are you looking forward to Wild West Days, Marley?" Gary Thornbrook asked as I set plates of blueberry pancakes in front of him and his friend Ed.

Despite the full house, the two men had managed to snag their favorite table. They showed up at the pancake house at least twice a week and always ordered the same meals. They'd been doing so for years, starting long before I'd inherited the business from my grandmother's cousin.

"I'm definitely excited," I said. "It sounds like it's going to be a fun event. I hear the two of you will be taking turns playing the part of the sheriff."

"You heard right." Ed grinned. "You should see our costumes. We went all out."

"We've got the clothes and pistols," Gary said. "Just props, of course, but they look good."

"What about the shiny badge?" I asked.

Ed poured syrup over his pancakes. "Of course. Can't forget that."

"Sounds like you're all ready to go," I remarked.

"We're hopin' to have us a hog-killin' time," Gary said with a phony drawl.

I couldn't help but laugh.

Ed cut into his stack of pancakes. "Hopefully we'll do the real sheriff proud."

"I'm sure you will." I checked their mugs and noticed that they could do with a refill. "Let me grab the coffee pot."

On my way back to their table, I made a couple of stops to refill a few other diners' mugs. I loved how many familiar faces I saw at the pancake house each day. Working there had allowed me to connect with the community when I'd first moved to town, and my roots were now firmly planted.

"How are things going at the museum?" Gary asked when I returned.

"Everything's been moved to the new location," I said as I topped up their coffee mugs. "Now it's just a matter of getting everything organized and set up."

"Squatters!"

I nearly jumped out of my skin when a man at the table behind me practically spat out the word. If the coffee pot hadn't been nearly empty by then, I would have spilled the hot liquid all over myself. When I took in the sight of the man's angry scowl, I edged away from him, not sure if he was in his right mind or not. I was pretty sure I'd seen him at The Flip Side before, but I didn't know his name. He was short and stout, with thinning dark hair and beady eyes.

"Hardly," Ed said to the man, unfazed by his ire. "You know the court held that the house belongs to the museum fair and square, Angus."

The man stood up like a shot, his chair skittering across the floor. "There's nothing fair about it! That house should be mine!"

"But it isn't," Gary said calmly.

"Thanks to that woman's funny business," Angus grumbled. "She's a crook, and she's going to wish she'd never crossed me."

He stormed off toward the cash register, where Sienna was counting change for an elderly couple.

"Which woman?" I whispered, keeping an eye on Angus as he handed money to Sienna.

Fortunately, he didn't give her any trouble. He paid quickly and stomped out of the restaurant.

"Jane Fassbender," Gary replied, his voice as low as my own.

Several diners were waiting for their meals, so I couldn't linger, but I desperately wanted to talk more about what had just transpired.

I got my chance to do so about ten minutes later when I stopped by Ed and Gary's table to refill their coffee mugs again.

"What was all that about earlier?" I asked as I topped up Ed's coffee.

"You mean with Angus?" he asked.

Joan Crenshaw, another senior citizen who was also a frequent customer, spoke up from a nearby table. "Sour grapes."

Her breakfast companion, Eleanor Crosby, nodded in agreement, as did Ed and Gary.

"Gwyneth McIvor, the woman who bequeathed the house to the museum, was Angus's aunt," Eleanor explained.

"Angus thought he should inherit the house," Joan added.

"An unjustified sense of entitlement, if you ask me." Eleanor shook her head before cutting into her breakfast frittata.

"You're not wrong." Gary nudged his mug closer to me so I could refill it.

"He wasn't close to his aunt?" I guessed.

"He barely had anything to do with her," Joan said. "Even when her health took a sharp downward turn in the last couple months of her life. I think it was more than generous of Gwyneth to leave him the ten thousand dollars that she did."

The others all nodded in agreement again.

Ed took a sip of coffee and set down his mug with a thud. "If Angus Achenbach wants a house and more money, he should work for it."

I glanced around the pancake house, noting that I wasn't needed elsewhere at the moment. "He doesn't have a job?"

"Can't seem to keep one for more than a few weeks at a time," Gary said. "It's always been that way. It got so no one would hire him here in town."

Ed speared a piece of pancake with his fork. "Probably because he's so lazy."

That statement elicited sounds of agreement from the others.

"He'll get over the situation with Gwyneth's house," Joan said. She paused with her coffee mug halfway to her mouth. "Eventually."

I left them to finish their meals, attending to the other diners in the restaurant. The rush tapered off not long after, but we didn't have much of a lull before things picked up again around lunchtime. When two o'clock rolled around, I shut and locked the front door with a small sigh of relief. As much as I loved running the pancake house, I'd been on my feet since six in the morning, and they were letting me know that they wanted a rest.

Leigh and Sienna were still cleaning up the tables, so I ignored the aching in my feet and gave them a hand. Leigh headed out soon after, wanting to get home so she could keep her promise to her three daughters to take them to the beach that afternoon. I wished I could spend some time on the beach too, preferably with a good book, but I knew I likely wouldn't have a chance to do that today. I'd get my beach time another day, though. That was one of the many perks of living right next to the ocean. All I had to do was step out my back door to hit the sand and surf.

I loaded the last of the dirty dishes into the dishwasher and turned the machine on, then pulled a stool up to the island in the middle of the kitchen and sat down, finally giving my feet a rest.

"What a day," I said as I watched Ivan and Tommy do the last of their cleanup.

Tommy shut a cupboard door. "I think we fed an entire army."

I tugged the elastic out of my hair, releasing my ponytail. My curls were probably all frizzy, but I didn't care. "It sure feels like it."

"You work too hard," Ivan grumbled, his characteristic scowl firmly in place.

"The rest of you work just as hard as I do," I said. "Maybe even harder."

Ivan pinned me with his dark stare.

"But you're right," I added before he could lecture me. "I need to hire more staff. I think it would be good to have someone part-time to help you guys in the kitchen, someone who can step in if either of you get sick. What do you think?"

I directed the question to Ivan. The kitchen was his domain. Even though I was his boss, I didn't want to step on his toes, and I respected his opinion.

"It's a good idea," he said as he hung a pot on a hook above the island.

I shifted my gaze to Tommy.

He turned on the faucet at the large sink so he could wash his hands. "I wouldn't say no to extra help."

"We need another server, too," Ivan reminded me in his gruff voice.

"Sooner rather than later," I agreed.

Sometime in the next few days, I needed to get busy and draft help-wanted ads to put in the local newspaper. Not today, though. I had to swing by the grocery store on the way home. Brett was having a rare poker night at our place, and I'd promised to pick up some snacks to feed our guests.

After saying goodbye to Ivan and Tommy, I made my way down the hall toward the office, where I'd left my tote bag. Before I got there, I spotted Sienna hovering inside the small break room.

"Hey," I said. "I thought you'd already gone." I realized that she seemed anxious, her teeth worrying her lower lip. "Is everything okay?"

She hesitated for half a second before smiling, although the expression didn't reach her eyes. "Everything's fine. See you soon!"

She zipped past me and out the back door, barely giving me a chance to say goodbye.

I remained standing in the middle of the hallway, puzzled and a bit worried.

Sienna might have claimed that everything was fine, but she wasn't quite herself.

Chapter Three

I consulted my phone as I pushed my cart down an aisle of Wildwood Cove's only grocery store. I'd texted Brett earlier, asking if there was any specific type of snacks he wanted me to pick up for his poker night. I smiled when I read his reply.

Nachos. And nachos.

I wasn't planning to take part in the poker game, but I did intend to enjoy some of the food, and I was completely behind Brett's request. Cheese-laden nachos were one of my weaknesses, along with chocolate, sweet tea, and anything cooked by Ivan. I'd definitely have to go running tomorrow, especially since Brett and I had eaten pizza the day before, but tonight I would indulge.

Adding two large bags of nachos to the grocery cart, I moved along to the potato chips and grabbed some of those as well. We had ripe avocados at home for the guacamole, but I filled my cart with veggies, dip, salsa, black olives, and two types of soda.

I maneuvered down the next aisle, heading for the dairy products. I scanned the baking supplies as I made my way to the back of the store, trying to think if we needed anything from the shelves I was passing. I didn't think we did, so I picked up my pace. When I reached the refrigerated display of dairy products, I parked my cart off to the side and checked out the yogurt selection. A woman a few feet away from me was standing in front of the milk and cream, her grocery cart filled halfway. She wore black yoga pants and a hot pink top. Her long, dark hair was tied back in a high ponytail, which she flipped over her shoulder while she held her cellphone to her ear.

"I can't believe they gave her the promotion," she was saying into her phone, indignation underscoring her words. "I'm way more suited for the position." She paused and placed a hand on her hip, presumably listening to the person on the other end.

"I know!" she said after a moment. "And she's been such a pain about Wild West Days. *She* didn't volunteer to be on the organizing committee, and yet she has the gall to tell those of us who did that we're doing things wrong! She thinks everything needs to be *historically accurate*. Nobody cares about that! The town just wants to have fun!"

I selected a carton of strawberry yogurt from the shelf. I couldn't help but hear the woman's side of her conversation, but I tried to act like I wasn't paying any attention. That became harder when she mentioned a familiar name.

"But everyone thinks Jane Fassbender is the greatest thing since sliced bread." She finally chose a jug of milk and plunked it into her cart. Still holding her phone to her ear, she steered her cart around me.

"You're right," she said after a pause. "Things will turn out as they should. One day soon, that job will be mine."

She disappeared down the canned goods aisle, her voice fading away.

Whoever she was, she sure didn't think much of Jane. From what she'd said, I figured she worked at the local community center. Although Jane was overseeing the museum's operations at the moment, that was a volunteer position. She also worked full-time at the community center. I thought I remembered hearing that Jane had recently been promoted to the position of director. That had to be what the woman on the phone was talking about.

Maybe she was just bitter about getting passed over for the promotion, but she didn't seem to be a fan of Jane. If she worked at the community center, she probably knew Jane far better than I did, but since volunteering at the museum over the past few weeks, I hadn't found any real reason to dislike her. Still, I could see how she might rub some people the wrong way. She was a woman who knew how she wanted things done, and she wasn't afraid to voice her opinion. She'd been a bit bossy at times during the museum's move, but I'd figured she just wanted to keep things running smoothly. It was entirely possible that I hadn't yet experienced all aspects of her personality.

Shrugging off what I'd overheard, I grabbed a block of cheddar cheese and headed for the checkout counter, eager to get home to spend the evening with Brett and some of our closest friends.

* * * *

"I think I've got a full house." Brett's younger sister, Chloe, spread her cards out on the kitchen table.

The four guys sitting at the table with her leaned forward to inspect her hand. They all groaned and threw down their cards in defeat.

"I thought you'd never played poker before." Her boyfriend, Kyle Rutowski, eyed her with suspicion.

"I haven't." Chloe smiled like the cat that got the canary as she swept the money on the table over her way.

They were only playing for small amounts, but it looked like she'd managed to win several dollars.

"Beginner's luck," Brett grumbled.

"Which I don't want to wear off." Chloe scooped up the money. "That's why I'm bowing out now."

"You can't do that," Brett protested. "You have to give us a chance to win our money back."

Chloe smiled sweetly. "Maybe another time."

The guys muttered half-heartedly as she left the kitchen table and came over to join me on the couch, where I was reading a mystery novel. My orange tabby cat, Flapjack, was asleep on my lap. Bentley, the goldendoodle Brett and I had rescued shortly after I'd moved to town, was curled up on his bed across the room, snoring quietly.

As Chloe sat down next to me, I tucked a bookmark between the pages of my paperback and set it on the coffee table. "You know they'll never let you play with them again, right?"

"That's okay," she said, unconcerned. "It really was beginners' luck. I'd be pretty much guaranteed to lose any future games." She lowered her voice as if sharing a secret. "And I don't like losing to my brother."

I laughed. "I'm pretty sure that goes both ways." This time I lowered my voice. "How are things going with you and Kyle?"

A hint of pink showed on Chloe's cheeks. "Really good." She glanced over at her boyfriend, a smile lighting up her face. "I've never felt this way about any of the other guys I've dated. He makes me so happy."

I threw my arms around her and gave her a squeeze. "I'm so happy for you."

She and Kyle had started dating shortly before Christmas, but they'd known each other since they were kids. I was glad that their relationship kept getting stronger as the weeks passed. Chloe deserved a good guy, and Kyle, a sheriff's deputy, definitely qualified.

"What are you two whispering about over there?" Brett called out from the kitchen table.

"None of your business," Chloe said, her smile transforming into a sassy one.

Brett was about to say something in response when Lonny Barron spoke up. "How are things going at the museum?"

"Moving along," Brett said. "The renovations are pretty much finished inside, except for refinishing the floors in two of the rooms upstairs. I've got the yard all fixed up now."

Manny Lopez, who'd recently started working for Brett, fanned his cards out in his hand, studying them. "I rode my bike past there last night. It looks great."

"When's the reopening party?" Chloe asked.

"At the end of the month," I said. "On the final evening of Wild West Days. Evangeline Oldershaw-Hobbs stopped by to talk to Jane about it yesterday. Apparently, Evangeline is paying for the party and wants to have a hand in organizing it."

Chloe raised her eyebrows. "I bet that didn't go over well with Jane."

"She didn't seem too pleased," I said, remembering the way Jane had rolled her eyes. "I figured that was because Evangeline was a bit... overwhelming."

"That's one word for it," Lonny said with a grin as he added some money to the small pile in the middle of the table.

Chloe stroked the fur on Flapjack's head. "It's probably partly that, but both those women like to be in charge and have a habit of stepping on other people's toes. I can't imagine the two of them getting along."

"I haven't had any problems with Jane myself," I said. "But I overheard a woman today who didn't seem to like her much. She thought she should have been awarded the promotion Jane got at the community center, and she seemed to think Jane was interfering with the planning for Wild West Days."

Chloe twisted her long blond hair and flicked it over her shoulder. "I bet that was Adya Banerjee. She works at the community center, and she's on the planning committee for Wild West Days."

"Yeehaw, me hearties!" Manny bellowed from the kitchen.

Chloe rolled her eyes. "I think you're getting your cowboy talk and pirate talked mixed up."

"Pirate Days—that should be an event too," Kyle said. He shifted his gaze away from his cards long enough to send a grin Chloe's way.

She smiled in return. "Actually, that's not a bad idea."

The guys returned their attention to their game, and Chloe got back to our conversation.

"Adya might not like Jane," she said, "but she's usually nice."

I tucked my feet up on the couch, careful not to jostle Flapjack too much. "Maybe Jane rubs some people the wrong way, but I don't mind her. Whatever differences she and Evangeline have between them, I hope they can work together to get the museum's party organized."

"I hope so too," Chloe said, an ominous note creeping into her voice, "but I wouldn't hold my breath."

Chapter Four

The Flip Side was closed on Monday, as usual, so I started the day with a long run along the beach. Bentley kept me company, although he didn't always keep pace with me. He liked to stop and sniff at driftwood and clumps of seaweed that had washed ashore. Then he'd charge off along the water's edge, passing me with ease before stopping again to hunt out more interesting smells.

The fresh air and exercise left me feeling energized. After a quick shower, I headed over to the museum to see if there was anything I could help with. I recalled Jane mentioning that she wouldn't be working at the community center until the afternoon that day, so she'd have time to spend at the museum. I wasn't sure what time she planned to show up, but I figured there was a good chance she was already there. She answered the front door within seconds of my knock, proving me right. She seemed glad to see me and quickly put me to work, first moving furniture with Frankie Zhou's help and later shifting some of the archive boxes onto the recently installed shelves.

After hearing about Jane from others, I noticed her bossiness more than I had before. She told us what to move, where to move it, and sometimes how to move it, but she never lifted a finger to help. I didn't want other people's opinions of her to color my own, so I tried not to hold it against her. For all I knew, she could have had a bad back and wasn't able to lift boxes or shift furniture.

About an hour later, my own back was beginning to protest. I stepped out into the hallway, wanting to get out of Jane's line of sight so I could rest for a moment. I'd learned that if anyone seemed idle in her presence, she'd quickly find a way to make them busy.

I stretched my arms above my head and then let them drop to my sides. As I shook them out, the back door opened, letting in a shaft of bright sunlight. Dean Vaccarino, the man who was refinishing the floors, sauntered in, not bothering to shut the door behind him.

"Morning," I said, trying not to let my wariness show.

I'd met Dean on the first day I'd volunteered to help with the museum's move. He'd given me the creeps then, and nothing had changed. He acknowledged my greeting with a barely perceptible nod, his eyes appraising me in a way that made my skin crawl.

To my relief, Jane appeared in the hallway, diverting his attention. "Oh, good. You're here. You'll be able to finish sanding the floors today, right?"

"Sure," he said in a lazy drawl.

"Let's go up and have a look at the state of things." Jane didn't wait for any agreement, already leading the way to the stairs.

Dean followed after her, in no hurry. He gave me a last long look, accompanied by a hint of a smirk, as he passed by me.

Once he was out of sight, I made a face and rubbed my arms, as if that could rid me of the creepy feeling he'd left on my skin. It didn't work all that well. At least I didn't have to spend any real time with him. Most of my volunteering shifts were spent working with Frankie or Jane. Frankie was a quiet guy and not all that easy to get to know, but he seemed nice. I suspected the reason he was spending so much time at the museum was that he had a crush on Jane, even though she was likely several years older than him.

I returned to the archive room and worked with Frankie for a while longer, placing boxes on the shelves in the order Jane had requested. In time, Dean faded from my thoughts, even though I could hear the floor sander he was using upstairs. Jane soon came down to check on our work. She scrutinized everything with sharp eyes, but fortunately had no complaints.

Once we had all the boxes of archives on the shelves, I slipped down the hall to the kitchen to get myself a glass of water. The window over the sink offered a view of the backyard, where the grass was neatly trimmed, and the flower beds weeded, thanks to Brett. As I stood there sipping my water, a familiar red Ferrari drove along the back alley and pulled up outside the gate.

It wasn't hard to guess who was about to pay a visit to the museum.

Sure enough, Evangeline got out of the passenger seat. This time, Richard stayed in the vehicle, leaving Evangeline to head this way on her own. I wondered if I should warn Jane but decided to stay put. Evangeline had almost reached the back porch, and maybe Jane was expecting her.

I refilled my water glass from the kitchen tap as the back door opened.

"Hellooo! Jane!" Evangeline's voice rang out through the Victorian.

I winced at the shrill sound. It wouldn't have surprised me if even Dean heard her over the noise of the floor sander.

"I'm in the office," Jane called back, not so loudly and without a shred of enthusiasm.

Evangeline strutted off down the corridor without a single glance in my direction.

A plate of oatmeal cookies sat on the counter, baked and brought over the day before by one of the neighbors. I knew they were meant for the volunteers, so I helped myself to one. I was ready for a snack, but most of all, I wasn't ready to join Jane and Evangeline. For a second, I considered slipping quietly out of the museum and heading home, but I didn't want to leave without letting Jane know that I was going.

I lingered in the kitchen, daring to hope that things were going fairly smoothly in the other room. After all, Jane had managed to be mostly civil to Evangeline when she stopped by two days earlier, or at least she had in the short time before I left with Brett.

Evangeline's voice drifted my way, though I couldn't hear what she was saying—until she raised her voice a few minutes later.

"Do I have to remind you who's paying for this party?" She sounded haughty and annoyed.

"You've already done that many times over," Jane said, her voice rising in volume to match Evangeline's.

"You act like you own this museum, but really you're just standing in for Nancy Welch. *Temporarily.*"

"And you act like you own this town," Jane shot back. "When really, everyone thinks you're ridiculous!"

I could hear Evangeline's huff of indignation from the kitchen.

"I've done nothing but good for this town," she said. "I've half a mind to take back my offer to pay for the party, but I won't because that would disappoint the town, and the rest of the town doesn't deserve to be punished because you're an insufferable control freak."

I crept closer to the corridor, wondering if I would have to intervene to prevent a brawl. As I peeked around the corner, Evangeline stormed out into the hallway.

When she'd almost reached the back door, she came to an abrupt stop and spun around to face Jane, her head held high. "I'll have the caterer contact you. I'm going over the menu with her soon."

"I'm capable of lining up a caterer," Jane said, standing in the middle of the hallway.

Even from where I stood, I could see the storminess in her gray eyes.

"I've already booked this one," Evangeline said. "The same one who will be catering my upcoming charity gala. If you fight me on this any further, Jane, I'll have to go to the Board."

"You don't want to do that." Jane spoke calmly now, but there was a dangerous glint in her eyes. "I know things about you, Evangeline. Things you wouldn't want getting out. Your precious reputation might get tarnished."

Evangeline stared at her. "What in the world are you talking about?"

"I'm talking about last October," Jane said. "At the Sea Spray Cottage Resort in Port Angeles."

Despite all the makeup Evangeline wore, I could tell that her face had gone pale. A second later, her cheeks flushed, and her blue eyes flashed with anger.

"It's never advisable to threaten an Oldershaw. Anyone who does lives to regret it." She pierced Jane with one last glare and then stormed out the door. It slammed shut behind her.

I returned to the sink so I could see out the window. Evangeline stomped down the walkway to the back gate, throwing it open with such force that it nearly got knocked off its hinges. She climbed into the Ferrari, and it zoomed off down the lane.

Jane threw her hands in the air. "That woman is intolerable!" She marched off in the opposite direction, toward the front of the house.

I wanted to let her know I was leaving for the day, but I decided to give her a few minutes to cool off first. I was afraid of the reception I might get right at the moment.

Frankie poked his head into the kitchen a moment later as I washed up my water glass. "Is the coast clear now?" he asked.

"Seems so," I said. "You weren't stuck in the office with them, I hope."

"No way." He was clearly horrified by the mere thought. "I was upstairs with Dean. I decided to hide out there while the battle raged. Cowardly, I know."

"I'd say it was smart, not cowardly. Where's Jane now?"

He shrugged. "I'll go find her."

I almost called out to him not to bother, but maybe he wanted to find her for his own reasons. After drying my glass and putting it back in the cupboard, I made my way down the hall toward the front of the house, where I could hear Jane's and Frankie's voices.

Before I reached the foyer, the front door burst open. Angus Achenbach, the man who'd made a scene at The Flip Side on the weekend, stood in the doorway, backlit by the bright sunshine. His thinning hair stood up on end as if it had been ruffled by the spring breeze. The intensity of his glower nearly sent me back a step.

"Where's Jane?" He shot the words at me, his voice almost a growl.

Jane appeared in the arched doorway that led to one of the rooms off the foyer. "I'm right here, Angus." She folded her arms across her chest. "What are you doing here?"

"I have every right to be here."

The gentle, sweet-scented breeze that drifted in through the open door provided a stark contrast to his hostile demeanor.

"You don't, actually." Jane sounded matter-of-fact, but I thought I detected a hint of wariness in her eyes. "This house is the museum's private property."

"You and your ridiculous museum!" Angus sneered. "This house is rightfully mine!"

Jane let out a long-suffering sigh. "So you told the court, but the judge didn't agree with you, remember? Gwyneth wanted the house to belong to the museum after she died, and now it does. If you keep up this infantile behavior, Angus, I'll have to get a restraining order."

Angus's upper lip curled back, and his nostrils flared. He resembled a wild and ferocious animal preparing to attack.

Frankie appeared from behind Jane, stopping by her side, his muscles tense. Although he had a wiry build, I knew from helping him move furniture that he didn't lack strength. He'd likely have no trouble taking on Angus, who carried several extra pounds and didn't strike me as the least bit athletic.

"Everything all right here?" he asked, flicking his gaze Jane's way before staring hard at Angus.

"You stay out of this!" Angus turned on Jane again. "My aunt left you this house because you bamboozled her before she died. She wasn't in her right mind, and you took advantage of that. You can stand there and threaten me with your restraining order, but I'll be the one who gets the last laugh. Just you wait and see."

Frankie took a step toward him but didn't have a chance to do anything. Angus turned around and thudded his way out the front door, his feet pounding against the boards of the porch. He left the door open behind him, and I heard him bellow at a rollerblading kid to get out of his way before he disappeared down the street.

Jane released another loud and dramatic sigh. It was only then that I realized I'd been standing frozen in the same spot since Angus had appeared in the doorway.

"Are you all right, Jane?" Frankie asked, his dark eyes full of worry.

She waved off his concern. "I'm fine. Don't mind Angus. He's always having a tantrum about something. He'll get over it."

She returned to the front room, and Frankie followed her.

I wasn't so sure that Jane was right. Angus struck me as the type of person who could hold onto a grudge like a dog with a bone, and I couldn't help but worry that he might turn out to be far more of a problem than Jane thought.

Chapter Five

The Flip Side and life, in general, kept me so busy that I didn't return to the museum until Saturday afternoon. I'd heard that all of the renovations were now complete and that Jane and some of her helpers set up most of the displays. I wanted to get a quick peek at what the place looked like now that everything was coming together.

I didn't go empty-handed. When I closed up the pancake house, we had four maple pecan sticky buns left over—Ivan and Tommy had made an extra batch to keep up with the demand—so I put two in one paper bag to take home to Brett and two in another bag to take to Jane.

I made my way across town on foot, enjoying the beautiful afternoon. I admired several blooming rhododendrons during my walk, including one in front of the museum with bright pink flowers. Port Townsend's annual Rhody Festival would be taking place soon, shortly before Wildwood Cove's Wild West Days. I'd never been to the festival, but I knew it was popular.

No one answered when I knocked on the front door, so I headed around back, where I had more luck. The door stood open and Frankie was on the porch, sweeping it clean with a broom.

I wasn't surprised to see him there. He worked for his family's moving company, but he always seemed to be at the museum lately. I knew Jane appreciated his help, but I didn't think she took as much notice of him as he hoped she would.

He paused his sweeping as I climbed the steps.

"Is Jane here?" I asked after saying hello.

"Upstairs, the last I saw her."

"Thanks."

He resumed sweeping as I entered the museum.

Aside from the swishing of Frankie's broom, I couldn't hear a sound inside the Victorian. I called out Jane's name, in case she'd come downstairs. I received no response, but a floorboard creaked above my head.

Instead of heading upstairs right away, I took the time to peek into both front rooms. The news I'd heard at The Flip Side was accurate. The museum's artifacts were now on display, ready for visitors. One room showcased old photographs of Wildwood Cove, Native American baskets, and information about the area's maritime history. The other room displayed clothing from the nineteenth and early twentieth centuries as well as old household items like a wood-burning cookstove, early clothes irons, and an old gramophone. There was plenty more to see, but I figured I'd browse the exhibits more closely another time.

I ran my hand along the polished banister as I took the stairs to the second floor. Everything was spick and span and gorgeous. The renovations had breathed new life into the old house, and yet I could almost feel the history of the place in the air. It made for a perfect atmosphere for a museum.

"Jane?" I called out as I reached the top of the stairway.

She poked her head out of a room to my right. "Hi, Marley. Come on in."

I stepped into the room, which had a large table in the middle, and shelves lining the wall. Although the shelves weren't completely full, they held several boxes. Jane grabbed one of them and shifted it over to the table.

"I took a quick peek at the front rooms downstairs," I said. "Everything looks great. Up here too." As much as I disliked Dean, he'd made the original hardwood floors look as good as new.

Jane smiled at the compliment. "Thanks. It wouldn't have happened without all the help of the volunteers, including you."

"I'm glad I was able to help." I held out one of the paper bags I'd carried over from The Flip Side. "I brought you a couple of sticky buns from the pancake house."

Jane opened the bag and took a quick look inside as she thanked me. "They look delicious." She sniffed the contents. "And they smell even better. I've heard great things about The Flip Side's sticky rolls." She set the bag aside. "Is there anything I can help you with?"

"No, I just dropped by to see how things looked. I don't want to get in the way."

"You're not in the way." She removed the lid from the box on the table. "I'm taking advantage of the fact that we now have room to sort through some of the donations we've received over the past couple of years."

I stepped closer, my ever-present curiosity perking up. "What's in this one?"

"Looks like documents, mostly." She pulled on a pair of cotton gloves and carefully lifted out a sheaf of papers. "These look like old receipts of some sort." She set those aside and reached into the box again, this time producing a small leather-bound volume. She gently opened the cover and turned the first few pages. "A journal. That could be interesting."

"Whose journal?" I asked, peering at the faded, spidery handwriting. I couldn't read any of it from my vantage point.

Jane returned to the front page, where she found a name. "Douglas Maxwell. That makes sense. This box was donated by his daughter, Dolly Maxwell." She carefully flipped through some of the pages again. "The entries date back to the 1930s."

"Sounds like it could be fascinating," I said.

"It very well could be, although you never can tell until you actually read such things. I once got excited about an old journal, only to discover that the author had just noted down what he ate each day. And he didn't exactly have a varied diet."

I hoped that wouldn't be the case with Douglas Maxwell's journal, even though I probably wouldn't have a chance to read it.

I peeked into the box as Jane set the journal on the table. I spotted a small roll of papers tied with a ribbon. The ribbon had likely once been white with red polka dots, but the white parts had yellowed with age.

"Do you think those might be letters?" I pointed to the roll of papers, not wanting to touch anything without gloves.

"They might be."

Jane untied the ribbon, and it slithered away, falling to the table. Carefully, she unrolled the papers. I held my breath, hoping they wouldn't crumble to pieces. We both breathed a sigh of relief once they were lying intact on the tabletop. Jane had to hold them down to keep them from rolling up again, but aside from a few creases and small tears, the papers appeared to be in relatively good condition.

My first guess appeared to be right. The handwriting of the letters was faded, but not so much as to make it illegible. I could tell right away that the letters had been penned by someone other than Douglas Maxwell, the owner of the journal. The handwriting was markedly different, loopier, and less of a spidery scrawl.

"What've you got there?"

Jane and I both jumped at the sound of Frankie's voice. He stood in the doorway, focused on Jane.

"Some documents donated by a local family," Jane replied.

"Need any help with them?" Frankie sounded hopeful.

"No, thank you." Jane smiled at him. "I'm fine here, and you've done so much already."

He returned her smile. "Call me anytime you need another pair of hands around here."

Jane thanked him, and he disappeared down the hall. A few seconds later, I heard him descending the stairs, his footsteps getting quieter and quieter until they faded away. I was more certain than ever that he had a crush on Jane. It was clear from the way he looked at her. I didn't know if she was aware of his feelings or not, but I sensed that she viewed him as nothing more than a helpful volunteer.

We turned our attention back to the letters.

Jane set the top pages aside and carefully looked through the others. "There are several letters here. No obvious indication of whom they were written to. They're all addressed to 'my beloved.'"

I leaned in for a closer look at the first letter's top page as Jane smoothed it out again. It was dated 1907.

"They're more than a hundred years old," I said, excitement stirring.

I loved getting a glimpse into the lives of people from the past. I wondered if Jane would let me read the letters.

She studied them intently and then sifted through the papers until she found the end of the first letter, which appeared to be three pages long.

"Does it say whom it's from?" I asked.

"There's no name, but…" Jane froze, staring hard at the yellowed sheet of paper in her hands.

"What is it?" I moved closer so I could see over her shoulder.

To my disappointment, there was no name signed at the end of the letter. Instead, there was simply a J with a diamond drawn around it.

A glance at Jane's face made me wonder if my disappointment was premature. A light of excitement shone in her eyes.

"Do you know what that means?" I asked, pointing to the J without touching the paper.

Instead of answering, Jane sifted through the other papers. All of the letters were signed in the same way.

"Jane?" I prodded, the suspense becoming too much for me to take.

She set down the papers and raised her gaze to meet mine. A smile broke out across her face.

"This is incredible!" She looked ready to jump with joy. I'd never seen her so excited.

"What's incredible?" I asked, quelling my growing impatience. "I'm still in the dark here."

"It's the Jack of Diamonds," she said, her whole face shining with excitement now.

"That's a person?" I still didn't know what she was talking about.

"You don't know about the Jack of Diamonds? He's only one of the peninsula's most notorious figures from the past."

"I didn't grow up here," I said. "I don't know a whole lot about the town's history."

Before I'd finished speaking, she was waving off my words as if anxious to explain. "The Jack of Diamonds was a thief. He plagued the Olympic Peninsula in the early twentieth century. He broke into the homes of the rich and middle-class, stealing jewelry and other small but valuable items. It's estimated that he stole thousands of dollars' worth of goods. These days that would translate to tens of thousands. Maybe even hundreds of thousands."

She paused for a breath, still smiling. "His real name was Jack O'Malley, but not a whole lot is known about him. He was shot and killed in 1908. It's thought that he might have come to the Pacific Northwest from Colorado, but no one knows for sure. Anyway, he got his nickname from the calling card he left whenever he committed a robbery."

"Let me guess," I said. "A Jack of Diamonds playing card."

"Exactly." She beamed at the letters lying on the table.

"And you really think these letters could be from him?" I asked.

"It's very possible. This was his stomping ground, and it's unlikely anyone back then would have pretended to be him. He was one of the most wanted men around." She went back to studying the letters. "I wish I knew the name of his beloved."

"Maybe there's a clue in the letters," I suggested.

"Let's hope so." She checked her phone.

I noticed that the lock screen displayed cover art from one of *Pride and Prejudice*'s many editions. I'd heard that Jane was a huge Austen fan. Apparently, so was her mother, which was how Jane got her name.

She set her phone aside and carefully stacked the letters back together. "We'll have to flatten these out, but that will have to wait." She tied the ribbon around them loosely.

"You're putting them away?" I couldn't keep the surprise and disappointment out of my voice. I really wanted to know more about Jack O'Malley and the letters. Whom he'd written to was a bit of a mystery, and I hated leaving mysteries unsolved.

"Believe me, I don't want to," Jane said. "I can't wait to read them. But I've got an appointment. If I don't leave now, I'll be late."

I followed her as she left the room, the letters still held reverently in her gloved hands. "Are you leaving them here at the museum?"

"Absolutely," she said on her way down the stairs. "I don't want to risk any damage to them by taking them with me. I'll lock them in my office for safekeeping."

I stayed on her heels as she entered her office and unlocked the top drawer of her desk, setting the letters inside.

"When will you be back to read them?" I asked. "And can I be here? I'd love to know what's in the letters and who the recipient was." A thought struck me. "If Dolly Maxwell donated the letters, isn't it likely they were written to someone in her family?"

"Probably. If the recipient isn't named anywhere in the letters, it shouldn't be hard to come up with a list of possibilities. And, of course, I'll start by asking Dolly about the letters. Hopefully, she'll know something about them." She shut and locked the drawer. "I'm not sure exactly when I'll be back to read them, but I could certainly let you know what I find out when I do."

It wasn't hard to read between the lines of what she'd said. She was willing to tell me what she found, but reading the letters was something she wanted to do on her own.

I had no choice but to stifle my disappointment and wait until she was ready to share.

* * * *

"At least she's willing to let you know what she finds out," Brett said to me that evening.

We walked hand-in-hand along the streets of Wildwood Cove, enjoying the perfect evening weather. Bentley trotted along beside us, Brett holding his leash.

"I hope she doesn't change her mind," I said.

Brett squeezed my hand. "I doubt she'd be able to keep the information all to herself even if she wanted to. People around here love stories about the Jack of Diamonds. Once word gets out that the letters exist, everyone's going to want to know what's in them. And they belong to the museum, not Jane. She might be in charge of them at the moment, but she doesn't own them."

We stopped at a street corner to wait for a car to pass by.

"You're right," I said as we crossed the road. "I guess I just have to be patient."

I didn't miss Brett's quiet rumble of laughter. "Not exactly your strong point. Not with mysteries, anyway."

I couldn't argue with him. I knew as well as he did how true that was. "I don't have much choice in this case." I stepped up onto the sidewalk. "At least I have plenty to keep me busy in the meantime. I won't have much chance to think about the letters and what might be in them."

"How are the help-wanted ads coming along?" Brett asked.

"They aren't. Not yet. But I really need to work on them soon."

"Tourist season will be in full swing before we know it."

"It's right around the corner," I agreed. "And Sienna will be leaving for college in no time. I'll make sure I get the ads written up by the end of the week. That way, they can go in next week's paper."

Brett slowed his steps. "Maybe we should have gone in a different direction." His words held a note of gentle teasing.

The museum was up ahead of us, at the end of the street.

"It might be hard for you to keep the letters off your mind if we walk right past the place where they're stored," he said.

"Too late. Although really, they weren't yet *off* my mind," I admitted, "so there's no real change."

"But even if there's a light on inside, we'll keep walking?" He was still teasing. He knew how hard it would be for me to resist knocking on the door to see if Jane was reading the letters.

"We'll keep on walking, even if there's a light on," I promised.

I was determined not to be a pest. As long as Jane didn't hold out on me too long.

As we drew closer to the museum, I noted the dark windows. At least that meant I wouldn't even be tempted to knock on the door. That made it easier to keep my promise.

Bentley, however, wasn't interested in walking straight past the museum. He stopped at the base of a tree, sniffing around, intensely focused on whatever scent he'd found.

We paused, giving him a chance to enjoy his sniffing. Brett tugged on the leash a moment later. Bentley snuffled at the tree again and then reluctantly tore himself away.

We'd taken two steps along the sidewalk when he stopped again.

"What's up, buddy?" Brett asked.

Bentley stood frozen on the sidewalk, his body tense, his gaze fixed on the shadowy space between the museum and the neighboring house.

"Come on, Bentley," I called, letting go of Brett's hand as I continued along the sidewalk.

I glanced back, but Bentley hadn't moved. Brett tugged on the leash again. Bentley resisted and let out a low growl, still fixated on the shadows next to the museum.

A chill skittered through me. Bentley rarely growled. Brett and I followed his fixed gaze. Murky shadows filled the museum's narrow side yard. It wasn't yet completely dark out, but daylight was fading fast.

"Do you see anything?" I asked Brett.

"No." He took a step along the sidewalk. "Come on, Bentley."

I grabbed Brett's arm. "Hold on." Something moved in the shadows. "Someone's there." I took hold of Brett's hand and tugged him toward the museum.

Bentley surged forward with us.

"Marley, wait." Brett drew us both to a halt.

I knew charging into the shadows wasn't the smartest idea, but I didn't plan to go all the way there.

"Jane?" I called out from where we stood on the front lawn.

The shadowy figure froze.

"Jane?" I said again, even though I knew it wasn't her. The person was too tall, but I was hoping to flush out whomever it was.

It worked. A second later, the figure stepped forward, out of the shadows.

"Dean?" I said with surprise as I recognized the man. "What are you doing here?"

He didn't answer right away. His gaze moved lazily from me to Brett and then back again.

"I've been working here," he said finally. "Remember?"

Brett glanced at the darkened windows of the museum. "After hours?"

Dean smirked. "I lost something earlier today. I came by to look for it."

I was glad I wasn't alone with him. His whole demeanor made me uneasy, but that wasn't unusual.

"Did you find it?" I asked.

"Nah," he said.

"Want some help?" Brett offered, but his voice wasn't as friendly as usual.

Dean shrugged. "I'll try again tomorrow." His gaze lingered on me. "Maybe I'll see you then."

I suppressed a shudder as he sauntered off down the street.

"I don't like that guy," Brett said in a low voice, watching him go.

"You're not the only one."

Just like earlier in the day, Dean had made my skin crawl.

But that wasn't what really had my attention.

Dean might have claimed he was looking for something he'd lost, but I had no doubt in my mind that he'd lied to us.

Chapter Six

Within minutes of arriving at The Flip Side the next morning, I knew something wasn't right. I entered the kitchen to find Ivan grimly chopping up zucchini for the frittata we'd named Thyme for Breakfast. Although Ivan often had a surly expression on his face, this one was more dour than usual. Something else was even more obvious, though.

"Where's Tommy?" I asked as soon as I'd greeted Ivan.

I almost always found the two of them working in the kitchen when I arrived at the pancake house. I would have assumed that Tommy was in the washroom or breakroom if I hadn't passed both walking from the office to the kitchen.

"He's late." Ivan kept chopping, the blade of his knife moving swiftly.

"He's never late." I amended my statement. "At least, not this late."

"He's never arrived more than ten minutes after me," Ivan said.

Which probably meant that he was always on time.

A tiny flame of concern flickered to life in my chest. "Have you heard from him?"

"I texted him." Ivan set down his knife and wiped his hands before retrieving his phone from his pocket.

He usually kept his phone in his locker while working, so I knew he was worried too.

He checked the device. "No reply."

"Maybe he's sick." I thought that was the most likely explanation.

If he was really unwell, he might not have woken up yet, or he might not have been able to get in touch with us.

"I'll try to reach him too." I darted out of the kitchen and down the hall to the office. Grabbing my phone, I sent a text message of my own to Tommy.

Everything okay? You're usually here by now.

I tucked my phone in my pocket, making sure the sound was on so I'd know as soon as I received a response. I scanned the dining room, checking that everything was ready for the day's customers.

I straightened some napkin dispensers and salt-and-pepper shakers, knowing that I was just giving my anxious energy an outlet rather than accomplishing anything.

Once I could no longer deny the fact that everything was ready to go, I returned to the kitchen, pulling my phone out again, even though it hadn't made a sound. I checked it anyway. As I already knew, I had no new messages.

Ivan's dark gaze followed my every move.

"I'll try calling him," I said.

If Tommy was asleep, maybe that would wake him up. As long as his phone had the sound turned on.

While Ivan cracked eggs into a bowl, I put a call through to Tommy's number. Even though Ivan kept working, I knew his attention hadn't really left me.

The small flame of worry inside of me danced higher when the call went to voicemail after three rings.

"Tommy, we're worried about you. Please let us know if you're all right."

I hung up and met Ivan's gaze.

"Something's not right," he said, voicing the thought that had circled around in my head a dozen times since I'd arrived at the pancake house.

I checked the time on my phone. "Half an hour until we open." I bit down on my lower lip, trying to figure out what to do. "Do you need me to help you here in the kitchen?"

"I can manage for now," Ivan assured me.

He'd worked on his own in the kitchen before, but with business as brisk as it had been lately, I knew it would be hard for him to shoulder the entire burden of kitchen duty for the whole day.

I came to a decision. "If we don't hear back from Tommy by the time Leigh and Sienna arrive, I'll swing by his place and see what's up."

Ivan indicated his approval of that plan with a curt nod. He got back to whisking the eggs in the bowl, but the set of his mouth, more downturned than usual, told me he was as worried as I was about Tommy.

I tried to keep my anxiety from escalating by settling in at my desk, checking The Flip Side's email, and making myself a to-do list of administrative tasks for the coming week. I made sure to include writing a couple of help wanted ads.

As much as I tried to distract myself, I couldn't stop worrying about Tommy. The minutes ticked by slowly, but I eventually heard voices coming from out front.

I jumped up from my desk and reached the office door in time to see Leigh and Sienna heading for the breakroom.

They both greeted me cheerily, unaware that anything was amiss.

I followed them into the breakroom. "Have either of you heard from Tommy this morning?" I knew it was unlikely, but I figured I should check before running off in search of him.

They both answered in the negative.

"Isn't he here?" Leigh asked as she hung her jacket in her locker.

"Tommy's always here when we arrive," Sienna said, a hint of worry beneath her words.

"Except that one time when he was sick with the stomach flu," Leigh reminded her.

I clutched my phone, which still had no new messages. "But that time he got in touch and told me and Ivan that he wouldn't be in."

"You haven't heard from him?" Now Leigh sounded worried too.

I quickly explained the situation to them.

"He must be really sick," Sienna said, the concern in her eyes changing into fear.

"I'm going by his place to see what's up." I looked at my phone yet again. Nothing had changed other than the time, which had advanced by one minute. "Are you okay to open without me?"

"Yes, of course. Go on," Leigh urged me.

I didn't need to be told twice. Leaving everything behind but my phone, I dashed out the back door and across the parking lot. Tommy and his roommates lived in a house located only a few minutes away from The Flip Side. That was good, since I was eager to get there, and I didn't have my car with me. I walked to and from work each day whenever the weather was good.

I jogged all the way to the street where Tommy lived before slowing to a walk. I'd never been to his house before, but I'd gone walking and jogging along the street many times, and I knew he lived in the blue two-story house in the middle of the block.

As I approached the front steps, I glanced at my phone once more. No one had texted me to say that Tommy had shown up in my absence. Anxiety swirled in my stomach. I took the steps two at a time and knocked on the front door. I could hear music playing somewhere inside the house.

It must have covered the sound of approaching footsteps because the door opened without warning, startling me.

One of Tommy's roommates stood before me in jeans, a T-shirt, and bare feet. His brown hair was almost as curly as mine.

"Hi. It's Keegan, right?" I said. Tommy had introduced us once at a community event.

It took him a second, but then recognition flashed in his eyes. "You're Tommy's boss."

"Marley."

He nodded. "Right. What's up?"

"Is Tommy here?"

Keegan rubbed his jaw. "Shouldn't he be at work?"

"He should be, but he's not," I said. "That's why I'm here. I haven't been able to get in touch with him, and I'm worried he might be sick or something."

"He must be. He's no slacker." Keegan stepped back to make room for me to enter the house. "Come on in. I'll go see what's up."

After Keegan shut the door, I waited in the foyer while he headed up the stairs to the second floor. An Arrowsmith song played on a stereo somewhere at the back of the house, but otherwise, everything was quiet. Keegan and Tommy had two other roommates, but there was no sign of them at the moment.

Keegan reappeared, running a hand through his curly hair as he descended the stairs. "He's not here."

My worry intensified, sending uneasy sparks through my body. "Where else could he be?"

My mind immediately conjured up images of Tommy lying injured at the side of a road. But if he'd been struck by a car or collapsed while on his way to work, surely I would have seen him on my way to his house. Unless an ambulance had whisked him away to the hospital. I hadn't heard any sirens, but that didn't mean there hadn't been any.

I fought back the panic that was trying to claw its way up through my chest. There was a good chance that there was a perfectly reasonable, unfrightening explanation for Tommy's absence.

"When's the last time you saw him?" I asked Keegan.

"Yesterday." He shoved his hands in the pockets of his jeans and rocked back on his heels as he thought. "Early evening."

"Did he go out somewhere?"

"To some charity gala."

"Right." I remembered Tommy mentioning that. "He was hired to take photos."

"Maybe he's with a girl." Keegan didn't sound too sure about that scenario.

"Has he been seeing anyone recently?" I asked.

"Not that I know of, and he probably would have mentioned it if he was."

"Even if he had spent the night at a girlfriend's place, it's still not like him to miss work and not answer his phone," I said.

"Yeah. You're right." Keegan's brown eyes were troubled. "Do you think something bad has happened?"

"I'm trying not to jump to that conclusion." I was fast losing that battle, though. I tried to think clearly and logically. "So you don't know if he ever came home after the gala?"

"If he did, it was after I'd gone to bed. I was asleep by eleven."

"Did you see his camera in his room?" I asked.

Keegan stood up straighter. "Good thinking. I didn't look for it." He jogged up the stairs again, calling over his shoulder, "Come on up."

I followed him up the creaking stairs.

At the top, Keegan turned left and entered the first room on his right. I trailed after him and stopped just inside the doorway.

It felt like an invasion of Tommy's privacy for me to be in there without his permission, but I hoped he'd understand. His room wasn't the tidiest place ever, but it also wasn't a complete mess. His dark blue bedspread was pulled up, although not with the greatest care, and a pair of jeans and the T-shirt I'd seen him in the day before hung over the back of a chair. Two pairs of sneakers lay haphazardly next to the door, along with an empty water bottle.

Beneath the window was a desk holding a laptop computer, a tablet, a phone charger, wireless earbuds, some spare change, and a couple of science fiction novels. His body board and skateboard leaned up against the wall next to the desk.

I swept my gaze over the room for a second and third time while Keegan moved around the space, taking a closer look at the desk and bedside table.

His camera's usually on the desk," he said. "I don't see it anywhere. Same with his phone."

I pulled out my own phone and dialed Tommy's number. The only ringing I heard came through my phone's speaker. Tommy's phone either wasn't here, or the sound was off. My money was on the first possibility.

As with my previous call, this one went to voicemail after a few rings. I hung up without leaving another message.

Keegan rubbed the back of his neck. "What should we do now?"

That was the same question going through my mind.

"Do you know anyone else who was going to be at the gala?" I asked.

"No. I think it was mostly rich people who were going. Not really my circle."

"I don't know anyone who was going either, but Evangeline Oldershaw-Hobbs and her husband hosted the event."

"I know who they are," Keegan said, "but I've never said two words to them."

"I can probably find out how to get in touch with Evangeline." I figured Jane might know. Otherwise, I could ask Sienna's mom, Patricia. She seemed to know everyone in Wildwood Cove. "If I can talk to Evangeline, at least we can find out if Tommy ever showed up to take the photos. But before I do that, I think I'll retrace his steps. He went on foot, right?"

"Yep." Keegan nodded at Tommy's skateboard. "He left his wheels behind, and he goes everywhere on foot or on his skateboard."

"Okay. I know the charity gala was being held at the local banquet hall," I said. "There are a couple of routes he could have taken to get there and back. I'll walk both of them and see what I can find."

I desperately hoped I wouldn't find something terrible. I was still wishing that Tommy would turn up unharmed, apologizing profusely for having lost track of time or over-sleeping somewhere other than at home. I had a bad feeling that wasn't going to happen, though, no matter how hard I wished for it.

Keegan checked his phone. "I'm supposed to be heading to work in a few minutes, but I can call in sick and help you look if you want."

"That's okay." I wanted company, but I didn't want him to miss work if it wasn't absolutely necessary.

"Can you let me know if you find him?" Keegan asked. "Or if you don't."

"Of course." We exchanged phones so we could enter our contact information.

Once I had my phone back, I didn't linger any longer.

A lump of dread sat heavily in my stomach, and anxiety tightened my chest, but I set off along one of the two routes Tommy might have taken to the banquet hall. I was terrified of finding him hurt—or worse—but I was also scared of not finding him.

I paused on a street corner, just long enough to send a text message to Leigh, letting her know what I was doing. I knew she'd share the information with Sienna and Ivan.

I longed for Brett's company. He'd most likely left for work already, and I hated to interrupt his day, but I really wanted to talk to him. Maybe he'd offer up some completely logical explanation for Tommy's absence that I'd yet to contemplate. Even if that wasn't the case, I still wanted to hear his voice. If he offered to help me look for Tommy, I probably wouldn't turn him down because my dread was growing heavier with every step.

I was about to phone Brett when I reached the end of the next street. Emergency lights flashed up ahead. I froze, my heart dropping before pounding against my ribcage. The next second, I broke into a run.

Chapter Seven

As I charged along the street, I counted the emergency vehicles. There were three sheriff's department cruisers and an ambulance. As I drew closer, I realized that they'd all parked in front of the museum. Could they still be there for Tommy?

I ran full tilt until I reached the museum. Then I stopped and looked around, my heart still racing in my chest. I recognized the sheriff's deputy talking to a paramedic on the front lawn. I jogged over his way.

"Deputy Devereaux!" I called, his name little more than a gasp. My lungs and chest ached, not so much from the exertion of running as from panic.

Devereaux said a final word to the paramedic and broke away from her, coming to meet me.

I had to draw in two ragged breaths before I could speak again. "What's happened? Is it Tommy? Is he okay?"

"Hold on," the deputy said. "Who are you worried about?"

"Tommy Park. He works at The Flip Side. He's missing, and when I saw all the emergency vehicles…"

"They're not for him," Devereaux said. "There's been an incident at the museum, but Tommy's not here."

A wave of relief crashed over me, but it retreated almost as quickly. Tommy was still missing.

A van slowed on the road and parked across the street from the emergency vehicles. When I took a closer look, I realized it was the medical examiner's van.

"Somebody's dead?" I asked with apprehension. "Who? What happened?

"I'm afraid I can't say," Deputy Devereaux replied.

On any other day, that might have driven me crazy. My curiosity would have jumped into overdrive, wanting to know who had died and how, but at the moment, I was far too concerned about Tommy.

Devereaux excused himself and walked with the medical examiner around to the museum's back yard. I stood there, feeling completely lost for a moment, trying to gather myself together. The panic that gripped me at the sight of the emergency vehicles had unraveled me. I needed to keep looking for Tommy, but now I wanted Brett's company more than ever.

Before I could phone Brett, I spotted his uncle, Sheriff Ray Georgeson, striding across the lawn from the direction of the backyard.

"Marley?"

He changed course and headed my way. He didn't look all that pleased to see me. Most likely, he thought I was trying to meddle in his investigation. I couldn't really blame him for assuming that was the case. I did have a history of getting involved in murder investigations.

Was *this* a murder investigation? Or a natural or accidental death?

I didn't pursue those questions any further. I was still too worried about Tommy.

"It's not what you think," I said quickly as Ray approached. "Tommy's missing, and when I saw all the emergency vehicles, I panicked. Deputy Devereaux says this has nothing to do with Tommy."

"That's right." The suspicion in his eyes had morphed into concern. "This is Tommy Park you're talking about?"

When I nodded, he asked, "How long has he been missing?"

"I'm not exactly sure. He was taking photos at the charity gala at the banquet hall last night. He left his house with his camera, but I don't know if he ever made it to the gala. All I know is that his camera and phone aren't at his house, and he didn't show up for work this morning. He's not answering his phone or replying to text messages."

"So he's been missing"—Ray checked his watch—"about twelve to sixteen hours?"

"You're going to tell me it's too soon to file an official missing person report, aren't you?" I guessed. "But this is so unlike him. I'm worried something terrible has happened. I'm retracing his steps between his house and the banquet hall. At least, that's what I was doing when I saw all this." I gestured at the emergency vehicles.

"Hold on," Ray said. "It's not too soon to file a report. One of my deputies will come by the pancake house to do that as soon as I can spare someone. In the meantime, go back to retracing Tommy's steps. If you don't find him, call the hospitals."

That was a job I dreaded. I desperately hoped it wouldn't be necessary. "And if he still hasn't turned up after all that?" I asked.

Ray removed his hat and ran a hand through his brown hair. "Let me know whether you find him in the next hour or so. If you don't, we'll get an official investigation underway."

Deputy Eva Mendoza appeared on the front porch of the museum, disposable booties covering her footwear. "Sheriff!" she called to get Ray's attention.

He glanced her way and then returned his attention to me. "I'm sorry, Marley. I've got to take care of this. We're really tied up at the moment. But keep looking. And let me know what happens. If I don't answer my phone, leave a message. If I don't hear from you, a deputy will be by to see you soon."

I nodded, suddenly unable to speak. Whatever was happening here at the museum was clearly taking up the attention of Ray's department. I was glad that he and his deputies would launch an investigation as soon as they could, but I wished they could start right away. By the time they finished up at the museum, it might be too late.

No, don't think like that, I scolded myself. *Stay positive.*

The more time that passed, the more difficult that was to do.

I turned my back on the museum and continued along the street, my feet so heavy they felt as though they were made of lead. I took only a few steps before stopping and putting my phone to my ear.

"Tommy's missing," I blurted out as soon as Brett answered the call.

Three seconds of silence followed.

"For real?" Brett asked.

The whole story poured out of me in a rush. By the time I reached the part about seeing the emergency vehicles by the museum, I was almost in tears.

"Where are you now?" Brett asked as soon as I'd finished speaking.

"I'm still at the museum. Out front."

"I can be there in fifteen minutes."

"Thank you." I nearly sagged with relief as I ended the call. I'd feel much more capable of facing whatever lay ahead once I had Brett by my side.

I paced along the sidewalk, unable to stand still while I waited. I stopped when I noticed Deputy Devereaux reappearing from around the far side of the museum. Winnifred Woodcombe had her arm hooked around his. She held her silver-handled cane in her other hand, and she leaned on both it and the deputy for support.

Desperate for a distraction, I tried to focus on what was happening before me. Somebody had died, and that knowledge added to my trepidation. The person who spent the most time at the museum these days was Jane

Fassbender, but she wasn't that much older than me, and she seemed healthy. Maybe someone else had died. But who? There couldn't be a good answer to that question.

Deputy Devereaux walked Mrs. Woodcombe over to one of the parked cruisers. He opened the door and helped her get settled in the front passenger seat. He leaned down and said a few words to her before crossing the lawn again, leaving the cruiser door open.

I glanced around. No other deputies were nearby.

I slowly approached the cruiser, my nerves so frazzled that I didn't know if I could handle any more bad news. At the same time, I wanted to talk to Winnifred.

"Mrs. Woodcombe?" I said as I approached the passenger side of the cruiser.

The pallor of her skin and the shock in her blue eyes startled me.

Despite her obvious distress, she offered me a hint of a smile. "We met the other day."

"That's right." I stepped closer. "Marley Collins." I hesitated before speaking again, not sure if she'd want me asking questions. "Are you all right? What happened? Deputy Devereaux said somebody died."

Mrs. Woodcombe blinked away tears. She looked years older than she had a few days ago. "Jane contacted me last night. She said she found something interesting and thought I'd want to have a look for myself."

"The letters?" I guessed.

She seemed surprised that I knew about them. "Yes."

"I was here when Jane found them," I explained.

Winnifred nodded, but I wondered if she'd really heard me. Her gaze had gone unfocused.

"I came by this morning to meet her." Winnifred's voice trembled, and she stopped speaking, her right hand gripping the handle of the cane that lay across her lap.

I did my best to steel myself for the bad news. "Is it Jane?" I asked. "Is she the one who died?"

Winnifred nodded. She drew in a shaky breath and sat up straighter. I got the sense that she was gathering her strength. "I'm afraid so. I found her inside the museum...lying on the floor."

My heart ached for both her and Jane. "That's terrible. I'm so sorry."

Winnifred shook her head. "I'm afraid it's even worse."

"Worse?" I asked, wondering how that could be.

Winnifred closed her eyes for a moment. "Jane is dead, and not from natural causes."

Chapter Eight

"Are you saying it was murder?" I asked once I'd recovered from the worst of my shock. Another possibility crossed my mind. "Or an accident?" I hoped that was the case.

Winnifred shattered that hope with her next words. "Murder, I'm afraid." She shook her head as if unable to believe it. "How could this happen?"

I didn't have an answer to that question.

"I'm sorry you had to see something so terrible," I said. My next words came out before I could stop them. "Are you *sure* it was murder?"

"I don't see how it could be anything else. There was blood on her head." She closed her eyes briefly. "And there was an antique clothes iron on the floor next to her. There was blood on it too." She fingered her gold necklace. "Someone must have hit Jane with it. Who would do such a thing?"

"Hopefully, the police will have an answer to that question soon if they don't already."

I glanced toward the museum. Ray and his deputies remained indoors or around the back.

"Did you notice anything else?" I asked.

Winnifred released her hold on her necklace. "Such as signs of a robbery?"

"Anything."

"There wasn't anything else amiss. Except…there was a ribbon in Jane's hand, but I don't see how that could be significant."

"What kind of ribbon?" I thought I might already know the answer.

"It had red polka dots," Winnifred said, confirming my suspicion.

"Did you see any letters?" I asked.

"Letters? Do you mean the ones Jane was planning to show me?"

"Yes. They were tied together with a ribbon with red polka dots."

An extra line appeared across Winnifred's already creased forehead. "I don't remember seeing any letters or papers of any sort. Jane was in one of the exhibit rooms, but everything was neat and tidy. Except for the clothes iron. And the blood."

The hint of color that had returned to her face drained away again.

I rested a hand on her shoulder, knowing I shouldn't bother her with any more questions. "Is there anyone I can call for you?"

She reached up and patted my hand. "Thank you, dear, but it's all right. The deputy already contacted my grandson. He'll be here to pick me up soon."

Brett's work van turned onto the street and drove slowly past the emergency vehicles. My drooping spirits lifted slightly at the sight. He parked across the street from the cruiser.

"That's my husband," I said as Winnifred's gaze drifted toward the van. "Would you like us to stay with you until your grandson gets here?"

"That's not necessary, but thank you. Perhaps I'll stop by your pancake house sometime soon."

"I'd like that."

I said goodbye and walked toward the back of the cruiser. Brett jogged across the street and met me on the sidewalk. I wrapped my arms around him, and he held me close.

"Jane's dead," I said, still having trouble believing it.

"What?" Brett pulled back so he could see my face. "How?"

"She was murdered. Winnifred Woodcombe found her."

It took a second or two for Brett to digest that information. "Have the police arrested anyone?"

"I don't think so." I hugged him again. "This is the worst day in a long time."

He rubbed my back. "No further news of Tommy?"

I shook my head as I released him. "Ray said he'll send a deputy to The Flip Side later so I can file an official missing persons' report."

"Let's hope it won't come to that." Brett took my hand. "Are you ready to start looking?"

Although I was terrified of what we might—or might not—find, I didn't want to delay the rest of the search any longer.

"Let's go," I said.

I kept a firm grip on Brett's hand as we set off down the sidewalk. It was easy to see on the residential streets that there wasn't anyone lying injured on or near the road. Still, we made sure to scan every front yard and check between parked cars.

As we drew closer to the Wildwood River, we reached a stretch of road without any houses. Instead of a sidewalk, there was only a grassy verge between the road and a ditch, which was currently dry. The other side of the road was the same. Beyond the ditch, trees and thick underbrush made it unlikely that Tommy could have wandered far in that direction.

We rounded a gentle bend in the road, and my heart slammed against my chest.

There was something in the ditch up ahead.

"Oh no." I dropped Brett's hand and ran forward. "Tommy!"

The crumpled form in the ditch didn't move. I nearly fell as I scrambled down the bank. I ended up on my knees next to Tommy at the bottom of the ditch. I could barely draw in a breath. Fear had a tight grip around my rib cage.

"Tommy?" I said, scared that I wouldn't receive any response.

Brett dropped to his knees on Tommy's other side and checked for a pulse.

Tommy's eyes flickered open. Relief hit me with the force of a rogue wave, leaving me lightheaded.

At first, Tommy's gaze was unfocused, but then he met my eyes.

"Marley?"

"You're going to be okay," I said through tears. I desperately hoped I was speaking the truth.

"Marley, call 911, okay?" Brett said to me.

I nodded and pulled out my phone.

Brett had first-aid training, so he spoke to Tommy, assessing his injuries, while I made the phone call.

The ambulance that responded must have been the one that was parked at the museum because I heard its approaching siren less than a minute after I placed the call for help. A moment later, the ambulance came into sight.

I stood up and waved to get the driver's attention. The siren cut off, and the ambulance pulled to the side of the road. Chloe's boyfriend, Deputy Kyle Rutowski, arrived next in a sheriff's department cruiser.

While the paramedics were getting out of the ambulance, I knelt beside Tommy again and gently squeezed his hand.

"Help is here, Tommy," I said.

Since our arrival, he hadn't moved much other than his eyes and his fingers.

Now he cracked the faintest of smiles. "I knew you'd find me."

Choking back a sob, I let go of his hand and backed away so Kyle and the paramedics could move in. Brett spoke with them for a moment while I clambered my way out of the ditch to stand on the grassy verge. Brett soon joined me, putting an arm around me.

I held onto him like he was my life preserver in a stormy sea. "How badly is he hurt?"

"I'm pretty sure he's got a broken leg," Brett said. "And he says it hurts to breathe. Could be broken ribs. Maybe a collapsed lung."

I closed my eyes and buried my face in Brett's chest.

He put a hand to my hair. "He's going to be all right, Marley."

I looked up at him. "Really?" I needed to know he wasn't just saying that to make me feel better.

"I really believe he will."

I held on tightly to both Brett and that assurance.

We stood there at the side of the road while the paramedics assessed Tommy and loaded him onto a stretcher.

"I'll come by the hospital soon," I said as the paramedics wheeled Tommy past us.

It lifted my spirits when he cracked another smile and gave me a thumbs up.

Even so, when the ambulance pulled away, my knees buckled.

Brett tightened his hold on me as I sagged against him. "Whoa. Sit down for a moment, Marley."

"I'm all right," I protested, but Brett had already lowered me to the grass.

I sat there, with my forehead resting against my knees, while Brett rubbed my back.

"I'm sorry," I said before slowly raising my head.

"Don't be. Just take a minute."

I did as he suggested, while he filled Kyle in on what we knew about the accident. Kyle assured us that he'd tell Ray that we found Tommy.

As soon as I'd stopped feeling light-headed, I carefully climbed to my feet, Brett helping me with a hand on my arm.

I needed to get to the hospital, but first, I had to break the news to my Flip Side family.

Chapter Nine

Brett dropped me off at the pancake house and headed out to finish off the job he'd been in the middle of when I'd phone him. We planned to cut our workdays short so we could head to the hospital in Port Angeles. I knew I wouldn't be able to relax until I'd seen Tommy again and received confirmation that he'd be okay.

I entered The Flip Side through the back door, not wanting all the customers to see my red eyes. I'd already texted Keegan to let him know we'd found Tommy, so I bypassed the office and headed for the kitchen. On my way down the hallway, Sienna spotted me and rushed over to meet me.

She grabbed my arm. "Did you find him? Is he okay?"

I stopped just inside the dining area and waved to get Leigh's attention. "Yes, he's okay," I said to Sienna as I gestured for Leigh to join us in the kitchen.

As soon as we were all gathered together, I told them about Tommy. "We found him in a ditch at the side of the road. Brett's pretty sure he's got a broken leg and maybe some other injuries, but we think he's going to be okay."

Sienna burst into tears. I pulled her into a hug.

"When they were loading him into the ambulance, he gave me a smile and a thumbs-up," I told her. "He'll be fine."

"But what happened?" Leigh asked. She had tears in her eyes.

"He was hit by a car," I said.

Tommy had told Brett that while I was on the phone.

"And the driver didn't stop?" Ivan practically bellowed the words.

His grip on the ladle in his hand was so tight that his knuckles had gone white. I was surprised the ladle didn't snap in two.

"I guess not," I said, "because Tommy was there all night."

Leigh put a hand over her mouth. "Poor Tommy. If it had been colder last night..."

She didn't need to finish her sentence. If not for the nice spring weather, Tommy could have died from exposure. That frightening thought had already gone through my head many times.

Sienna cried harder in my arms.

"The important thing is that he's in good hands now," I said. "I'm going to close early, and Brett and I are going to the hospital." I gave Sienna a squeeze. "Do you want me to call your mom? You can go home now if you want."

She shook her head and stepped back, wiping her eyes. "I want to stay."

"Leigh?" I checked with her as well.

She blinked away the tears in her eyes. "I'm staying too."

When I glanced Ivan's way, he glared at me before ladling crêpe batter onto the hot pan.

We were all staying.

While Sienna made a quick trip to the restroom to wash her face, I headed out into the dining room, determined not to give away that I was upset. Hopefully, my eyes weren't quite as red now. I smiled and greeted some of our regular customers on my way to the door, where I flipped the sign, so the closed side faced out. We still had a decent crowd in the restaurant, enjoying brunch, but I wasn't going to let any more customers in. When our current diners were done, I'd close up for the day.

Somehow, we all managed to get through the next hour or so. Some of our regular customers realized that something was up after I flipped the sign on the door, so I gave them a brief explanation. Everyone was shocked and worried about Tommy.

After the last diner left the pancake house, I locked the front door and leaned against it. Time had moved so slowly since I'd arrived back at The Flip Side, and the strain of worrying and holding myself together had left me exhausted. I couldn't give into my fatigue yet, though.

I helped Leigh and Sienna clear and clean the tables. The two of them left shortly afterward, once I'd promised to text them with an update as soon as I'd seen Tommy. I planned to help Ivan in the kitchen, but he wouldn't hear of it.

"Go to the hospital." It sounded like an order, but that was just Ivan's way. "Tell Tommy we're all thinking of him."

"I will," I assured him.

I texted Brett, and he replied right away, telling me that he was at home, letting Bentley outside. He said he'd be by to pick me up in a matter of minutes. He was true to his word. I didn't have to wait long outside the pancake house before he drove up in his truck. Half an hour later, we pulled into the hospital's parking lot.

Anxiety squeezed my stomach on our way into the building. I'd assured Ivan, Leigh, and Sienna that Tommy would be fine, but until I knew that with absolute certainty, I couldn't stop worrying.

We asked about Tommy at the information desk and found out that he'd been admitted. That heightened my anxiety. In the elevator, Brett calmed me down a bit by pointing out that Tommy wasn't in surgery or the intensive care unit. That meant he couldn't be too badly off.

Still, I couldn't relax entirely, and my stomach twisted as we stepped off the elevator.

We found Tommy in a room with one other patient—an elderly man who was currently asleep. I thought Tommy was sleeping too, but when we reached his bedside, he opened his eyes.

"Hey," he said, his voice croaky.

"Hey," I returned, taking his hand. I kept my voice low so we wouldn't disturb his roommate. "How are you feeling?"

As I asked the question, my gaze swept over him, taking in details I'd missed at the roadside. He had bruising and abrasions on his other arm, and his lips were dry and cracked. There was also a large bruise and a bright red scratch over his left cheekbone. Although he had a blanket covering him, I could tell that his left leg was in a cast.

"I've been better," he said, "but it could have been way worse."

"Your leg didn't need surgery?" Brett asked.

"Nope. Just a cast." He managed a tired grin. "I'll be zooming around on crutches in no time."

That got a smile out of me. He was probably right.

"What about your chest?" Brett asked.

"My lungs are all good," Tommy said. "I've got three cracked ribs, though. That's why it hurts to breathe deeply."

Blinking back tears, I squeezed his hand. "We're so glad it wasn't any worse."

"Hey." He noticed the tears in my eyes and gave my hand a squeeze in return. "I'm going to be fine, Marley. I promise."

I nodded and tried to get my emotions under control.

Tommy looked at both of us. "I wanted to thank you guys. If you hadn't come looking for me, who knows how long I would have been lying in that ditch?"

I didn't even want to think about that. "Of course, we came looking for you."

This time his grin was livelier. "I figured once you realized I was missing, you wouldn't rest until the mystery of my disappearance had been solved. I knew I could count on Wildwood Cove's Nancy Drew."

"Even if I didn't have a penchant for solving mysteries, we would have come looking for you," I assured him.

He squeezed my hand again. "I know. Thank you."

I blinked back another round of tears and cleared my throat. "What about your family? Has anyone contacted them for you?"

"The hospital did. My parents are on their way. My sister and brother-in-law will look after the restaurant for a few days."

Tommy's parents owned a Korean restaurant in Seattle. That's where he'd learned to cook.

With his free hand, Tommy reached for the plastic cup of ice water on the bedside table. Brett grabbed it and handed it to him. Tommy took a long sip through the straw before passing it back to Brett. Once the cup was back on the bedside table, I couldn't wait any longer to ask my next question.

"What happened, Tommy? Do you have any idea who hit you?"

He shifted against his pillows, and I finally relinquished his hand so he could move his weight more easily.

"I haven't got a clue," he said once he seemed comfortable. "The car came from behind me, so it crossed onto the wrong side of the road. One second I heard an engine and saw lights on the road, and the next I was flying through the air into the ditch. When the driver was out of the car, all I saw was a shadowy figure."

"Hold on," Brett said before I had a chance. "The driver stopped?"

Tommy rubbed his forehead. "For a moment. But not to help me."

"What do you mean?" I asked.

"Whoever it was, they climbed down into the ditch and went through my pockets. I was face down at the time and not really with it. I managed to roll over, but by that time, the driver was getting back in the car. Then they drove off."

"Why did the driver go through your pockets?" That baffled me.

"I guess I was an easy target. They took my wallet, my phone, and my camera." He frowned as he finished his sentence.

I knew how much his camera meant to him. Photography was a passion of his.

"That's why I couldn't call for help," Tommy said. "No phone. I tried crawling out of the ditch, but the bank was too steep, and I rolled back down. The pain in my leg and chest made me pass out." He seemed embarrassed by that admission.

"I'm not surprised," Brett said. "I'm impressed you were even able to try to get out."

"Me too," I added.

My heart ached, knowing what he'd gone through before we'd found him. A rush of anger swirled through me too. It was bad enough that someone had hit Tommy and driven away without getting help for him. Taking advantage of his injuries to rob him was about the lowliest thing the driver could have done.

"What about the car?" I asked, fighting to keep my anger contained. "Did you get a look at it?"

"Only as it was driving off, and it was so dark that I couldn't see much."

That stretch of road had no streetlights, so the car's headlights would have been the only illumination.

"I know it was a car, rather than a truck or van," he continued. "Average size and shape. But that's about it."

I could tell that our conversation had sapped him of energy, and I knew we needed to wrap it up soon.

"Maybe the police will find the car's paint chips on your clothes, or maybe they'll be able to narrow down the make of the car from the skid marks."

If there *were* skid marks. We had to hold onto any hope we could. The thought of the driver getting away with what they'd done was too bitter a pill to swallow.

"Maybe," Tommy said, exhaustion weighing down the smile he tried to give us.

Brett noticed that too. "We should let you rest."

"Thanks for coming. And thanks again for finding me."

"Any idea when you'll be discharged?" I asked.

"Tomorrow, probably. My parents will drive me back to Wildwood Cove. Once I'm home, I'll have my tablet and laptop, so I'll stay in touch by email until I get a new phone."

"All right." I kissed him on the forehead. "Get some rest. We'll all be thinking of you."

On our way out of the room, I glanced back. Tommy's eyes had already closed.

I hoped he'd sleep well. After what he'd told us, I knew I wouldn't.

Chapter Ten

I was right about not sleeping well that night. I tossed and turned, my mind going around in circles. Whoever had struck Tommy had to be cold-hearted. No decent person could have hit him, robbed him, and left him there at the side of the road.

Had the driver hit Tommy on purpose, planning to rob him?

That seemed unlikely. There was no guarantee that Tommy would have anything on him worth stealing. I doubted the driver could have seen Tommy's camera, considering how dark it was and the fact that the car approached him from behind. So maybe the decision to steal Tommy's belongings was a spur of the moment one. That didn't change the fact that the thief was heartless and cruel.

My thoughts were so wound up in what happened to Tommy I almost forgot about the murder. That sent a wave of guilt crashing over me. Poor Jane was dead, *murdered*, and I'd hardly spared her a thought all day.

As my mind turned over the events at the museum as well as what had happened to Tommy, the chance of getting any real sleep drifted further out of my grasp.

Eventually, I got out of bed and curled up on the window seat, a blanket wrapped around my shoulders. At least I wouldn't be disturbing Brett's sleep that way. He'd already woken up a couple of times and tried to comfort me.

Sitting by the window and gazing out into the darkness didn't stop my mind from spinning. It was only once I cracked open the window to hear the rhythmical sound of the waves crashing ashore that I finally relaxed. Flapjack hopped up onto the window seat with me and curled up on my lap. I stroked his fur as I listened to the ocean. My thoughts slowed, and my mind grew hazy.

When I crawled back into bed a while later, leaving Flapjack on the window seat, I finally fell asleep. I didn't wake up until Flapjack walked onto my stomach and lay down, purring. Sunlight streamed in through the gap in the curtains, which fluttered slightly in the breeze. I hadn't shut the window when I'd returned to bed, and I could hear the crashing surf and the cry of a seagull.

Brett's side of the bed was empty. No wonder, I realized, when I glanced at the clock on the bedside table. It was nearly nine o'clock. Brett and I were both early risers, and even though The Flip Side was closed on Mondays, I usually got up by seven.

My day got off to a slow start and never really picked up speed. I heard from Tommy in the afternoon via email, which perked me up a little bit. His parents had arrived from Seattle a few hours after Brett and I visited him. At the moment, he was staying with his parents in a ground-floor room at the motel by the Wildwood River. His roommates were in the process of converting a tiny room on the main floor of their house for Tommy to use as a temporary bedroom, so he wouldn't have to take the stairs so much while on crutches. When the room was ready, he'd move back home, and his parents would return to Seattle. He felt bad about the fact that he wouldn't be back at work anytime soon, but I assured him in my reply that we'd manage, although we looked forward to having him back with us.

Losing Tommy temporarily did leave us in a bit of a bind, though I downplayed that in my email. I needed to get busy hiring more staff, now more than ever, so I drafted help-wanted ads that evening and sent them off to the local newspaper, the *Wildwood Cove Weekly*. When I arrived at the pancake house on Wednesday morning, a small stack of newspapers sat waiting for me by the front door. I moved them to the rack inside the restaurant and checked out the one on top. Both the murder and the hit-and-run had made the front page.

First, I read the article about Tommy's accident, hoping for new developments in the case that had made it into the paper. There didn't seem to be any. The article outlined what I already knew and included a couple of quotes from Tommy. In one, he mentioned how grateful he was to Brett and me for finding him. My eyes grew misty as I read the article, mostly because it caused me to relive the moment of discovering Tommy in the ditch.

At the time the paper was printed, the driver still hadn't been identified. I hoped that would change soon, but I knew it likely wouldn't be an easy investigation with so little to go on. Not to mention the fact that the sheriff's department also had a murder to investigate.

I read that article next, but again the paper didn't tell me anything I didn't already know. I flipped through the pages and confirmed that the help-wanted ads for the pancake house were there, letting people know we needed a server and a cook. Hopefully I'd receive some responses soon.

Dropping the newspaper onto the top of the stack, I joined Ivan in the kitchen and helped him with some of his prep work. I'd texted everyone after visiting Tommy, but Ivan still asked after him, and I filled him in on what Tommy had told me. I filled in Leigh as well, once she arrived. We were so relieved that Tommy was safe and would recover from his injuries, but we'd all miss him terribly in the meantime, and not just because of our staffing shortage. Tommy was part of our family, and his easygoing, upbeat personality made him a joy to work with.

Around midmorning, Sienna's mom, Patricia, arrived at The Flip Side with her friend Sue.

"How's Sienna doing?" I asked when Sue headed for the washroom. "I know the news about Tommy really shook her."

Patricia wrapped her hands around her mug of tea. "She's still shaken, but it helped her settle down when she knew you'd visited him and said he was doing as well as could be expected."

"Hopefully she'll have a chance to visit him soon," I said. "Then she can see for herself that he's going to bounce back."

Patricia nodded, but she had a frown on her face.

"Is anything else wrong?" I asked.

Patricia let out a barely perceptible sigh. "Sienna hasn't been herself lately. And it started before Tommy's accident."

"I noticed that the other day," I said. "Do you know why?"

"When I asked her, she said she's just stressed about school and graduation."

"It can be a tough time." I rested the coffee pot on the table. "Final exams and college on the horizon."

"That's true." Her frown hadn't disappeared.

"How are *you* doing?" I asked. "It can't be easy for you either, knowing your only child will be leaving home in a few months."

Patricia managed a weak smile. "I've been trying not to think about it too much, but of course, that's impossible. Over the past eighteen years, Sienna and I haven't been apart for more than a week at a time. I have a feeling she'll handle it far better than I will."

"It'll be an adjustment, for sure, but at least she's not going to be too far away."

Sienna would be attending my alma mater, the University of Washington in Seattle.

"You're right," Patricia said. "I never said anything, but I was a bit worried that she'd set her heart on going somewhere all the way across the country. I'm relieved that's not the case. I'm sure we'll get used to the new normal in time."

"You will," I said as her friend returned to the table.

I took their orders and then left them to chat while I headed for the kitchen.

Shortly before the start of the lunch rush, I emerged from the office to see Winnifred Woodcombe sitting at a table by the window, a cup of coffee in front of her. I checked in with Ivan to make sure he wasn't too swamped at the moment, and then I delivered plates of Thyme for Breakfast Frittata and churro waffles to a middle-aged couple on the far side of the dining room.

On my way back, I paused by Winnifred's table. "Good morning, Mrs. Woodcombe. I'm so glad you stopped by."

She returned my greeting with a smile. "I decided I really shouldn't wait any longer to visit your pancake house. I've been here before, of course, but not since Jimmy passed away. I'm meeting a friend for an early lunch."

"Is there anything else you need while you're waiting?" I asked.

"No, thank you, dear." She tapped her mug. "I'm fine with my cup of coffee." Her smile faded. "I was so sorry to hear about your employee. What a terrible thing for the driver to hit him and leave him lying there in the ditch."

"I don't know how anyone could have done that," I said with a brief flicker of anger at the unknown culprit. "I'm just so thankful that Tommy will recover."

"That's a blessing," Winnifred agreed. "But I don't know what's happening with this town. A hit-and-run *and* a murder!"

"I know. It's terrible. How are you holding up?"

"I'm managing," she said. "It's hard to get the picture of poor Jane out of my head, but I'm doing my best to remember her as she was when she was alive. And while there's no way I could possibly fill her shoes, I hope I'll do a decent job of taking the helm until Nancy Welch returns in a couple of months."

"You're taking over at the museum?"

"I volunteered, and the Board agreed. Of course, it will be better for everyone when Nancy's back in charge. She knows everything about the museum. I'll do my best to hold things together until her return."

"I'm sure you'll do a great job," I said. "Have you had a chance to see the letters Jane wanted to show you?"

Winnifred pursed her lips. "It's a funny thing about that. The police allowed me to enter the museum this morning to see if I could tell if anything was amiss."

I guessed what she was going to say next. "And you couldn't find the letters?"

"Not a single one. Of course, I didn't have a chance to go through the boxes upstairs, so if Jane packed them away again, they could still be up there."

"She told me she was going to keep them in her office," I said. "I saw her lock them away in her desk drawer. And at the time, they still had the ribbon around them."

Winnifred's expression grew puzzled. "I checked every drawer of her desk, even the locked one, but I didn't find any letters. Apparently, Jane's cell phone is missing too. The police haven't been able to locate it."

"That's odd, on both counts," I said. "And too bad about the letters. I was hoping to learn more about them, and I'm sure you were too."

"Very much so," Winnifred agreed.

Her friend showed up then, so I got back to work, even though my mind didn't stray far from thoughts of the letters. As I helped Ivan in the kitchen between serving meals with Leigh, questions swirled around in my head.

Did the presence of the ribbon with Jane's body mean that she'd had the letters out when she was killed? And if the letters were truly missing, had the killer taken them?

I couldn't think of a reason why the person who'd killed Jane would steal some old letters, as interesting as they might be. Maybe Jane had moved the letters to a new location in the museum right before she was killed and didn't bother to leave the ribbon with them. That seemed a more likely explanation. She'd mentioned that she planned to flatten them out. Perhaps that was why she'd moved them. Hopefully they were still at the museum, and Winnifred would find them soon.

By the time I closed The Flip Side in the afternoon, Leigh and I were both worn out. Ivan probably was too, but he didn't show it, aside from allowing me to help him in the kitchen for a short while after closing. Eventually, however, he shooed me out of his domain and insisted that I go home.

I didn't have it in me to argue. Not that arguing with Ivan was something I would normally want to do anyway. Even though I knew he had a heart of gold beneath his scowling and tattooed exterior, I found it hard to withstand his intimidating glare.

I stopped in the office and checked The Flip Side's email account. So far, no one had replied to the help-wanted ads in the paper. Hopefully tomorrow would be a different story.

After shutting down the computer, I grabbed my tote bag and headed out the front door, planning to walk home along the beach. I locked the door and then turned around, nearly crashing into someone who loomed over me. My heart almost stopped.

"Dean?" I took a step back, which left me pressed up against the door. "You startled me."

Dean moved closer, crowding into my personal space. His dark eyes bore into me. "You need to keep your mouth shut." His voice was low and menacing.

My heart hammered in my chest. "Excuse me?"

"I don't need any trouble from the cops. You didn't see me at the museum the other night. Got it?"

I slipped my hand into my tote bag, hoping I could find my phone by touch alone. "You want me to lie to the police?" Somehow, I kept my fear out of my voice.

My hand closed around my phone, and I gripped it like it was a lifeline.

Dean leaned in closer, so his face was mere inches from mine. I smelled stale cigarettes on his breath.

"I want you to keep your mouth shut." He smirked, his eyes cold. "If you don't, you might find out that rats have short lives."

Chapter Eleven

"He threatened you?" Brett halted the motion of the porch swing with his foot. A mixture of anger and concern had clouded his blue eyes as I told him about my encounter with Dean. "What else did he do?"

"Nothing," I assured him. "He walked away."

Brett's frown didn't ease up. "You should tell Ray."

"I left a message for him as soon as I got home." I'd been tempted to phone Brett at the time, but I'd decided to wait until I saw him in person and phoned the sheriff—Brett's uncle Ray—instead, leaving a message for him at his personal number. "I told him about the threat and how we saw Dean at the museum the night before Jane's body was found."

Little did Dean know that I hadn't given him a thought over the past few days. When he threatened me at The Flip Side, he'd reminded me about his shifty behavior when Brett and I had seen him while we were walking Bentley. There was no way I was going to withhold that information from the sheriff, so really, Dean had achieved the opposite of what he'd hoped.

Brett put an arm around me and started the seat swinging again. "I don't want that guy coming near you again."

"Neither do I." I rested my head on his shoulder. "I'll watch out for him, but hopefully he won't bother me anymore."

"If you see him hanging around the pancake house, get Ivan to deal with him," Brett suggested.

"Good idea."

Ivan could scare away just about anyone when he put his mind to it, and even sometimes when he didn't intend to.

"Do you think Dean could have had something to do with Jane's death?" Brett asked as we enjoyed the view of the ocean from our back porch.

Flapjack jumped onto my lap and curled up, purring.

I stroked his orange fur. "I've been wondering about that since he threatened me. He wasn't up to anything good when he was at the museum that night. I'm sure of it. I don't know exactly when Jane died, but it could have been that evening." I shuddered. "What if he killed her right before we saw him? She could have been inside, bleeding on the floor..."

Brett kissed the side of my head. "If that's the way it happened, we had no way of knowing."

He was right, but it still unsettled me to think that we could have run into Jane's killer right after he'd struck her in the head. Even worse was the thought that we could have tried to help Jane if we'd known she was hurt.

The sound of a vehicle crunching along the gravel driveway reached our ears.

"That's probably my dad," Brett said, getting to his feet.

My father-in-law, Frank, was coming over to help Brett work on one of the building façades for Wild West Days. The event would take place mostly at Wildwood Park, and the town was setting up a wild west town of sorts. Volunteers like Brett and his dad were constructing and painting various faces for the different stores and establishments. At the moment, Brett and Frank were working on a façade for the saloon, complete with batwing doors.

I shifted Flapjack onto the seat of the swing, so I could get up. Bentley was sniffing around the logs at the top of the beach, but when a car door slammed, he raced around the house to greet our visitor.

As I stood up, I spotted Sienna down near the water's edge, skipping stones.

"I'll be around to say hi in a few minutes," I told Brett.

I followed him as far as the bottom of the porch steps and then turned the opposite way, heading down to the beach. Sienna was on her own, searching the rocks at the water's edge. As I approached her, she picked one up and flicked it out over the ocean. It skipped across the water four times before sinking out of sight.

The evening sun still had some warmth, and I breathed in the familiar smell of the sun-baked seaweed that clung to the shore.

"Sienna!" I called as I drew closer to her.

She brushed her hair out of her face and turned my way. As long as I'd known her, she'd always had colored streaks in her dark brown hair. At the moment, they were turquoise. She used to have a pierced lip, but a few months ago, she'd removed that silver ring, leaving only the piercings in her ears.

"Hey, Marley." She stuffed her hands in the kangaroo pocket of the white hoodie she wore with her denim shorts and flip-flops.

As had been the case lately, she didn't seem her usual chipper self.

"Everything all right?" I asked her.

"Sure." She didn't move as a wave lapped over her feet.

I almost shivered at the sight. Despite the warm spring weather, the water was still too chilly for me.

"I talked to Tommy today," she said, her face brightening slightly. "Well, not *talk* talked, but online."

"How's he doing today?" I asked. I'd sent him a quick email to check up on him while I was waiting for Brett to arrive home from work, but I hadn't yet received a reply.

"He says he's good. He's moving from the motel to his place today. His parents are heading home in the morning, though they might be back next week sometime. It'll be ages before Tommy can work again, right?"

"It'll be a while," I said. "Doing his job on crutches wouldn't be easy, but I'll make sure he gets his benefits."

Before I'd inherited the pancake house from my cousin Jimmy, he'd set up benefits for The Flip Side's full-time employees. Now I was more glad than ever to have them in place.

"By the time he gets back, I might already be gone." Tears pooled in Sienna's eyes and trickled down her cheeks.

I put an arm around her, surprised by her tears. "What's wrong? Tommy's going to be okay."

She brushed at her cheeks with the back of her hand. "I know, but everything's changing." Another round of tears escaped her eyes.

"Hey." I gave her a squeeze. "Is that why you haven't been yourself lately? Because of all the changes ahead?"

She stared down at her feet. "Kind of. This will sound dumb, but…I'm scared about going away to college."

"That doesn't sound dumb at all."

Her eyes still shone with tears when she raised them to meet mine. "It doesn't?"

"Of course not. It's going to be a big change for you—leaving home, being in a new environment with new people."

She scuffed the toe of one flip-flop in the wet sand. "Most of my friends can't wait to go away. They think Wildwood Cove is too small for them. They'd probably think I'm weird if they knew that I really love it here."

"I can't say what your friends would think, but you're definitely not weird," I assured her. "It's totally normal to feel both those ways. Some kids can't wait for the freedom and excitement of leaving home after high school, but you have a great family, and you've lived in this beautiful town your whole life. I promise you that it's not strange to have reservations about leaving."

"Really?"

I gave her another hug. "Really."

When I pulled back, she still looked sad, but her eyes were free of tears.

"Have you told your mom about this?" I asked.

She shrugged. "I just told her I'm stressed about school and stuff. I don't want her to know I'm scared because then she'll worry."

"She already knows something's not quite right. I think you'd both feel better if you talked to her about it."

Sienna nodded glumly. "Maybe." She stared out over the ocean. "Do you think I'll be able to come home? After I'm finished with college, I mean."

"Sure," I said, "if that's what you want. Some professions might require you to live elsewhere, but there are lots of things you can do here in Wildwood Cove. Do you have any idea what you want to do after college?"

"Maybe," she said again. She bit down on her lower lip. "Thanks, Marley."

I sensed she'd been about to say something else but changed her mind. I didn't push her to tell me.

"You're welcome," I said. "You can talk to me anytime about anything, okay?"

She managed a small smile when she nodded. A split second later, her eyes brightened. "What we *should* be talking about is the murder. We need to solve it!"

It didn't surprise me that she'd had that thought. Sienna was almost as good as me at getting involved in murder investigations. Although I was certain that "good" was not a word the sheriff would have used.

"Who are your suspects?" Sienna asked.

"Suspect. Singular," I said. "Probably because I haven't thought much about it. I've had so much else on my mind."

Sienna hooked her arm through mine as we walked slowly along the beach in the direction of her house. Bentley appeared, bounding along beside us.

"I get that," Sienna said, "but now that we know Tommy's okay, we should put our heads together. Who's your one and only suspect?"

"Dean Vaccarino, but you have to promise me you won't go anywhere near him." I told her how Dean had threatened me earlier in the day. "Even if he's not the killer, he's dangerous."

"Don't worry. I'll steer clear of him." When I shot a sidelong glance her way, she added, "I promise."

I stopped short and smacked a palm to my forehead. "I can't believe it."

"What?" Sienna asked.

"I actually have two suspects, but I'd forgotten about the other one." Apparently, I'd been even more distracted than I'd thought in recent days.

"Who is it?"

"Angus Achenbach."

"I don't know him," Sienna said with a hint of disappointment.

"He's the nephew of the woman who bequeathed her house to the museum."

"Oh, okay. Now I know who you're talking about. The guy who had a tantrum at The Flip Side. Wasn't he ticked off that he didn't inherit the house?"

"More than ticked off," I said as we resumed walking. "Apparently, he took the matter to court and lost, but he still came by the museum and accused Jane of influencing his aunt when she was making her will. His temper's a bit frightening."

"Definitely a suspect, then," Sienna agreed.

And one I needed to tell Ray about.

Another memory surfaced. "And there was a strange moment between Jane and Evangeline Oldershaw-Hobbs."

"Evangeline is super-rich," Sienna said. "You know about her family's candy company, right?"

I nodded. "Oldershaw Confections. Evangeline donated money to cover the cost of the museum's reopening party. She and Jane were butting heads over organizing the event."

"That doesn't seem like enough of a reason to kill someone."

"It doesn't," I agreed. "But I overheard Jane say something strange to Evangeline. It sounded like a threat. She said she knew something about Evangeline. When Jane brought it up, Evangeline went as pale as a ghost."

Sienna considered that. "So, Evangeline might have wanted to keep Jane quiet. To keep some dark secret from coming to light."

"It's possible," I said. "I have trouble picturing Evangeline killing someone, though. I don't think she'd want to risk getting blood on her designer clothes."

We drew to a stop, now in line with Sienna's house, a yellow and white Victorian.

She surprised me by changing the subject. "Has anyone applied for the job postings?"

"Not yet," I said with a sigh. "Hopefully soon, otherwise we're going to be run off our feet."

She looked thoughtful. "Maybe Logan can help out in the kitchen temporarily."

"You think he'd be interested?"

Logan was a friend of Sienna's and my next-door neighbor. He planned to attend culinary school in the fall.

Sienna shrugged. "He might be. He worked at a restaurant in Port Townsend last summer. He'd only be available on weekends until school's out, though."

"We're busiest on the weekends, so that would still help," I said.

"I'll text him, and if he's interested, I'll tell him to get in touch with you." Sienna already had her phone out.

"Perfect. Thank you, Sienna."

"Thank *you*. You know, for talking with me."

I gave her a quick hug. "Any time."

She took a couple of steps up the beach but then glanced back over her shoulder. "Don't forget to do some snooping," she called with a mischievous smile.

"I prefer to call it sleuthing," I called back.

"Potayto potahto," she said in a sing-song voice. Then she waved and ran up the beach to her house.

I didn't mind letting her have the last word. I was just happy to see her smiling again.

Chapter Twelve

Ray showed up at The Flip Side in his sheriff's uniform the following morning. I'd left another message for him after talking to Sienna, telling him about Angus Achenbach's visit to the museum and Jane's threat to Evangeline.

"Could we talk for a moment?" he asked when I greeted him by the front door.

I glanced around the crowded dining room. I didn't want to leave Leigh working on her own for too long, but I also didn't want to decline Ray's request.

"Sure," I said. "Let's go to the office. Would you like some coffee?"

"That's all right, thanks." He removed his hat and tucked it under his arm. "I'll only keep you a minute or two."

"Have you found the driver who hit Tommy?" I asked as I led the way into the office.

"Not yet, but we're still working on it."

"Have you got any leads?" Even before I asked the question, I knew what his response would be.

The corners of his mouth twitched, almost turning up into a smile. "You know I can't talk about an ongoing investigation, Marley."

Exactly as I'd expected.

"I know." I leaned against the desk. "But it's hard knowing that the driver is still out there, enjoying their freedom after what they did to Tommy."

"I understand that," Ray said. "I promise you that my deputies and I are determined to solve the case."

"I don't doubt that for a second," I assured him. "Are you here about the messages I left for you yesterday?"

"Particularly the first one."

That was the one about Dean.

"Do you think Dean could have killed Jane?" I asked.

"I don't like that he threatened you."

I didn't fail to notice that he hadn't answered my question.

"I don't like it either," I said. "He creeps me out."

"He's got a record, Marley, and he's got a history of violent behavior."

That didn't surprise me, but hearing it from Ray sent a shiver down my back.

"Do you think he'll try to hurt me?" I couldn't keep the alarm out of my voice.

"He might be content with the threat he already delivered, but I want you to be extra vigilant, just in case. If he comes near you again, call 911."

"I will," I promised.

Ray asked me a few questions about my encounters with Dean and Angus and what I'd overheard between Jane and Evangeline. Then he took his leave, but not before I put a maple pecan sticky roll into a paper bag so he could take it with him.

I got back to work after Ray left, but whenever I wasn't chatting with customers or taking orders, my thoughts zipped back to Dean. His history of violence made him a strong murder suspect in my mind. It wasn't hard for me to picture him grabbing the antique clothes iron and smashing it into Jane's head. In fact, I could picture it so clearly that my stomach twisted into a knot.

What wasn't so clear was his possible motive. While I volunteered at the museum, I never witnessed any arguments or altercations between Dean and Jane. Of course, there were probably times when Dean was there when I wasn't. Still, I'd never detected any animosity or tension between them.

Brett and I had caught Dean skulking around the museum the night before Winnifred found Jane's body. Whatever his reason for being at the museum that evening, I didn't think it was an honorable one. Maybe Jane had interrupted whatever he'd shown up to do. There was a good chance Dean thought the museum would be empty at that time of day. Jane's presence could have surprised him, and if she'd caught him in the act of... *something,* maybe he'd decided to silence her.

That theory wasn't much more than speculation, though. I needed to find out more about Dean and why he might have been at the museum that evening if I wanted to figure out if my theory held any water. The problem was that I didn't want to go anywhere near Dean. Anything I could dig up about him would have to come either from the Internet or people who knew him.

I'd still have to be careful. I didn't want anyone reporting back to Dean that I suspected him of killing Jane. Even if he wasn't the murderer, I didn't doubt that such information would put me in danger.

I also needed to find out more about Angus Achenbach. He was angry enough to lash out at Jane physically. What I needed to know was whether he had the opportunity to commit the crime.

The same was true with Evangeline. She'd hosted the charity gala that night, but since I didn't know exactly when Jane was killed, I couldn't say if the gala provided Evangeline with an alibi or not. I still had trouble picturing Evangeline getting her hands dirty by killing someone, but I couldn't discount her entirely. Maybe she'd hired someone to murder Jane. That seemed unlikely as well. A hired killer probably would have taken a weapon to the museum rather than grabbing whatever was on hand. I figured the murder probably wasn't planned in advance.

As the lunch rush dwindled down, a welcome distraction arrived at the pancake house in the form of my friend Lisa Morales. When I saw her come in the door, I rushed over to greet her with a hug.

"I was going to head home for lunch," she said as she returned my hug, "but I had a sudden craving for Ivan's mocha mascarpone crêpes."

"Can't Ivan make crêpes for you anytime?" I asked as she took a seat at a free table.

Lisa and Ivan had been dating for a while now.

"He could," she said, tucking her wavy, dark hair behind her ear, "but this way I get to visit you."

I smiled. "I like your reasoning."

I relayed Lisa's order to Ivan and returned with the coffee pot. I glanced around and decided I could spare a few minutes to sit and chat.

"How have you been?" I asked. Although we exchanged text messages regularly, I hadn't seen my friend face-to-face in nearly a week.

"I've been fine, but how about you? Are you feeling better now that Tommy's safe?"

"Much better." I'd filled her in on that story during one of our text exchanges. "And if I can find a new server and someone to help Ivan in the kitchen, things should be good."

"You'll find someone soon."

"I hope so. I know it's hard for Ivan to take on the whole workload himself. How is he handling it?" I knew Ivan would never complain to me, even if things were getting to be too much.

"He's mostly been concerned about Tommy. I think he's finding work more tiring than usual, but he can handle it for the time being." She frowned, her dark eyes growing troubled.

"What is it?" I asked, worried.

She hesitated before speaking again. "It's probably nothing."

"But?" I prodded.

"The other day, I asked Ivan if he wanted to have dinner together after I'd finished work. He said he couldn't because he needed to go to Port Angeles."

"Okay." I didn't see why any of that would trouble her.

"He didn't say *why* he was going. Normally he'd tell me. This time he seemed...a bit mysterious."

"Did you ask him why he was going?"

"No," Lisa said. "I had a feeling he didn't want to tell me, so I didn't push."

"But now you're worrying about it."

"I can't help but wonder if he was going to the doctor or the hospital. What if something's wrong and he hasn't said anything because he doesn't want to frighten me?"

"Is this the first time he's gone somewhere without telling you why?" I asked.

"Yes."

"Then it's probably nothing to get worked up about." I reached across the table and squeezed her hand. "If you're really concerned, ask him about it."

"I don't want him to think I don't trust him because I do."

"I think he knows that."

She sighed. "I'll try to let it go. If it happens again, then I'll ask him and see what he says."

"I'm sure it's nothing you need to worry about," I said, hoping that was true.

"You're probably right." She didn't sound entirely convinced, but she also didn't look quite as troubled as before. She rested her arms on the table, leaning in closer and lowering her voice as she changed the subject. "How's your murder investigation coming along?"

"I haven't made much progress, and I feel a bit guilty about that," I confessed. "I was so concerned about Tommy that I didn't give Jane's murder much thought until yesterday."

"Don't feel guilty," Lisa said. "That's totally understandable." She regarded me closely. "But now that you *have* started thinking about it?"

I spoke quietly so that no one would overhear me. "I have a few suspects. Do you know Dean Vaccarino or Angus Achenbach? They're at the top of my list."

"I know who they are, but that's about it." Lisa took a sip of coffee. "We don't move in the same circles."

"Thank goodness for that. Neither one is a nice guy." I thought back over everything I'd heard or witnessed in the past week or two. "How about Adya Banerjee? Do you know her?"

"She's in the Zumba class I've been taking on Tuesday evenings." Lisa dropped her voice to a whisper. "You think *Adya* could be a killer?"

"I'm not sure," I said, "but I saw her at the grocery store last week. She was on her phone, complaining to someone about Jane."

"Right. They both work at the community center." Lisa frowned. "Well, *worked*, in Jane's case."

A bell dinged in the kitchen. I told Lisa I'd be right back and hurried to the pass-through window to fetch her crêpes.

My stomach grumbled as I set the plate in front of her. I hadn't yet had a chance to eat lunch myself.

Lisa must have heard my stomach's complaint. She pointed her fork at me. "You should grab something for yourself."

The pancake house would close for the day in about half an hour, and the crowd of diners had thinned considerably. I decided I could take Lisa's advice, so I made another quick trip to the kitchen, returning with a slice of the frittata and a fruit salad for myself.

Thyme for Breakfast Frittata featured zucchini, mushrooms, and bell peppers, as well as feta cheese, dill, and thyme. Ivan cut it into generous slices, and it made for a delicious and satisfying meal.

"I was going to say that I think Adya is harmless," Lisa said once I was sitting down again, "but she did gain from Jane's death."

"How so?" I asked before taking a bite of my food.

"She got Jane's job at the community center."

"Did she?" That was interesting. I speared a piece of cantaloupe with my fork. "That's one of the things Adya was complaining about when I saw her at the grocery store. She thought the promotion should have been hers."

Lisa picked up her coffee mug and met my gaze. "And now it is."

Chapter Thirteen

Lisa didn't stay at The Flip Side much longer. She finished up her crêpes and then stopped by the kitchen to see Ivan. Soon after, she returned to her job at a lawyer's office on Main Street.

I now had three solid suspects and a possible fourth in Evangeline Oldershaw-Hobbs. Maybe I even had five suspects. I considered whether Frankie Zhou deserved a closer look, but I soon discounted the idea. For the moment, anyway. I didn't think he would have wanted to harm Jane.

Impatience hummed through my bloodstream. I'd told Lisa that I felt guilty about not giving much thought to Jane's murder, and that was true, but I also felt guilty for not doing much to try and *solve* her murder. It wasn't my job, of course, but normally mysteries attracted me like a powerful magnet, and I couldn't stop digging until I found the answers I was looking for. With Jane's murder, I'd been too distracted to do much sleuthing, but she deserved justice, and if there was anything I could do to help, I wanted to do it.

As I closed up the pancake house at two o'clock, I resolved to start my investigation that very afternoon. My plans got derailed almost right away. I was finishing up the last of the cleaning in the dining room when someone knocked on the front door.

The interruption disappointed me until I recognized Logan on the other side of the glass. I hurried over to let him inside.

"Logan, thanks for coming by," I said as I opened the door for him. "I gather Sienna talked to you?"

Logan pushed his sandy blond hair off his forehead. "She said you could use some help in the kitchen."

"That's right. Ivan's assistant is injured, and I was hoping to hire more staff even before that happened. I take it you're interested?" I figured that was a safe assumption since he'd shown up at The Flip Side.

"Definitely." He held up his phone. "I've got a copy of my resume. You can look at it on my phone, or I can email it to you."

"Emailing it would be great." I rattled off The Flip Side's address. "Do you have some time right now?"

"Sure," he said as he tapped his phone, sending the email. "I'm free for the rest of the day."

"Great. Do you know Ivan Kaminski?"

"I know he's your head chef, and he was one of the judges at the amateur chef competition last spring." Logan had competed in that event. "I've never actually met him, though."

"Why don't we change that right now?"

I led the way into the kitchen. Ivan was cleaning the grill, but he looked up when the door swung open.

"Ivan, this is Logan Teeves. Logan, Ivan Kaminski."

Ivan wiped his hands on a towel before holding one out to Logan.

"Nice to meet you, chef," Logan said when he shook Ivan's offered hand.

"Could you give Logan a quick rundown of how you do things here?" I asked Ivan.

He gave a curt nod. I hoped Ivan's gruff ways wouldn't put off Logan.

"Thank you," I said. "I'll leave you to it, then. I'll be in the office."

I headed out of the kitchen, listening as Ivan's deep voice faded to a rumble on my way down the hall.

In the office, I accessed The Flip Side's email account and scanned Logan's resume. I knew he was a good kid, and, as Sienna had told me, he already had experience working in a restaurant. As far as I was concerned, he could start work at the pancake house on the coming weekend, but I wouldn't make that decision official until Ivan had a chance to weigh in. He was the one who'd be working closest with Logan.

I rejoined Ivan and Logan in the kitchen, and Logan left a short while later after I promised to be in touch with him about the job soon.

"So?" I said to Ivan once we were alone. "What do you think?"

"He'll do," Ivan said as he hung pots on their hooks above the large island.

"That's all?" I wasn't sure if he was just being Ivan, or if he wasn't all that impressed with Logan.

"He'll do well," Ivan amended.

The answer wasn't any less brusque, but this time I detected a hint of approval in Ivan's expression.

Relief eased the tension that had gathered in my shoulders.

"Thank goodness," I said. "Hopefully, he can start on Saturday. And I have more good news."

"About the pancake house?" Ivan guessed.

I nodded. "When I checked The Flip Side's email to download Logan's resume, I found two responses to our job postings, one for the kitchen opening and one for the server position."

Ivan hung the final pot. "Everything will work out fine."

Now that things were finally in motion, I could cautiously agree with him.

Before leaving the pancake house, I phoned Logan and officially offered him a part-time job at The Flip Side. He accepted readily, allowing me to breathe easier. When I left the restaurant, I even had a spring in my step. Lately, I'd had a lot of plans for the future formulating in my head. At times I found it overwhelming to think about all the possibilities that lay ahead of me, but now that I was putting some of the plans into motion, I felt more in control, more relaxed.

I really wanted to talk to Brett, though. In between thoughts of Tommy's accident, Jane's murder, the missing letters, and pancake house business, I'd revisited the conversation I'd had with Sienna the night before. Listening to her voice her fears about the changes she faced in the near future had given me some new insight into things I'd been thinking about in recent weeks. Things I really wanted to talk to Brett about.

He wouldn't be home from work for another couple of hours, so I decided to kill some time by heading into town to pick up some bread at the bakery. When I reached Wildwood Road, I paused to wait for a couple of cars to drive by. I was about to cross when another vehicle came zooming along at high speed. I quickly hopped back onto the grassy verge as a flashy red convertible shot by with a toot of its horn and a wave from the driver.

By the time I registered that it was Richard and Evangeline in the Ferrari convertible, the car had already disappeared around a bend in the road. Richard had been driving way too fast, but that wasn't unusual. I remembered what Brett had said about the couple enjoying the attention they got from speeding around town in such an expensive car. I didn't doubt that was true.

It wouldn't have surprised me if Richard had been the one to run Tommy down, considering his careless driving, but the Ferrari didn't match the description Tommy had provided of the suspect vehicle.

Pushing thoughts of Richard and Evangeline aside, I crossed the now-clear street and resumed my journey to Marielle's Bakery. When I arrived, there was one customer at the counter and two others seated at one of the small round tables off to the side, enjoying coffee and some freshly baked goodies. Marielle was busy serving the woman ahead of me, but she sent me a quick smile, which I returned. I realized a second later that the customer in front of me was Winnifred Woodcombe.

When Winnifred had paid for her purchases, I spoke to her.

"Good afternoon, Mrs. Woodcombe," I said as she picked up her bag of bread and croissants.

"Marley," she said with a smile as she faced me. "It's nice to see you again."

"You too," I returned.

"Do you have a moment to talk after you place your order?" she asked.

"Sure," I said, my curiosity awakening.

"I'll wait over here then." She nodded at one of the vacant tables.

I chatted with Marielle as she fetched me a loaf of brown bread and placed half a dozen of her scrumptious butter tarts in a small box. On the spur of the moment, I asked her to add two croissants to my order. Seeing Winnifred buying some had given me a sudden craving.

After I'd paid for my purchases, I joined Winnifred at the table by the window. She'd leaned her silver-handled cane against the wall. Now that I saw it up close, I realized the handle was in the shape of an eagle's head.

"I wanted to chat with you," she said, drawing my attention away from her cane, "because when we last spoke, you seemed so interested in the letters Jane found."

I almost cringed. "I'm sorry. I didn't mean to be nosy."

"Oh, no, dear." Winnifred waved off my concern. "You weren't at all. I take a great interest in things from the past myself, whether they're related to my family or not."

I relaxed into my seat, relieved that my curiosity hadn't annoyed her. "Did Jane tell you she thought the letters were written by Jack O'Malley?"

"She did. If she was right, that makes the finding all the more exciting. I can't even imagine which one of my ancestors he could have been writing to."

"I didn't know about Jack O'Malley before," I admitted, "but he sounds like an interesting character."

"He certainly was. He was a thief—and a very successful one—but also a charming and handsome fellow, by all accounts."

"I'd like to learn more about him," I said. "I love stories from the past."

"We have that in common. Which is why I wanted to invite you to come with me to visit my cousin Dolly this afternoon. You see, Dolly is the one who donated the box that the letters were in. Jane told me as much over the phone before her death."

I sat up straighter. "So Dolly might know what was in the letters?"

"That's what I'm hoping. Although Dolly has always been a bit... scatterbrained, so we mustn't get our hopes up too high."

I tried to rein mine in, but they'd already taken off toward the sky. "I'd love to go with you."

"Wonderful," she said with a smile. "Are you free right now?"

"Absolutely."

Winnifred pushed back her chair. "Then let's go pay Dolly a visit."

* * * *

Dolly Maxwell lived in a cute, powder blue Victorian not far from Main Street. White wicker furniture sat on the front porch, and wind chimes tinkled in the gentle breeze. Winnifred rapped on the front door with the head of her cane and opened the mail slot.

"Dolly, it's Winnifred," she called out.

"Coming," a thin voice replied from somewhere within the house.

"She doesn't move as fast as she used to," Winnifred said to me as we waited on the porch.

Several seconds later, the lock turned, and the door opened.

Although the two elderly women were cousins, I couldn't see much in the way of a family resemblance. While Winnifred was tall, with blue eyes, straight hair, and a regal bearing, Dolly couldn't have been much taller than five feet. Her eyes were brown, and she had a head of curly gray hair. I guessed that Dolly was in her eighties, a few years older than Winnifred.

"Come on in, Winnie." Dolly moved back so she could open the door wider. "I see you've brought a friend."

"This is Marley," Winnifred said as she stepped over the threshold. "She owns the local pancake house."

I said hello and followed Winnifred into the foyer.

Dolly shut the door. "My Harold used to make the most delicious pancakes." She slowly made her way into the living room to the left of the foyer. "Come in, come in. Make yourselves comfortable. Shall I make tea?"

"Leave that to me." Winnifred leaned her cane against the wall and strode toward the back of the house.

Dolly sat down in an armchair and peered at me through the lenses of her round, wire-rimmed spectacles. "Do sit down, dear. Are you Frances Whittle's granddaughter?"

I sat on a pale peach loveseat. "No, ma'am. No relation."

"Who's are you?"

"I'm not from Wildwood Cove originally," I said. "I moved here from Seattle a couple of years ago. Jimmy Coulson was my grandmother's cousin, and I'm married to Brett Collins."

Dolly smiled. "I remember Jimmy. Always a fun fellow." Her gaze became unfocused. "Collins...that rings a bell."

"Brett's parents are Frank and Elaine Collins. Sheriff Ray Georgeson is his uncle."

"Ah." Dolly nodded. "The sheriff is a good man. My Harold thought of running for sheriff at one time. Unfortunately, his ticker was never all that sound. It took him away from me far too soon."

"I'm so sorry," I said.

"I'll have the tea ready in a moment," Winnifred called out from the kitchen.

I jumped up. "Is there anything I can help with?"

Winnifred appeared carrying a tray laden with a teapot, cups and saucers, and cream and sugar. I quickly freed her of the burden.

"Thank you, Marley," Winnifred said. "Just set it on the coffee table."

I did as she requested. Winnifred pulled up a straight-backed chair and poured the tea. When we all had a cup in hand, with cream and sugar added, we got down to the reason for our visit.

"Marley and I would like to know more about the letters you donated to the museum," Winnifred told her cousin.

"I donated letters to the museum?" Dolly took a sip of her tea. "How lovely."

I wasn't sure if she was referring to the donation or the tea.

"You donated a box full of papers several months ago," Winnifred reminded her. "There was a stack of letters, tied with a ribbon. Jane Fassbender believed they were written by Jack O'Malley."

"Jack?" Dolly repeated vaguely. "Is that the same Jack who used to tug on your pigtails?"

"That was Jack Haversmith. Jack O'Malley lived before our time. You remember, he's more commonly known as the Jack of Diamonds. The thief."

Dolly smiled. "The Jack of Diamonds. There are some great stories about him."

"Likely with a liberal dose of fiction mixed in with the facts," Winnifred said, "but, yes, we did enjoy those stories as youngsters." Winnifred took a drink of her tea and then set the cup back on the saucer resting on her lap. "Do you know why you would have had letters from the Jack of Diamonds?"

"Dear heavens," Dolly said. "I have no idea."

My hopes of finding out more about the letters withered away. Dolly was a sweet old woman, but it didn't seem like her memory was sharp enough to help us.

If Winnifred was exasperated with her cousin, she didn't let on. "Where did you find the box that you donated?" she asked.

"Hmmm." Dolly thought over the question while sipping at her tea. "The attic. Krista was cleaning up there and brought it down one day. She thought the people at the museum might find the papers interesting, and I certainly had no use for them."

"Krista is Dolly's granddaughter," Winnifred said for my benefit.

"Did you read the letters before the box was donated?" I asked Dolly, my hopes fighting to resurface.

"Oh no. My eyesight isn't great, I'm afraid. I have to get the large print books out of the library. Anything else is simply too small for me to make out."

Winnifred let out a small sigh. It was the first sign of any disappointment on her part. "Do you remember where the box came from in the first place?"

"Goodness." Dolly took a moment to think. "I don't know. The attic hadn't been cleaned out in decades. Maybe generations. It could have been sitting up there since before I was born."

"This is the house Dolly grew up in," Winnifred said to me.

Dolly smiled. "And my mother and Winnie's father before me." Her smile faded. "I'm sorry I'm not more helpful."

"Don't worry about it," Winnifred said.

We finished our tea while chatting about unrelated topics. I kept my disappointment hidden, but when I parted ways with Winnifred on the front porch a while later, I wondered if we would ever know the contents of the missing letters.

Chapter Fourteen

After closing The Flip Side the next day, I put two leftover sticky rolls in a paper bag, and Ivan cooked up a stack of bacon cheddar waffles, which I then placed in a take-out box, along with smaller containers of butter and maple syrup. Armed with the food, I set off on the short walk across town to visit Tommy.

As I walked along Wildwood Road, a dark blue car approached. The driver slowed down and waved at me. It took half a second for me to realize that the driver was Frankie Zhou. I'd only ever seen him driving the white cube truck he'd used to help move the museum's furniture. I'd heard it belonged to his family's small moving company.

I waved back as the car picked up speed again, but my feet had become rooted to the spot. Right before Frankie had captured my attention by waving, I'd noticed a good-sized dent in the front bumper of his vehicle. Now my mind was spinning. I'd discounted Frankie as a murder suspect, but could he be the one who'd hit Tommy and left him at the side of the road?

Another car sped past me, pulling me out of my thoughts, at least enough to get me walking again. When I arrived at Tommy's place a few minutes later, the image of Frankie's dented bumper was still imprinted on my mind.

I knocked on the front door and heard Tommy call out, "Coming!"

Several seconds passed. I heard some shuffling noises, and a moment later, Tommy opened the door, bringing a smile to my face.

"You're looking better," I remarked.

He laughed but cut off abruptly with a wince. "I'm pretty sure I could get hired as an extra on a horror movie with this face."

The bruising on his left cheekbone had changed from blue-black to greenish-yellow.

"I still think you're looking better," I assured him. "Definitely more alert."

"That much I'll agree with." He slowly backed up on his crutches so I could enter the house.

"You're getting around on those, okay?" I asked with a nod at the crutches.

"I'm more of a tortoise than a hare these days, but I'm managing. Come on in."

I shut the front door and followed as he made his way carefully into the living room.

"I've brought gifts," I said as Tommy lowered himself into an armchair and eased his broken leg up onto a footstool.

He eyed the packages I'd brought, his expression hopeful. "Of the edible variety?"

"Of course," I said. "The waffles are probably cold by now, though."

His eyes lit up. "Bacon cheddar waffles?"

"Ivan said they're your favorite."

Tommy grinned. "The man knows his stuff."

"Do you have a microwave?" I asked.

"It's the only kitchen appliance my roommates know how to use. Well, that and the coffeemaker."

"I'll heat them up then." I headed toward the kitchen at the back of the house. "Where do I find a plate?"

"In the cupboard to the left of the sink," Tommy called out.

I found a clean plate easily, which was fortunate, considering how many dirty ones were stacked haphazardly in the sink. The kitchen was actually tidier than I'd expected, knowing as I did that four guys in their twenties lived in the house.

"What about cutlery?" I called over my shoulder.

"The drawer to the right of the stove."

I grabbed a knife and fork and tipped the waffles from the take-out container onto the plate. After zapping the waffles in the microwave, I added the small cups of butter and maple syrup to the plate and carried it all back to Tommy in the living room.

"Can I get you anything to drink?" I asked as I handed him the plate.

"I wouldn't say no to an orange crush. Grab one for yourself too, if you want."

I fetched two cans of soda from the fridge and returned to the living room.

"You're the best, Marley," Tommy said as I gave him one of the cans. He set it on the small table next to his chair and started spreading butter over the waffles. "I didn't eat much for a couple of days after the accident, but my appetite has come back with a vengeance."

I sank down on the couch across from him. "I'm glad to hear that. I also brought you two sticky buns."

"You're spoiling me."

"Hardly," I said, popping open my can of orange crush. "It's the least I can do."

Tommy poured the maple syrup over his waffles. "Help yourself to one of the sticky buns."

"That's okay, thanks. I ate not too long ago, and I brought them for you."

"I'll have to hide them," Tommy said after enjoying a large bite of his waffles. "They won't be safe once my roommates get home."

"Will there be any left by the time they get home?" I asked with a smile.

"Good point. It's not likely."

"Is Ray keeping you informed about the hit-and-run investigation?" I asked once Tommy had eaten a few more bites. "Has there been any progress?"

"He called this morning, actually. A guy was out walking his dog yesterday and found my wallet and phone. Lucky for me, he turned them in to the sheriff's office."

"That's good news," I said. "Is your phone still in working order?"

"Sheriff Georgeson said it seemed to be. I guess I'll find out for sure once I get it back. He said he'd bring it by this evening on his way home."

The sheriff's office was located in Port Angeles, but Ray and his wife lived in Wildwood Cove.

"What about your wallet?" I asked. "Was it cleaned out?"

Tommy shook his head as he swallowed. "That's the weird thing. The cash is gone—just forty bucks, so it's not a huge deal—but my credit cards are still there. Unfortunately," he added, his face falling, "my camera is still missing."

"I'm sorry." I knew how much his camera meant to him, and I was sure it was worth a pretty penny.

"I wish whoever it was had taken my phone instead of my camera," Tommy said morosely before digging into his waffles again.

"It's odd that the driver only kept the cash and camera," I said. "But they probably weren't a seasoned thief, and there's a good chance they weren't thinking clearly after hitting you."

Tommy shrugged. "I don't know what to make of it. I'd like to hope that there's still a chance of getting my camera back, but I don't think it would be a good idea to hold my breath."

Unfortunately, I had to agree with him.

Tommy had already polished off the waffles, so I took his plate and added it to the stack in the sink.

"Did Ray say where the dog walker found your phone and wallet?" I asked when I'd returned to the couch.

"In some bushes at the side of Wildwood Road, not far from where it joins up with the highway."

"So the driver must have stopped and tossed out your phone and wallet a couple of minutes after leaving the scene." I had to swallow back a wave of emotion when I thought about the driver leaving Tommy lying injured in the ditch. "Is Ray any closer to figuring out the identity of the driver?"

"I don't think so. There's not much to go on. I'll be surprised if the driver ever gets tracked down."

I wasn't sure if I should say anything more on the subject or not. My uncertainty must have shown on my face.

"What's up?" Tommy asked.

I played with the tab on the top of my soda can. "The car that hit you… could it have been a Ferrari convertible?"

"No, I don't think so. It wasn't the right shape."

That was the answer I'd expected.

"Could it have been a two-door, dark blue sedan?" I asked.

"It could have," Tommy said slowly. "Why?"

"I don't know if it means anything, but there's this guy who's been helping out at the museum a lot lately. On my way over here, I saw him in his car—dark blue, two doors—and there was a dent in the front bumper."

"So, you think this guy could be the one who hit me?"

"It's a possibility," I said. "I'll report it to Ray, and he can figure that out."

Tommy ran a hand through his short dark hair. "So maybe there is a chance the driver will be identified. Did you get the plate number?"

"No, but I recognized the driver," I said. "I don't want to get your hopes up too much, but I wanted to check and see if you thought it was possible."

"Don't worry," he assured me. "My hopes aren't flying off in any direction. Who's the driver you saw?"

"His name is Frankie Zhou. He's in his late twenties, and…" I trailed off as Tommy shook his head.

"No way. I know Frankie. He's not the guy who hit me."

"How can you be sure?" I asked. "I thought you didn't get a good look at the driver."

"I didn't, but I know Frankie from the skate park. He's a good guy. If he'd hit me—or anyone—with his car, he wouldn't have taken off. And he wouldn't have robbed me."

Tommy seemed so certain that I knew I wouldn't be able to dissuade him, and I didn't try. As far as I knew, he could be right. There might be a perfectly innocent explanation for how Frankie got that dent in his bumper. At the same time, it was possible that Frankie had accidentally hit Tommy and then acted out of character because he'd panicked. It wasn't for me to decide whether Frankie should be arrested for the crime, but I did feel I had a duty to tell Ray what I'd seen. He'd take the matter from there.

"You're probably right," I said, hoping that was the case.

Frankie seemed like a nice guy. Even though I didn't know him well, I didn't want him to be the guilty party.

Tommy took a long drink of his orange crush before setting the can on the table next to his chair. "I'm preparing myself for the possibility that the driver will never be found. I think that's the most likely scenario."

It probably was, though that thought didn't sit well with me. The driver should have to pay for his or her crimes, and Tommy deserved both closure and justice.

I didn't voice those thoughts. "The important thing is that you'll be okay," I said instead.

Tommy grinned. "I'm pretty good at bouncing back."

I returned his smile. "Thank goodness."

"Tell me about the murder case," Tommy requested. "I'm sure you've got some theories."

"I do, but I don't know enough to finger the culprit yet."

I told him about my suspects and the information I'd gathered.

"Do you know anything about Angus Achenbach?" I asked after filling him in.

"Never heard of him before," Tommy said.

"I hadn't either, until recently."

Soon we turned the conversation to The Flip Side. After an hour had passed since my arrival, I decided to head out. Tommy seemed happy to have company, but I could tell he was getting tired. It couldn't be easy dealing with all those broken bones, no matter how well he'd bounced back.

"You don't need to get up," I said after I'd taken our empty drink cans to the kitchen. "I can show myself out."

"Nah." Tommy eased out of the chair and grabbed his crutches. "I'm going to lie down for a bit, and the front door is on the way."

He followed me out to the foyer.

"I'll keep in touch," I said as I opened the front door. "Maybe all of us from The Flip Side can get together sometime soon."

"That would be awesome," Tommy said. "I miss everyone already. Sienna is coming over tomorrow, but I'd love to hang out with all of you."

"We'll make it happen," I promised.

After exchanging a few more words, I set off for home, my enjoyment of the warm spring weather marred only by thoughts of Frankie's dented bumper and what it might mean. When I turned a corner a few minutes later, Jane's murder elbowed its way to the front of my mind.

Adya Banerjee stood out front of a white Victorian with a for sale sign on the lawn. I recognized the blond woman with her too. Chantel Lefevre was a local real estate agent and not exactly one of my favorite people. I'd met her shortly after my cousin Jimmy had died.

As I drew closer, I caught a snippet of the women's conversation.

"I'll call the seller's agent, and we'll get the offer in before the end of the day," Chantel said.

Adya thanked her, and they went their separate ways, Chantel heading for her banana yellow sports car and Adya climbing into a red, four-door sedan.

As the two women drove off, I realized that I'd slowed almost to a stop.

Lisa had mentioned that Adya had taken over Jane's position at the community center after the murder. There was a good chance that the promotion had come with a pay raise. Was that why Adya was now putting an offer on a house?

Maybe the real estate dealings had no significance, but what I'd overheard had reminded me that I needed to get to work on narrowing down my suspect list.

Chapter Fifteen

I called Ray while walking home. Often when I phoned him, I ended up having to leave a message, but this time he picked up. I told him about the dented bumper on the car I'd seen Frankie driving, and he promised he would look into it. I asked him if he thought it was strange how the driver who'd hit Tommy hadn't tossed the camera along with the phone and wallet—or at least not in the same place—but he wasn't willing to comment. That didn't surprise me. He had an understandable habit of remaining tight-lipped about his investigations. That didn't always stop me from trying to get information out of him.

When I arrived home, I greeted Bentley and Flapjack, and then opened the French doors to the back porch so Bentley could go out in the yard. Flapjack followed him outside and settled on the porch railing, where he liked to watch birds, butterflies, and any other creatures that might fly by. After pouring myself a glass of sweet tea, I joined the animals outside and took a seat on the porch swing.

The tide was working its way in over a sandbar, and several ducks paddled around in the shallows. A seagull landed on a log at the top of the beach, capturing Flapjack's attention. The tabby's tail swished back and forth, but he made no move to get up and stalk the bird. Bentley finished his investigation of some interesting scents at the edge of the yard and came bounding over our way, startling the seagull into flight.

The sky was a bright shade of blue, and the sun warmed my face. I hadn't yet gathered enough courage to swim in the ocean this year—the water was still a bit too cold for me—but if the beautiful weather continued, that would probably change soon. In the meantime, I'd continue to enjoy the light spring breeze from my porch swing.

As I relaxed and drank my sweet tea, my thoughts returned to Tommy's accident. He'd been walking home from the charity gala when the car hit him. None of Wildwood Cove's roads were particularly busy late at night. Traffic increased during tourist season, which was in its infancy, but I suspected that the stretch of road where we'd found Tommy hadn't been very busy that night. In fact, there was a good chance that many of the vehicles heading east along that road were driven by people who were returning home after the gala.

Maybe one of the guests had hit Tommy. I figured it was more likely than not that alcohol was served at the event. Perhaps someone had decided to drive home despite being impaired. That would explain why the car had crossed the centerline and struck Tommy from behind.

If that was the case, then maybe Frankie wasn't the culprit. I didn't know much about the guy, but he didn't strike me as the sort of person who would have received an invitation to the gala. As I understood it, the guests were mostly rich people from the peninsula and Seattle, many of whom were friends with Evangeline and Richard. Then again, maybe I was judging too quickly. Maybe Frankie's family business was prosperous, and he was plenty rich. Even if that were the case, though, he still didn't seem like the type to rub shoulders with Evangeline Oldershaw-Hobbs.

I figured it wouldn't be too hard to find out if Frankie had attended the event. Once I knew one way or the other, I could put my speculation to an end, in that regard at least. I could ask Tommy if he'd seen Frankie there. Otherwise, maybe I could get a copy of the guest list somehow. I wasn't sure how I'd go about that. Ray would have no trouble procuring one, but there was no way he'd share the list of names with me.

Hopefully the matter would soon be put to rest. If Ray managed to track down the driver or determined that Frankie was the one who struck Tommy, the case would be closed. Maybe it was purely wishful thinking, but I hoped that the hit-and-run and the murder case would both be solved in short order.

When Brett arrived home from work, I set aside my thoughts of sleuthing. I hadn't had the chat with him that I'd meant to the night before. We'd ended up having dinner with his parents, and afterward, we'd both gone straight to bed since we had to be up early in the morning. This evening, however, we had no plans.

While Brett showered, I started making some spaghetti sauce and returned to my spot on the porch swing while it simmered on the stove. Brett joined me soon after, and I shifted over so I could snuggle up against him. He rested his arm around my shoulders, and Bentley settled down at our feet. Flapjack remained on the railing, but he'd given up on watching the birds and was snoozing instead.

I filled Brett in on my day, and he told me about his. He got up to check on the spaghetti sauce. When he returned, I decided it was time to broach the subject that had been hovering at the edge of my thoughts for the past few weeks, and even more so since my chat with Sienna on the beach.

"You know how we've talked about starting a family?" I said.

Brett had been gazing out at the view of the ocean, but now he turned his full attention on me. "I definitely haven't forgotten."

"Silly question, I guess."

He grinned and kissed me. "Have you been thinking about it some more?"

"A lot," I admitted.

"I meant what I said before. We don't have to rush into anything if you're not ready."

"I know you meant it," I assured him.

Brett had no hesitation about having children together, and I wanted kids with him too, but I found the idea overwhelming, and he knew that. It would be such a big change to our life, and I had next to no experience with babies. The thought of being responsible for one made me more than a little nervous.

"I think I'm ready now," I said.

The shift in Brett's expression was subtle, but I could tell that what I'd said was welcome news.

"Are you sure?" he checked. "We can wait if that would make you more comfortable."

"We can't wait *too* long. I'm already thirty-five. But I don't need to wait any longer. If you're ready, I'm ready."

Brett pulled me onto his lap. I laughed, but only until he kissed me.

"You're going to be a great mom," he said before kissing me again.

I rested my forehead against his. "I don't know about that, but I know you'll be an amazing dad."

"How about we be amazing together, like we already are," he said.

I gazed into his blue eyes, and my heart swelled so much that I thought it might burst. "Together, I'm pretty sure we can do anything."

* * * *

Saturday morning brought a rush of customers that would have proved overwhelming without Logan's help in the kitchen. He'd settled in quickly, and so far, everything was running smoothly. During a slight lull after the breakfast rush, I stopped to talk to Marjorie Wells, who had dropped in for breakfast after walking the whole length of Wildwood Beach and back again with her friend Donna. Although Marjorie qualified as a senior citizen and had gray hair, she was one of the most active people I knew. She'd even competed in the Golden Oldies Games, a sporting competition that had taken place in Wildwood Cove the previous summer.

"Marjorie," I said while Donna crossed the restaurant to say hello to someone she knew, "don't you attend classes at the community center?"

"Sure. At the moment, I'm taking yoga and learning how to paint with watercolors, but I've taken several other classes in the past as well. Are you thinking of signing up for something?"

"Not at the moment." I lowered my voice so the other diners wouldn't overhear me being nosy. "Do you know Adya Banerjee?"

"I know who she is, but I've never exchanged more than a few words with her. Why do you ask?" A twinkle appeared in her eyes. "Is this part of one of your investigations?"

I glanced around and saw with relief that no one was paying us any attention. Donna was still across the room, chatting with two other women.

I slipped into the chair across from Marjorie. "I've been thinking about Jane's murder," I said in a voice barely above a whisper.

"Ah." She nodded with understanding. "Jane and Adya worked at the community center together."

"Jane received a promotion shortly before her death, one that Adya wanted. And guess who has Jane's job now?"

Marjorie considered that. "Do you think Adya really would have murdered Jane to get a promotion?"

I shrugged. "People have killed for less. It might not be the strongest motive ever, but I know that Jane was most definitely not one of Adya's favorite people."

Marjorie tugged her coffee mug toward her and wrapped her hands around it. "You know, my friend's granddaughter works as a receptionist at the community center."

I perked up at that news. "So she probably knows Adya."

"And she's a very observant young lady. If there's anything juicy to know about Adya, Desiree might be aware of it."

"Do you think she'd share that sort of information?" I asked.

"I think she would with me. I've known her all her life."

Out of the corner of my eye, I saw Donna heading toward us. Our private chat would have to wrap up.

"How about I talk to Desiree and report back to you," Marjorie suggested. "Is there anything in particular you'd like to know?"

"Not really. I'm just wondering if she has a temper or anything like that." I vacated the chair as Donna returned to the table. "Thank you, Marjorie."

"My pleasure," she said with a smile.

I stepped back and flashed a smile at Donna before heading for the kitchen to check on Ivan and Logan. Everything was still going well on their end, so I returned to serving meals and taking orders.

Business picked up again as the brunch crowd arrived, and the lunch rush followed right on its heels. Thankfully, Sienna and Leigh were both working that day, so we were managing the crowd of diners well between the three of us.

I grabbed two plates of raspberry orange pancakes from the pass-through window and spun around. I nearly dropped the plates when I noticed Dean Vaccarino sauntering into the restaurant. Pulling myself together, I adjusted my grip on the plates, avoiding disaster.

Across the restaurant, Frankie raised a hand to get Dean's attention. I hadn't noticed Frankie earlier, so he'd likely just arrived. Dean headed in his direction and claimed the chair across from him.

I wondered if they were friends. The fact that they'd met up for lunch suggested that they were. Before yesterday I would have thought that Frankie seemed too nice to be pals with Dean, but how nice could he be if he'd left Tommy lying injured in a ditch? Okay, so I didn't know for sure if Frankie was the driver who'd struck Tommy, but seeing him with Dean gave me another reason to harbor suspicions about him.

I didn't want anything to do with Dean and preferred to steer clear of him, but Leigh and Sienna were both serving other customers. I didn't want Sienna dealing with him anyway. It was bad enough when Dean leered at me. If he did that to Sienna, I'd be at risk of losing my temper.

I managed to greet Frankie and Dean politely, if not warmly, and I poured coffee for them without having to endure more than a hard stare from Dean. I figured he was attempting to intimidate me again, and I wondered if he knew I'd talked to Ray about him after he'd threatened me.

The two guys ordered right away, so I left them with their coffee and took refuge in the kitchen.

"Dean Vaccarino is here," I said to Ivan.

He glowered at me. "The man who threatened you?"

Logan glanced our way as he added a slice of breakfast frittata to a plate, but he stayed quiet.

"The one and the same," I said.

I'd filled Ivan in on my encounter with Dean not long after it happened.

Ivan flipped a pancake on the griddle and then wiped his hands. "You want me to kick him out?"

"No, no," I said quickly. "He's not causing any trouble. Not yet, anyway. He's here to eat."

"If he threatens you again..." Ivan didn't need to finish his sentence.

"I'll let you know right away," I promised.

I took the plates Logan had filled with food and left the kitchen.

As soon as the door swung shut behind me, I saw that Dean wasn't the only unexpected customer of the day.

Chapter Sixteen

Dean was the most unwelcome person to show up at the pancake house, but the title of most surprising customer went to Evangeline Oldershaw-Hobbs. My jaw nearly dropped to the floor when she walked into the restaurant. I recovered quickly and called out a greeting, letting her know she could choose any free table she wished. There were only a few to choose from, and she peered down her nose at each one before pursing her lips and choosing a small table by the window. She already looked as though she'd tasted something sour, and she hadn't even sampled the food yet. I figured that didn't bode well. Nevertheless, I was determined to remain cheerful and polite, no matter what complaints she came up with.

After grabbing the coffee pot, I headed over Evangeline's way. "Would you like some coffee to start?" I asked.

She sighed as she set her designer purse on an empty chair. "I suppose so."

She sounded as though she were making a great sacrifice. Maybe because The Flip Side's coffee didn't cost a fortune per pound.

I managed to keep a smile on my face as I filled her mug and handed her a menu. "Shall I give you a minute to decide?"

"I'm meeting someone," she said, setting the menu aside without so much as glancing at it. "I'll wait until she gets here." She made a show of checking the gold watch on her wrist. "*If* she ever gets here."

"Of course." I fought to keep my smile in place. "Let me know if you need anything in the meantime."

I made a quick escape. Less than five minutes later, a slightly plump, middle-aged woman with brown hair tied back in a messy bun arrived and scurried over to Evangeline's table. I was surprised that Evangeline's companion looked as ordinary as I did. She wasn't wearing designer clothes, and she had little to no makeup on. Several wisps of hair had come loose from her bun, and her cheeks were flushed as if she'd rushed to get to the pancake house.

When I returned to the table to take their orders, I realized why Evangeline was meeting with the woman. They were discussing the food for the museum's party. The brunette—Diana—was the caterer Evangeline had hired, and they were having a business meeting. I suspected Diana had chosen the location. I doubted Evangeline would have decided to come to my humble establishment otherwise. Then again, their options had likely been limited. I'd heard that CJ's Seafood—the most formal restaurant in town—was closed for a few days because an elderly member of the family that ran the establishment had passed away.

Although Evangeline spoke in a haughty voice and kept her nose in the air every time she spoke to me, I managed to get the two women settled with their meals without any complaints. I left them to their meeting and gathered up some dirty dishes from a recently vacated table, carrying them into the kitchen. I was putting the dishes into the dishwasher when Sienna poked her head into the kitchen.

"Marley, there's a woman out here asking to see you," she said.

I shut the dishwasher and moved over to the sink. "Do you know who she is?"

"She looks kind of familiar, but I don't know her name."

"Okay," I said. "I'll be there in a moment."

Sienna disappeared, and I quickly washed and dried my hands before leaving the kitchen.

When I returned to the dining room, Sienna pointed out a woman in her late twenties with dark blond hair that fell to her shoulders. She was sitting at a table for two in the far corner. I had to pass by Evangeline and Dean to get there. Fortunately, Dean was too busy eating his churro waffles to notice me, and Evangeline didn't wave me down to complain about something, as I'd feared she might.

The blond woman offered me a hesitant smile as I approached her.

"Hi," I greeted. "I'm Marley Collins, the owner of The Flip Side. I understand you wanted to speak with me?"

She hadn't been in the restaurant a few minutes ago, and she didn't have a meal in front of her yet, so I figured it was unlikely she had a complaint about the food.

"Yes," she said, her smile less hesitant now. "I hope I'm not bothering you. My name is Krista Maxwell. Dolly Maxwell is my grandmother. I understand that you and my great-aunt Winnifred met with her the other day."

"That's right," I said, intrigued. "How can I help you?"

"Aunt Winnifred thought I might be able to help *you*. Do you have a moment to talk?"

Fortunately, Leigh and Sienna had everything under control. The lunch rush was trailing off, and we'd be closing for the day in less than an hour.

"Of course." I noted that she had a cup of coffee in front of her. "Can I get you anything to eat first?"

"The girl with the turquoise streaks in her hair already took my order, thanks. I'm looking forward to trying the food here. I've heard nothing but great things about it."

"I'm glad to hear it." I sat down across from her. "Is this about the letters?"

"It is. Aunt Winnifred told me you were interested in learning more about them like she is."

"That's right. If you don't mind sharing what you know."

"I don't mind at all," she said, to my relief. "Unfortunately, I can't tell you all that much."

My hopes, which had started to rise, sank back down again. "So you didn't read them?"

"I read some of them," Krista clarified. "I was cleaning out my grandmother's attic a few months ago when I came across the box of documents. I took a cursory look at everything in that box, including the journal, before donating it, and I skimmed through a few of the letters. I asked my grandmother about them at the time, but she didn't think she'd ever seen them before. It's possible she did know about them once, but her memory's not as sharp as it used to be."

I nodded in understanding.

"I didn't grow up in Wildwood Cove," Krista continued. "So I didn't realize the significance of the signature on the letters. Aunt Winnifred filled me in on the story of Jack O'Malley. It's exciting to know he might have penned letters to someone in my family. I'm almost wishing we'd held onto them, although the museum will probably do a better job of preserving them."

"Do you have any idea who received the letters?" I asked.

My hopes started to rise again when Krista nodded.

"That's one of the few things I do know," she said. "I noticed in one of the letters I read that Jack used her name—Flora."

"And you have an ancestor name Flora?" I guessed.

"Flora Penrose. She was my great-great-grandmother."

"And she lived here in Wildwood Cove?"

"Yes. According to Aunt Winnifred, she was born here in town in 1888 and died in 1982."

I digested all that information while Krista took a sip of coffee.

Sienna arrived at the table with a smile and delivered Krista's raspberry orange pancakes and a side of fruit salad. I glanced around to make sure I wasn't needed elsewhere. Evangeline was alone at her table, focused on her phone. Diana hadn't finished her meal yet, so I assumed she'd gone to the restroom. Dean and Frankie were nearly finished with their food but hadn't quite emptied their plates. Dean caught me looking his way and his lip curled in a slight sneer. I ignored him and swept my gaze over the other remaining diners. Everyone seemed happy, so I turned my attention back to Krista as Sienna left us alone again.

"Was Winnifred surprised to find out that Flora had been the recipient of the letters?" I asked.

"I'll say." Krista added syrup to her stack of pancakes. "But she didn't have a chance to tell me anything else about her. She was on her way out to an appointment when we talked on the phone. She asked me to fill you in, since she wouldn't be around for the rest of the day."

"I appreciate that, and it was kind of Winnifred to think of me. I'm curious by nature," I admitted, "and I was with Jane Fassbender when she discovered the letters. Jack O'Malley sounds like he was an interesting character, so I was eager to know more."

"I'm told there are some great stories about Jack." Krista's face sobered. "I heard about what happened to Jane Fassbender. It's so sad. And scary."

I agreed with her. "Did you hear that the letters have gone missing from the museum?"

Krista washed down a bite of pancake with a sip of coffee. "I did. That's so strange. Do you think Jane put them somewhere else shortly before she was killed? Maybe she took them home with her."

"It's possible. If that's the case, hopefully someone will come across them while sorting through her belongings." I paused to consider that. "Do you know if she has any family members in town?"

"I have no idea," Krista said. "I didn't really know her."

Jane had likely taken the letters home, even though she'd said she'd keep them at the museum. The other possibility—which involved her killer or some third party taking them—seemed less plausible. I doubted that Jane would have willingly handed them over to anyone other than Winnifred or Dolly, and I couldn't see how the letters would be worth stealing. But if they *had* been stolen, was that why Jane was killed? It seemed even more farfetched to think that the letters could be worth killing for. Then again, I really didn't know much about their contents.

Maybe I could still find out more from Krista.

"Do you remember anything else about the letters aside from Flora's name?" I asked.

"Mostly, they were expressions of Jack's love for her. He mentioned them being together one day. I got the feeling they were planning to run away together, which apparently never happened."

I recalled what Jane had told me. "Because Jack was shot and killed not too long after the letters were written."

Krista nodded as she speared half a strawberry with her fork. "I know he was a criminal, but I still can't help but feel sad that their love story was cut short so tragically."

"It must have been hard for Flora." I wondered if she had to grieve in silence or if anyone else knew about her relationship with Jack. I redirected my attention, reminding myself that I wanted to know if the letters could somehow be connected to Jane's death, even if that did seem unlikely. "Do you remember anything...I don't know...scandalous about the letters?"

"Scandalous?" Krista seemed surprised by the question. "How so?"

I shrugged, not entirely sure what I was searching for. "I guess I'm wondering if there was anything in the letters that made them worth stealing."

"Not that I recall," she said. "Although I didn't read all of the letters. I was running late for a date with my boyfriend at the time."

Maybe I was heading toward a dead end. It really didn't seem like the letters would have been worth stealing. "Do you think there could be any more letters at your grandmother's house?" I asked, not quite willing to give up hope of learning more about what Jack had written to Flora about.

"That's a possibility. There's still a bunch of stuff up in the attic." Krista thought for a second. "I can have a look around and see if I can spot any more. That could take me a while, though. There's still a lot of boxes up there."

"I guess there's no reason to rush," I said, even though I was itching to know if there were more letters or not. "But if you do find more, I'd love to hear about them."

"I can keep you in the loop."

We exchanged phone numbers, and I thanked Krista for all of the information she'd shared. As she focused on her pancakes and fruit salad—which I'd insisted were on the house—I got back to work. While I remained hopeful that she would find more letters, I figured I needed to follow other avenues of investigation. As fascinated as I was by Jack O'Malley and Flora Penrose's love story, I was more interested in seeing Jane's killer behind bars.

Chapter Seventeen

To my disappointment, I didn't have a chance to talk to Diana, the caterer, before she left the pancake house. I knew she'd worked at Evangeline's charity gala, and I'd hoped to strike up a conversation with her and guide it in that direction. She might not have known who had attended the event, but I figured it was worth asking. I could have asked Evangeline, but I preferred to avoid that. I had the feeling she wouldn't be receptive to my questions. Even though I didn't know Diana, I thought I might have better luck with her.

Fortunately, when I asked Leigh if she knew Diana, she supplied me with her last name—Gladwyn—and she also told me that Diana had a website for her business. After closing the pancake house, I ducked into the office and did a quick Internet search using Diana's name. I easily found the website for Diana's Catering, and it took only another few seconds to find her contact information, including an email address and telephone number.

I dialed the number, but the call went to voicemail. I hung up without leaving a message and jotted down the contact information on a scrap of paper for future reference.

Leaning back in my chair, I considered how to move forward in terms of investigating Jane's murder. As Dean had left The Flip Side earlier, he'd stared at me one last time. Although that had sent a chill up my spine, I'd applauded myself for not allowing my reaction to show.

Dean was most definitely an untrustworthy and unsavory character. It really wasn't that hard for me to picture him killing Jane. I still didn't have a concrete motive to attribute to him, but he'd certainly been up to something shifty when Brett and I had walked Bentley past the museum. I didn't know how to find out if Jane had caught him in the act of something illegal or underhanded. Dean was probably the only one who knew if that had occurred.

I wanted to find out more about Dean, but in a way that kept him from knowing what I was doing. If he found out that I was looking into him as a murder suspect, I didn't doubt that he would step up his intimidation tactics, or worse. I didn't even like to think about that happening.

A quick Internet search didn't turn up much information about Dean. A couple of social media profiles popped up in the search results, but Dean obviously didn't use them much. The most recent activity dated back nearly two years.

I gave up for the time being. I'd have to figure out another way to find out more about Dean because he occupied the prime spot on my list of murder suspects.

I tried my best to focus on other things, but I wasn't very skilled when it came to forgetting about mysteries. I'd received two responses to the advertisements for the new positions at The Flip Side, so I contacted the applicants and set up interviews. That evening, after I'd returned home, I called Winnifred to thank her for asking Krista to share what she knew with me. Winnifred told me she was planning to search the museum for the missing letters, in case Jane had secreted them away somewhere other than her desk before her death. When I offered to help with the search, Winnifred readily accepted, and we arranged to meet at the museum on Monday.

I spent the rest of the weekend working at The Flip Side and helping Brett paint the building façades for Wild West Days. With the event less than three weeks away now, preparations had ramped up throughout the town. I hoped that by the time Wild West Days rolled around, at least one of the town's recent crimes would be solved.

* * * *

On Monday morning, I had some time to kill before meeting up with Winnifred at the museum, so I decided to go for a run. Brett had gone to his parents' house to help out with some yard work, so I decided to take Bentley with me as my running companion. The morning was cool enough that he wouldn't get too hot, and I didn't plan to go too far.

We set out along Wildwood Road, heading toward town. I decided we'd go that way first and then walk home along the beach later. When we reached town, we headed in the direction of the community center. That was intentional on my part. I'd texted a few friends the day before, asking if they knew Diana Gladwyn, the woman who'd catered the charity event. I wanted to know if she could help me figure out who'd hit Tommy.

It turned out that Lisa knew Diana. Not only that, Lisa had given me some valuable information. She said that Diana attended a spin class at the community center on weekday mornings, whenever she wasn't busy with a catering job.

I crossed my fingers that today was one of those days. I'd checked the community center's website before setting out and had timed my arrival to coincide with the end of the morning spin class. Bentley trotted beside me while I jogged, but I slowed our pace when the two-story building that housed the small community center came into view. I slipped my phone from my armband and checked the time. It was two minutes past the scheduled end of the class.

Two women dressed in exercise gear descended the front steps as I approached with Bentley, but I didn't recognize either of them. Bentley and I paused at the base of the steps for a couple of minutes and watched the door. Two men and another woman exited the building, but Diana had yet to make an appearance.

Bentley grew bored, whining as he looked up at me from where he sat at my feet. I decided it would be best if it didn't look like we were lying in wait for Diana, anyway, so I walked with Bentley to the end of the street, glancing over my shoulder now and then to make sure I didn't miss the caterer.

When we reached the corner, we turned and headed back. I wondered how many times we'd have to walk up and down the street before I decided it was time to give up and move on. On my third pass by the front steps, the door opened, and the woman I was hoping to see appeared. She paused at the top of the steps and chatted with another woman dressed almost identically to her, in leggings and a tank top. They said goodbye after a moment, and Diana's friend jogged down the steps and off down the street. Diana descended more slowly, and I gave Bentley a pat on the head as he sat on the sidewalk.

"Diana?" I called out when she was halfway down the steps.

She looked my way without recognition.

"I'm Marley Collins," I said. "I own The Flip Side pancake house."

She stopped on the bottom step and smiled. "Right! I ate there on the weekend. The food was delicious."

"Thank you. I'm glad you enjoyed it."

"Your dog is so cute. Can I pet him?"

"Sure," I said with a smile.

Bentley wagged his tail as Diana fussed over him.

"I understand you're a caterer," I said as she gave him a smile and one last pat on the head.

"That's right." She turned her attention to me. "Are you looking for one?"

"Not at the moment." I hurried to get to the point of why I'd stopped to chat. "I understand you catered the charity gala at the banquet hall recently."

"That's right."

"Did you hear about the hit-and-run that happened that night?"

What remained of Diana's smile faded away. "I did. I couldn't believe it when I heard. I'd just met Tommy at the gala that night."

"He's a friend of mine," I said, "and he works at The Flip Side."

"Of course. I remember Tommy mentioning that. We chatted for a few minutes that evening. How's he doing?"

"He's got a broken leg and some broken ribs, but he's doing well, considering."

"I'm glad to hear that," Diana said. "I'm so relieved he wasn't hurt any worse."

Bentley nudged my hand with his nose, so I stroked the fur on his head while I continued my conversation with Diana.

"The driver who hit him hasn't been identified yet, and I was wondering if it could have been someone who attended the gala. Maybe someone who had a bit too much to drink."

Diana's brown eyes widened. "Oh, my gosh. I never thought of that, but it's possible, isn't it? I heard the hit-and-run happened not far from the banquet hall." She paused to think for a second. "But I don't know who it could have been. The guests were definitely consuming alcohol, but I didn't notice anyone who was visibly impaired. Of course, that doesn't mean they weren't too impaired to be driving."

"Do you know who all was at the event?" I asked, knowing it was unlikely that she'd be able to provide me with a full guest list.

"I recognized a few people, but there was a decent crowd, and I was mostly focused on the food."

That was pretty much what I'd expected her to say. "That makes sense."

Diana continued unbidden. "Evangeline and her husband were there, of course. They hosted the event. I recognized Juliet and Desmond Harper, as well as Winnifred Woodcombe and Helena Angelopoulos."

I didn't know the Harpers or Helena Angelopoulos.

"Do you know Frankie Zhou?" I asked.

"Of course," Diana replied. "He was there too."

I perked up at that. "Really?"

"He was helping me with the food. He does that sometimes," she explained, "for my evening jobs, when my assistant is unavailable, or we need extra help."

"So, he was working, rather than attending as a guest."

"That's right."

"Which means he wouldn't have consumed any alcohol?"

Diana looked at me more closely. "Hold on. You can't be thinking Frankie was the driver who hit your friend."

"I'm just trying to consider every possibility," I said, avoiding a direct answer.

She shook her head. "Frankie definitely wasn't involved. He's a good guy. Even if he did accidentally hit someone on the road, he wouldn't have left them there. Besides, Tommy left the gala well before Frankie and I did."

"About how long before?" I asked.

She considered the question. "At least forty-five minutes, I'd say. Tommy left as soon as the guests started heading out. Frankie and I waited until all the guests had gone, and then we had to pack up the leftovers and clean up."

"Frankie was there with you the whole time?" I checked.

"He didn't leave until I did."

I wasn't sure whether to be relieved or disappointed. I didn't want Frankie to be the guilty party, but I did want the hit-and-run driver to be identified and brought to justice.

Clearly, the case wouldn't be so easy to solve. Despite the dented bumper, I had to strike Frankie's name from my suspect list. Even if Tommy had lingered outside the gala venue to chat with someone, it was unlikely that he'd been walking along the stretch of road where he was hit forty-five minutes after the end of the event.

Just to be sure, I sent a quick text to Tommy after thanking Diana for the information. In the message, I asked Tommy about the timeline.

By the time Bentley and I returned home from our outing, Tommy had replied. He'd headed for home as soon as he'd left the charity gala and was struck within fifteen minutes of leaving the banquet hall.

That left no room for doubt.

Frankie was in the clear.

And I was back to square one.

Chapter Eighteen

Marjorie phoned me shortly after Bentley and I arrived home. She'd spoken to her friend's granddaughter, Desiree, who worked at the community center, and asked if I wanted to meet up for lunch. Since I still had some time before meeting Winnifred, I readily agreed. I could meet up with Marjorie and then head straight over to the museum.

We arranged to meet at the local coffee shop, the Beach and Bean. In addition to coffee and other drinks, the Beach and Bean offered a small selection of sandwiches and baked goods. Marjorie was already at the coffee shop when I arrived. She sat at a table near the back, a sandwich and drink in front of her. I waved to her and got in line at the counter. After I'd purchased a matcha latte and a croissant sandwich, I joined Marjorie at the table she'd claimed for us.

The weather was gorgeous again, and I'd noticed lots of people out and about around town. It seemed that many had gravitated toward the coffee shop, as the place was crowded, with no free tables. I figured that might be for the best because the noise of the crowd made it less likely that anyone would overhear our conversation. Even if Marjorie didn't have anything juicy to report, I didn't need anyone else catching on to the fact that I was looking into Adya as a murder suspect. If any rumors ended up flying around town about her, I didn't want to be responsible for starting them, especially if she was innocent.

We spent the first couple of minutes catching up on one another's lives, but after Marjorie had finished half her sandwich, she got down to business.

"I spoke to Desiree the other day," she said, keeping her voice low. "She's known Adya for a few years now."

"Does she know her well?" I asked.

"They aren't friends or anything, and they don't hang out in the same circles. Desiree's in her twenties, and Adya is in her late thirties, I believe. But Desiree said that the two of them are on friendly terms at work."

I wondered if that would have colored Desiree's opinion of Adya, making her information less than impartial. It turned out that I didn't have to worry about that.

"Even so," Marjorie continued, "Desiree didn't hesitate in saying that Adya and Jane didn't get along in the least. I guess you already knew that, though."

"That seemed to be the case from what I'd already heard," I confirmed.

"What you might not have heard," Marjorie said, "is that the conflict between Adya and Jane recently heated up."

"Because Jane got the promotion?" I guessed.

"That was part of it."

"And the other part?"

Marjorie lowered her voice further. "After Jane received the promotion, she embarrassed Adya at a staff meeting, in front of all their colleagues."

I winced. "Embarrassed her, how?"

"Adya pitched some ideas for new classes for the fall season, and Jane tore each and every one of them apart. Desiree was taking notes at the meeting. She said it was painful to record what was going on."

"It sounds like Jane wasn't all that professional." I knew some people found Jane abrasive, but I had trouble picturing her being purposely cruel.

"I think it's more that she was insensitive," Marjorie said. "Desiree told me that Jane never seemed to be *trying* to be mean, but she also didn't seem aware of the effect her words had on people at times. Jane had some legitimate concerns about Adya's ideas, according to Desiree, but the way she went about sharing those concerns was tactless."

"Did Desiree say anything about how Adya responded?" I asked.

"Oh, yes. Adya sat quietly while all that was happening at the meeting, but Desiree was afraid she might spontaneously combust. Desiree was surprised there wasn't smoke pouring out of Adya's ears. Afterward, Desiree overheard Adya fuming to one of her other coworkers about what had happened. And, that's not all."

Marjorie lowered her voice so much that I had to lean forward to hear what she said next.

"Adya told her coworker that she wished Jane would drop dead."

* * * *

I mulled over everything Marjorie had told me as I walked from the Beach and Bean to the museum. If Jane were still alive and well, I would have written off Adya's wish for her to drop dead as words spoken in the heat of the moment, not truly meant. But since Jane had been murdered, I couldn't help but view Adya's words in a much more sinister light.

Fortunately, Ray was already aware of everything Desiree had passed on to me through Marjorie. As we'd finished up our lunches, Marjorie had mentioned that Ray and his deputies had questioned Jane's colleagues at the community center in the days following the murder. Desiree wasn't keen for Adya to find out that she'd shared what she'd overheard, both with me and the sheriff, but Marjorie had assured her that Adya wouldn't learn about that from me. That was the truth. I didn't want to get anyone in hot water. Plus, if Adya was the killer, I didn't want to paint a target on Desiree's back.

When I arrived at the museum, I checked around back to see if the door was open, as it had been several times when I'd come by to volunteer. The backyard was quiet and the door was shut, so I returned to the front of the building and knocked on that door. Winnifred must have been close by, because she responded to my knock within seconds.

"Marley, come on in," she said as she stood back so I could step into the foyer. "It's another beautiful day, isn't it?"

"Gorgeous," I agreed.

Once again, the sun was shining brightly, colorful flowers bloomed in gardens all across town, and birds twittered and sang in the trees.

"I was adding a few items to the exhibits Jane set up," Winnifred said as she shut the door.

"If you need any help with that, let me know," I said. "I have some time on Mondays and Tuesdays when The Flip Side is closed."

"Thank you, dear. That's very kind of you. We should be all right at the moment. Almost everything is in place now."

"Any sign of the missing letters?" I asked, wondering if they had turned up while Winnifred was sorting through the museum's artifacts.

"No sign at all, I'm afraid. Of course, I haven't carried out a thorough search yet. I checked Jane's desk again, as well as the filing cabinet in her office, but no luck."

"Hopefully we'll find them," I said, although I was trying to keep my hopes from climbing too high.

"Shall we start in Jane's office?" Winnifred suggested. "Once we finish in there, we can head upstairs to the storage rooms."

That sounded like a good plan to me, so we got to work. Aside from the desk and the filing cabinet in Jane's office, several shelves of boxes were full of documents. We started our search by going through those. Right away, it became clear that most of the boxes contained receipts and other papers related to the running of the museum, rather than documents of a historical nature. We decided to search every box, anyway, in case the letters had somehow made their way into one where they didn't belong.

"I enjoyed my chat with Krista," I said as we worked. "Were you surprised to find out that Flora Penrose was the recipient of Jack O'Malley's letters?"

"Surprise doesn't quite cover it." Winnifred lifted the lid off a box I'd shifted over to the desk for her. "I'd assumed that Jack had written to some distant cousin of my grandparents, not my grandmother. Flora's family was very well-to-do and held a position of prominence here on the peninsula. I always understood that Flora was a proper lady. But that's not all..."

I stopped searching through a stack of receipts I'd taken out of a box, eager to hear what she had to say next.

"My father was born about seven and a half months after Jack O'Malley was killed. Flora married my grandfather four weeks after Jack's death."

I turned that information over in my mind. It didn't take more than a second or two for me to catch on to the implication of Winnifred's words.

"You mean, Jack O'Malley is your grandfather?" I asked with surprise. I hadn't expected that twist in the story.

"I don't know for certain," Winnifred said quickly, "but the timing is suspicious. Although I have no idea how much time Flora would have spent with Jack. It must have been difficult for her to sneak away to see him. Even exchanging letters would have required some secrecy."

I set one box aside and opened another. "If it is true, how do you feel about it?"

"I suppose I have mixed feelings," Winnifred said. "On the one hand, I feel sorry for my grandfather—the one I knew as my grandfather—if he was deceived. He was such a kind man. Then again, it's possible he knew my father wasn't his child and raised him as his own regardless. Another part of me feels quite excited about the prospect. It certainly adds an interesting twist to my family's history."

"That's for sure," I said.

I finished searching another box. "No luck here."

Winnifred closed the box she'd checked. "I'm afraid I haven't found them either."

I returned everything to the shelves. We'd searched all of the boxes.

"Let's try upstairs in the storage room," Winnifred suggested.

As I followed her up the stairs, I tried to buoy my sinking hopes. I really wanted us to find the letters, but I couldn't think of a reason why Jane would have taken them back up to the storage room, especially since she'd planned to show them to Winnifred. We didn't want to leave any stone unturned, though, so we continued our search on the second floor.

First, I grabbed what I thought was the box we'd found the letters in originally. When I spotted the journal, I knew I had the right one.

Winnifred flipped carefully through the leather-bound volume. "I'd love to read this from cover to cover. Perhaps Krista could help me with transcribing it." She set the journal aside. "But that's for another time. I must remain focused if we're to find the letters."

It didn't take long to confirm that Jane hadn't returned the letters to the box. We moved on to the other boxes in the room, but all we turned up was a lot of dust, artifacts, and documents donated by other local families.

"That's the last one," I said as I hefted the last box back onto the shelf.

Winnifred picked up the journal again. "Thank you so much for helping me with the search, Marley."

"I was glad to help," I assured her. "I'm sorry we didn't find what we were looking for."

Winnifred sighed. "I am too. It's strange that the letters are nowhere to be found."

I wiped my dusty hands on my jeans. "Can you think of any reason why someone might have stolen the letters?"

"None at all." Winnifred seemed to reconsider the question. "If the letters had related to someone else's family, I might have said that perhaps someone didn't want the information contained in them getting out. But the letters are connected to my family, and I know that Dolly and Krista didn't take them. If they'd wanted the contents kept secret, they simply wouldn't have donated them in the first place."

That was a good point. Not that I'd suspected Dolly or Krista of stealing the letters.

"I guess we'll have to wait and see if they turn up sometime in the future," I said with disappointment.

"That does seem to be the case, unfortunately," Winnifred agreed.

I checked the time on my phone. "Do you need help with anything else?" I asked.

"No, thank you, dear. You've been such a great help already. You head on out. I think I'll have a look at this journal before I carry on with my day."

I tucked my phone back in my tote bag and left the room. When I was halfway down the staircase, I paused. I thought I'd heard a floorboard creak below me. I listened hard, but the only sound that met my ears now was a barely perceptible rustle of pages coming from the storage room where I'd left Winnifred.

I continued on my way down the stairs. When I reached the foyer, I stopped again. This time I was certain I'd heard something on the main floor. Another sound drifted out into the hallway from Jane's office. It sounded like somebody was opening and closing drawers. I wondered if I should retreat upstairs or call 911. I decided the latter might be overreacting. After all, maybe Winnifred was expecting someone else to turn up at the museum.

Again, I considered heading back up to speak with Winnifred. That was probably the best option. I took one step backward. A floorboard creaked beneath my feet. The noises coming from Jane's office ceased abruptly.

I cast around for something I could use as a weapon to protect myself, but there wasn't anything in the hallway. My heart beat painfully in my chest as I tried to work up the courage to move toward the office.

A shadow filled the doorway. Adya Banerjee appeared so suddenly that I almost yelped.

We stared at each other for two full seconds before she spoke.

"Who are you?" She managed to make the question sound casual, but I knew she'd been as startled as I was when we'd first laid eyes on each other.

"My name's Marley," I said, wondering why I wasn't the one asking questions. I decided to change that. "Are you looking for Winnifred?"

I knew she wasn't because that wouldn't explain why she'd been moving about in Jane's unoccupied office.

"Winnifred?" Adya seemed confused.

"Winnifred Woodcombe. She's in charge of the museum at the moment. I can get her for you if you'd like. She's upstairs."

Adya forced a smile that lacked any warmth. "No need to bother. I was just looking for a bracelet I lost."

"You lost it here at the museum?"

"I don't know where I lost it. That's why it's lost." She brushed past me, jostling my shoulder. "Clearly, it's not here, though. I'll be on my way."

She slipped out the front door and shut it behind her before I had a chance to say anything more.

Footsteps sounded on the stairs, and Winnifred appeared a moment later. "Did I hear voices?" she asked.

"Adya Banerjee was here," I said.

"That name rings a bell. She works at the community center, I believe."

"That's right. Were you expecting her?"

"Not at all," Winnifred said. "You're the only one I was expecting to show up today."

I headed into Jane's office, and Winnifred followed.

"She was in here." I couldn't see anything obviously out of place. "And I thought I heard her opening and closing the desk drawers." I moved around the desk to study it. Sure enough, one of the drawers was ajar. I opened it farther to take a peek inside, but it held office supplies and nothing else. I shut it and tugged on the top drawer, but it was locked.

"How strange," Winnifred said. "Did she explain herself?"

"She said she was looking for something she'd lost. A bracelet."

"Did she find it?"

"I don't think so."

I also didn't think Adya had been completely honest with me.

Chapter Nineteen

Winnifred didn't seem overly troubled by the fact that Adya had been sneaking around the museum, but she did mention that she'd make sure to keep the doors locked in the future. On my walk home, I replayed my conversation with Adya in my head. If, in all innocence, she wanted to search for something she lost on a previous museum visit, why hadn't she knocked on the door or at least announced her presence? Even though Winnifred and I had been up on the second floor, we left the storage room door standing open, and I was certain we would have heard anyone who knocked or called out from below.

Perhaps my pre-existing suspicions of Adya had influenced my view of her behavior at the museum, but when I added everything together, I couldn't help but conclude that she was a strong murder suspect. I wondered if Ray considered her to be one. The whole situation was still on my mind when Brett arrived home that evening.

"Maybe I should call Ray," I said after I'd filled Brett in on everything that had happened at the museum.

"I think that's a good idea," he said.

I hesitated with my phone in my hand. "He'll probably think I'm meddling."

"He might." Brett grinned at me. "Are you?"

"I didn't intentionally come across Adya acting suspiciously at the museum."

Brett gave me a quick kiss. "I know. And no matter what Ray thinks, I'm sure he'll appreciate you making sure that he has potentially useful information."

I hoped that was the case. I tried phoning Ray, but I hung up without leaving a message when I didn't receive an answer.

"No luck?" Brett asked as he put our dinner dishes in the dishwasher.

"No, and I wasn't sure how to explain everything in a message."

"Why don't you explain to him in person, then. He's supposed to help out tomorrow evening with the construction for Wild West Days. If he doesn't get called into work."

I agreed to that plan and hoped that Adya wouldn't get up to anything criminal in the meantime.

* * * *

When I closed The Flip Side on Wednesday afternoon, I asked Leigh if she could stick around for a few minutes.

"Sure," she replied, eyeing me as she stacked up some dirty plates. "Is everything okay?"

"Everything's fine. There's something I want to talk to you about, but it's nothing bad."

We finished cleaning up and then sat at a table by the window, Leigh with a cup of coffee in front of her.

"I'm dying of suspense here, Marley," she said before taking a drink.

"Sorry. Like I said before, it's nothing bad. I've just been doing a lot of thinking about the future."

Despite my previous assurances, an expression of alarm crossed Leigh's face. "Are you selling The Flip Side?" she asked with dismay.

"No, no," I rushed to say. "Not at all. I love this place."

Leigh relaxed. "Good."

"What I mean is, Brett and I are hoping to start a family soon."

A smile spread across Leigh's face. "That's fantastic!"

"I'm excited but nervous," I admitted.

She reached across the table and squeezed my hand. "That's totally normal. I think most people are nervous when they're about to become parents for the first time. But you and Brett will do great, and if you ever need any advice, give me a call."

With three daughters, Leigh had plenty of experience with children.

"Thank you," I said with a smile. "I'll most likely take you up on that." I tried to get back on track. "Anyway, before Brett and I have kids, I want to make sure that I have more flexibility with my schedule."

Leigh nodded with understanding. "That's a good idea."

"Which brings me to what I wanted to talk about. It's absolutely okay for you to say no, but I was wondering if you'd be interested in a promotion to the position of assistant manager."

She stared at me, holding her coffee mug an inch off the table. She set it back down with a thud. "Seriously?"

"You've worked here for years. Far longer than I've been around. You're reliable, trustworthy, and I know you've got what it takes to handle a bigger role here. But like I said, I don't want you to feel any pressure to accept. Your current job is still yours. No matter what."

"Wow." As some of Leigh's shock ebbed away, her smile returned. "Thank you, Marley. I appreciate your confidence in me. Can I take some time to think about it and talk it over with my husband?"

"Of course. There's no need to rush into a decision."

"I won't keep you waiting too long," she promised.

We spent a few more minutes going over the pay raise and the responsibilities that would come with the promotion if she chose to accept it. She gave me a hug before leaving, and I was pleased by her reaction to my offer. She clearly wasn't horrified by the thought of taking on more duties, so that was promising. If she ended up turning down the offer, I'd have to come up with another solution, but I wouldn't hold it against her in the least.

Satisfied with how that meeting had gone, I shifted my focus to the next ones I had scheduled. I had two interviews set up for the middle of the afternoon, and I looked forward to meeting the job applicants. With any luck, it would only be a week or two before I had all of The Flip Side's staffing issues taken care of, so I could focus on my future with Brett.

* * * *

I arrived home that evening to find Ray and my father-in-law helping Brett with the façades for Wild West Days. Bentley was lying in the grass, watching the men work, but he charged across the yard to greet me as soon as he spotted me on the beach. The saloon was all finished and looked fantastic. Now work had started on the general store and the sheriff's office. Other volunteers would take care of the remainder of the façades, which would include a music hall, a post office, a hotel, and a blacksmith's shop.

During the event, volunteers like Gary and Ed would dress up in period costume and stay in character while interacting with the crowd. I could already tell that the old town would look great, and I was sure everyone who attended Wild West Days would have a blast.

As soon as Brett saw me, he broke away from the others and greeted me with a kiss.

"How did the interviews go?" he asked.

"Not very well," I said, the disappointment still weighing heavily on me.

"What happened?"

"One applicant had a major attitude problem," I said. That interview had been painful. I didn't know why the young man had even applied for the job. He'd made it clear right from the start that he thought the position was beneath him. "The other showed up twenty minutes late, didn't bother to apologize, and then interrupted me every time I tried to speak."

Brett winced. "Okay, so they definitely weren't the right candidates."

"I'll say."

He kissed me again. "Don't worry. You'll find the right people."

"I hope so." At the moment, I wasn't feeling overly optimistic.

"You will," Brett said without a shred of doubt. "What about Leigh? Did you offer her the promotion?"

I brightened as I remembered that meeting. "I did, and she seems open to the idea. She's going to think about things and talk it over with Greg. I'm hopeful she'll say yes."

"I'm glad that part went well."

I took his hand as we walked toward the others. I called out greetings to Frank and Ray before asking Brett, "How are things going here?"

"We're making progress." Brett grinned at me. "I'm sure you're eager to talk to Ray."

"I don't have to corner him *right* away."

"Will you really be able to think about anything else until you do?" Brett asked.

I laughed. "You know me too well."

"Better than I know myself." He gave my hand a squeeze before letting it go.

I admired the general store façade that my father-in-law was working on, but then I approached Ray. He was painting the sheriff's office.

"New digs?" I asked as he added paint to his brush.

Ray stepped back to check his work. "I think I'll stick with my current office. It has heat and air conditioning." He glanced my way. "And before you ask, Frankie Zhou has an alibi for the hit-and-run."

"I know," I said before I could think better of it.

He looked skyward. "Of course you do."

I was about to speak again when he held up a hand.

"We haven't identified the driver, and you know I can't discuss ongoing investigations."

"I wasn't going to ask about your investigations," I said.

"No?"

I couldn't blame him for his skepticism.

"I want to," I admitted, "but I'm not going to. I do have something I want to tell you, though."

"Here we go."

I was relieved to hear a hint of good humor beneath his words. He'd lectured me more than once about staying out of his murder investigations, and I knew he wasn't about to change his opinion that I should leave all investigating to the professionals, but at least he wasn't mad at me.

I told him everything I knew about Adya, including my encounter with her at the museum.

Ray rubbed the back of his neck as he listened carefully.

"She didn't have permission to be in the museum?" he asked when I'd finished speaking.

"Not from Winnifred, and she's the one in charge at the moment."

He nodded, his expression giving nothing away. "Thank you for telling me."

As much as I wanted to know what he thought about the information, I knew he wouldn't share that with me. He surprised me with his next words, however.

"There is one thing I can tell you."

"What's that?" I asked with interest.

"I know you were worried about the way Angus Achenbach confronted Jane at the museum when you and Frankie were there," Ray said. "But, as much as he blamed Jane for the fact that he didn't inherit the Victorian, he's not the killer."

"How did you rule him out?"

"He was arrested for driving under the influence that evening and spent the night in a holding cell."

"I guess it's hard to get a more solid alibi than that."

Ray nodded as he got back to painting. "Iron-clad."

"What about Dean?" I asked. "Is he still a suspect?"

"We're looking into him."

I could tell he wasn't about to share anything more.

"Thank you for letting me know about Angus," I said.

At least I now had one less suspect to worry about.

I spent the next hour helping out and trying my best not to think too hard about Wildwood Cove's unsolved mysteries.

* * * *

By the time dusk had fallen, Brett and I were heading into town. The pieces for the saloon's façade were in the back of Brett's truck. We were transporting them to the community center, where they'd be stored until it was time to set up for Wild West Days in the park. The paint wasn't yet dry on the sheriff's office and the general store, so those façades would be brought over another day.

A man from the event's organizing committee met us at the center and helped move the pieces into the basement. Once that was done, Brett and I climbed into his truck again. I checked my text messages as Brett drove us away from the community center, and I tapped out a quick reply to one my mom had sent me earlier. After tucking my phone away in my bag, I sat back and watched the passing scenery.

The streetlights came on, and the windows in the houses that lined the street glowed with warm yellow light.

I sat up straighter as we passed Dolly's house. "Hold on. Can you pull over for a minute?"

"What's up?" Brett asked as he steered the truck into a free spot by the curb.

We'd stopped a couple of houses past Dolly's. I undid my seatbelt and shifted around so I could see back up the street.

"Remember how I told you about visiting Winnifred's cousin the other day?" I said.

"Sure."

I pointed. "That's her house back there. The front door is standing open."

Brett took a look for himself. "Maybe she wanted some fresh air?"

"Except it's not very warm anymore."

The temperature had dropped as the sun disappeared from the sky.

Brett offered up another possibility. "Maybe a neighbor stopped in to visit for a minute?"

"Maybe."

"Do you want to go check to make sure?" Brett asked.

"I'll worry if I don't." I unbuckled my seatbelt. "She's elderly, and I'm pretty sure she lives alone. It'll just take me a minute."

"I'll come with you."

I hopped out of the truck, and Brett joined me on the sidewalk. I kept expecting a neighbor or other visitor to appear in the doorway, but nobody did. Lights were on in the house, and some of the glow spilled out onto the front porch, but with the living room curtains drawn, I couldn't tell if anyone was moving about inside.

A trickle of unease worked its way down my spine as we jogged up the front steps.

"Dolly?" I called out from the porch. "It's Marley Collins. Are you all right?"

Nobody responded, and I couldn't hear any noise coming from within the house.

I knocked on the open door and leaned inside to peek into the living room. "Dolly?" I caught sight of a slipper-encased foot. "Dolly!"

"Marley?" Brett said as I dashed into the house.

"Oh no!" I choked out the words.

Dolly was lying on the floor, unconscious, wearing a pink bathrobe over a nightgown.

Brett had followed me into the house, right on my heels. He crouched down next to Dolly, his phone already to his ear.

My breathing hitched when I heard a scuffling noise coming from somewhere deeper in the house.

My eyes widened as footsteps pounded down the staircase from the second floor.

"Brett!" I said with alarm.

Before Brett had a chance to get to his feet, a dark figure bolted across the foyer and out the front door.

Chapter Twenty

I shivered as I stood on Dolly's front lawn, even though I wore a hoodie. Brett put an arm around me as we watched the paramedics load Dolly into an ambulance on a stretcher. Two sheriff's department vehicles were also parked on the street in front of the house. Deputies Devereaux and Mendoza had responded to Brett's emergency call, but by the time they arrived on the scene, the intruder was long gone.

Brett had dashed out of the house after the black-clad figure, with me right behind him, but the stranger had slipped through a gate into a neighbor's yard and disappeared within seconds. I wanted to continue the chase, but Brett had wisely dissuaded me. The trespasser had already harmed Dolly—we'd discovered that she'd taken a knock to her head—and there was absolutely no guarantee that he or she wouldn't hurt Brett or me as well if given a reason.

"I can't believe this," Winnifred said with a shake of her head as she crossed the lawn to join Brett and me. She'd just finished having a conversation with Deputy Devereaux. "Poor Dolly."

"How is she?" I asked.

Brett and I had vacated the house as soon as the paramedics had arrived, giving them room to work. We hadn't had a close look at Dolly since. I'd phoned Winnifred as soon as the deputies arrived, and she'd shown up within a couple of minutes. It turned out that she lived only four houses away from Dolly, so she didn't have far to come. She'd already conferred with the paramedics as well as Deputy Devereaux.

"She's conscious," Winnifred said, which brought me a rush of relief. "But she's woozy and confused. She doesn't seem to know what happened."

She shook her head again. "Who would do such a thing? It's appalling that anyone would attack such a vulnerable woman."

I didn't have an answer to Winnifred's question, and neither did Brett.

Deputy Eva Mendoza exchanged a few words with Devereaux at the base of the front steps and then headed our way.

"You say the intruder came down the stairs from the second floor?" Mendoza directed the question at Brett and me.

"That's right," Brett said as I nodded.

"Were they looking for something to steal?" Winnifred asked the deputy.

"Most likely," Mendoza replied. "Although it's strange that they apparently bypassed the main and second floors and went straight for the attic after attacking Mrs. Maxwell."

"The attic?" Winnifred echoed with confusion. "Why would any burglar go up there? Everything is boxed up, and I doubt there's anything of real value up there. The thief would have had much better luck on the other floors of the house."

"Was the attic tidy?" Mendoza asked.

"Yes," Winnifred replied. "Dolly's granddaughter, Krista, was sorting through things up there recently, but she left everything neat and orderly."

Mendoza glanced over her shoulder at the house. "It's not tidy anymore. The attic's been ransacked."

A chill settled into my chest. "Do you think the burglar was looking for something specific?"

"It's possible." Mendoza directed her next question at Winnifred. "Any idea what that might be?"

"None at all," Winnifred said.

"But the letters..." I trailed off.

Winnifred's thin eyebrows drew together. "Surely this isn't related."

"What letters?" Deputy Mendoza asked.

With help from Winnifred, I filled Mendoza in on the letters and their mysterious disappearance.

The deputy nodded as we finished speaking. "I remember hearing about those letters now. But even if Ms. Fassbender's killer stole them, why search Mrs. Maxwell's house? The killer would already have possession of the letters."

None of us could answer her question.

I shared one of my own. "Why leave the front door open if you wanted time to search the house? If the burglar took pains to get Dolly out of the way, why announce their presence with the open front door?"

"That may have been unintentional," Winnifred said. "That door can be quite finicky. If you don't give it a firm shove, it doesn't latch properly and tends to drift open on its own."

That was one thing explained, at least, but so much else remained unknown.

"This is probably unrelated to the murder," Deputy Mendoza told us.

"But isn't it at least possible that there's a connection?" Brett asked.

"It's possible," Mendoza said. "And we'll look into it."

She took statements from Brett and me, but we weren't able to provide much helpful information. Neither Brett nor I knew if the intruder had been male or female. He or she had appeared as little more than a blur. All we could really say was that he or she wasn't particularly overweight or particularly thin.

After we provided our brief statements, Deputy Mendoza told us we could head on home. By that time, the ambulance was long gone, and Krista had arrived, thanks to a phone call from Winnifred. The two of them had disappeared into the house, along with Deputy Devereaux.

It didn't take long for Brett and me to get home, and I was relieved to reach the comfort of our beloved beachfront Victorian and greet our animals. I was worried about Dolly and likely would remain so until I received news that she'd be okay.

Deputy Mendoza doubted that the events at Dolly's house were connected to Jane's murder, but because of the fact that the intruder had focused on searching the attic—where Krista had found Jack O'Malley's letters—I couldn't help but believe that Jane's killer had passed within feet of me and Brett that evening.

* * * *

At the end of the next workday, I packed up two leftover sticky rolls and took them with me to Tommy's house. We arranged to have another visit, and I didn't want to go empty-handed. He had his phone back, which made him happy, so we could stay in frequent contact now. Logan had turned out to be a great help to Ivan in the kitchen, and I enjoyed having him working at The Flip Side, but we all still missed Tommy. It wasn't the same without him at the pancake house each day.

"I come bearing gifts," I said, holding up the paper bag when Tommy opened the front door.

He grinned as he leaned on his crutches. "Music to my ears. And my stomach."

He offered me one of the sticky rolls, but I declined, having already indulged in one earlier in the day. I grabbed him a plate from the kitchen, and he dug in while we sat in the living room and got caught up. Once again, all his roommates were off at work, so the place was quiet.

"How's the sleuthing going?" he asked after we'd talked about The Flip Side and our co-workers.

"I wish it were going better," I said. "For both cases."

"Both? Marley, you don't have to look into what happened to me if that's what you mean."

"You really expect me to stay out of it?"

He grinned. "Okay, maybe that's like asking the sun not to rise."

"Pretty much."

His face sobered. "But I don't want you putting yourself in any danger, especially on my account."

"You can leave the lecturing to Ray and Ivan," I said with a smile. Then I also got more serious. "Don't worry. I intend to be careful. Last night the potential danger became all too clear."

"Last night? I must have missed out on something."

I told him what had happened to Dolly Maxwell.

Tommy set his plate aside, one sticky roll demolished. "What kind of scumbag would attack an old lady in her home?"

"One who's desperate to find something."

"What kind of something?"

I brought him up to speed on everything I knew about the missing letters.

"Dolly's granddaughter found them in Dolly's attic," I said to wrap up. "I really doubt it's a coincidence that the burglar focused his or her attention there."

Tommy thought that over. "How many people knew the letters came from Dolly's attic?"

"That's exactly what I spent half the night thinking about," I said.

I really had, which was why I'd had to stifle several yawns throughout the day. Winnifred, Krista, and I knew where the letters had come from. Jane might have known that the letters were stored in Dolly's attic, but with her gone, there was no way of knowing if she'd mentioned that to anyone else. It didn't seem likely that she would have told many people, but there was always a possibility that she'd mentioned it in passing to somebody.

Krista and I had talked about the letters at The Flip Side. There was a chance someone could have overheard us. Dean and Frankie had both been within possible earshot during that conversation. I'd struck Frankie from my suspect list for the hit-and-run, but now I had to consider him as a murder suspect, despite my original decision not to do so. Why he would have wanted to kill Jane, or why he would care about the letters, I really didn't know, but in my mind, I placed his name at the bottom of the list, just in case.

Aside from Dean and Frankie, Evangeline had also been sitting near Krista and me that day. I knew Evangeline had a connection to Jane, and Jane had made a veiled threat toward her, but I didn't know why Evangeline would care about letters relating to Winnifred and Dolly's family. Still, I couldn't discount the fact that she'd been within earshot. As for Diana, who was sitting with Evangeline at the time, I didn't think she warranted a spot on my suspect list. Not unless more information about her came to light, anyway.

I shared all those thoughts with Tommy

"I really don't think Frankie is your guy," he said.

"Probably not." Nevertheless, I wasn't ready to disregard him entirely.

"As for Dean," Tommy continued, "I've asked a few people about him."

I tensed. "That might not have been the greatest idea."

He waved off my concern. "Don't worry. I was discreet. I know it wouldn't be good if he found out we suspected him of anything."

He hadn't banished all my concerns, but I allowed myself to relax.

"Did you find out anything interesting?" I asked.

"He's done some time in jail, for assault, I think it was. And he was arrested for theft a few years ago, but the charges got dropped."

"Ray mentioned that Dean has a criminal record and a history of violence."

"And that's why I need you to promise me something before I tell you my next bit of intel," Tommy said.

"Promise you what?" I asked.

"That you won't intentionally go near Dean or his house without someone with you. Preferably someone bigger than Dean, like Ivan or Brett."

"I have no problem promising you that," I said. "Dean creeps me out, but he also scares me, if I'm honest."

"I think that's a healthy fear in this case," Tommy said.

"So what's the intel?" I asked.

"I found out where Dean lives. I don't know if that will be helpful at all, and I don't know the house number, but apparently it's a white house that's seen better days. On Sandpiper Road, near the river. It backs onto the woods and has a big stump in the middle of the front yard."

I made sure to memorize that description. "That information could come in handy. Did you find out anything else?"

"That's it," he said. "I'm a novice at this sleuthing thing. Not like you."

"Don't sell yourself short," I said. "You did great. Thank you."

"How will you figure out if Dean's the killer or not?" Tommy asked.

"I have no idea," I admitted. "All I know is I won't go near his house without Brett."

We chatted a bit longer about life in general before I decided I should be getting on my way soon.

"Did you have a good visit with Sienna the other day?" I asked as I headed for the door, Tommy accompanying me on his crutches.

He grinned. "I beat her at Mario Kart three times in a row."

I rested my hand on the doorknob. "And how many times did she beat you?"

"Four. But not in a row." His grin faded. "Has Sienna talked to you recently about...stuff?"

"You mean about going away to college and all that?"

Tommy shrugged, not meeting my eyes. I knew then that I'd guessed wrong.

"There's something else on her mind?" Worry tried to take root in my chest.

"Maybe..." Tommy shook his head. "Never mind."

"Are you sure?" I asked, feeling uneasy. "Should I be concerned?"

"No, definitely not," Tommy rushed to assure me. "Forget I said anything."

I didn't press the matter, but I knew I wouldn't be able to forget that he'd brought it up. Once my curiosity was piqued, there was no shutting it off.

Chapter Twenty-One

As much as I wanted to know what Tommy thought Sienna might want to talk to me about, I wasn't going to find out that afternoon, so I tried my best to focus on other things. After hearing Tommy's information about Dean, I was eager to take a closer look at him as a suspect.

I didn't know what good it would do to check out Dean's house, but I wanted to walk by it anyway. As I'd promised Tommy, though, I wouldn't do that alone. Brett wouldn't be off work for a while, so I couldn't rope him into tagging along with me quite yet. I had something else I needed to do first, anyway.

I had Winnifred's phone number, and I knew where she lived, but I was close to the museum, so I decided to stop and see if she was there. If she wasn't, I'd give her a call and ask how Dolly was doing.

As it turned out, I didn't need to bother with a phone call. When I knocked on the front door of the museum, Winnifred opened it within seconds.

She greeted me with a warm smile. "Marley, what a nice surprise. Come on in."

I stepped into the foyer, and she shut the door behind me. "I came by to ask how Dolly is doing."

"She's on the mend," Winnifred said, much to my relief. "She's still in the hospital and might be for another day or two because of the hit she took to her head. At her age, the doctors want to be extra careful."

"That sounds like a good idea," I said. "But I'm so glad to hear that she's on the road to recovery."

"I visited her this morning, and she wanted me to thank you and your husband for checking on her last night. If you hadn't noticed the open door, who knows how long she could have been lying there before somebody found her." Winnifred shook her head with a frown. "I can't even bear to think about it."

"Brett and I are glad we were able to help."

Winnifred smiled. "It's much appreciated. Would you like to join me on the back porch for a cup of tea? I was about to pour one for myself."

"That sounds great," I said.

I followed her to the kitchen at the back of the museum. Soon we each had a cup of tea in hand. We carried our drinks out to the back porch and sat at the wrought-iron table.

"Do you know if the burglar took anything from Dolly's house?" I asked once we were settled.

"It's so difficult to tell," Winnifred replied. "Krista went up there with one of the deputies last night, but she didn't know if anything was missing. The place was in complete disarray—boxes emptied on the floor—and there were so many odds and ends up there that I'm not sure we'll ever know for certain if anything was taken."

I thought back over the events of the previous night. "I didn't see the burglar carrying anything when he or she fled. It's still possible they had papers or something small tucked away out of sight, though."

"I can't make sense of it," Winnifred said before taking a sip of her tea. "Even if someone wanted more letters, the *why* of it eludes me."

"I can't make heads or tails of it either," I admitted.

We lapsed into a comfortable silence as we enjoyed our tea. My mind, however, never quieted.

"You mentioned that the attic is a mess," I said after a minute. "I'd be happy to lend a hand cleaning it up."

Winnifred had a twinkle in her blue eyes when she looked at me. "And to help figure out if the intruder took something?"

I gave her a sheepish smile. "Guilty as charged, but I really am happy to simply help out."

Winnifred patted my arm. "I know you are, dear. I'm just teasing. And I appreciate the offer on both counts. With my creaky old bones and joints, I certainly won't be of much help. I'm sure Krista wouldn't say no to an extra pair of hands."

"I'll get in touch with her then," I said.

After another brief silence, I steered the conversation in a slightly different direction.

"Do you find it surprising that no one in your family knew there were letters from the Jack of Diamonds in Dolly's attic for all those years? Or do you think Flora stashed them up there decades ago, and no one ever looked at them until recently?"

"I've been thinking about that," Winnifred said. "It's possible that Flora was the only one ever to see them and that she hid them up there in the attic a long time ago. It's also possible that someone else found them and read them at some point and decided to keep them hidden."

"But it's such an intriguing story." If I found out about such an interesting connection in my family, I never would have been able to keep quiet about it.

"I agree, but my family enjoyed a position of prestige here on the peninsula back in the day. The Woodcombe and Penrose names still carry weight, whether deservedly or not. To think that one of our family members had a relationship of a romantic nature with a criminal—and had possibly even given birth to his child rather than her husband's—would have seemed scandalous back then. It's not difficult at all for me to imagine anyone from my mother's or grandmother's generations keeping the letters hidden. In fact, I'm a bit surprised that no one destroyed them, though I'm very glad they didn't."

"I think the reason your name still carries weight in this town is because of all the wonderful things you've done for Wildwood Cove, not just because of your family's history."

"Thank you, my dear," Winnifred said with an appreciative smile.

"I get what you're saying about the rest of it, though. Things would have been viewed differently a hundred years ago, or even fifty years ago. There's something else that I don't quite get. If Jack O'Malley was such a skilled thief, couldn't he have committed much more lucrative burglaries somewhere else, such as in Seattle? I imagine the peninsula didn't have a large population during his day."

"I've considered that too. And I've heard that very question raised in the past, before I ever knew of his connection to Flora."

"Do you think that's it?" I asked. "Did he stick around this area because he was in love with a local girl?"

"That's exactly what I figure. He did start his career, if you can call it that, in Seattle, but for the last year or so of his life, all of the crimes attributed to him took place on the peninsula. I suspect he took a trip over here for some reason or other and met Flora and wanted to stay close to her. Another possibility is that they met in Seattle—my family did make trips there now and then—and he followed her back here."

"This is where he died?"

"Fairly close." Winnifred added more tea to our cups. "I believe it happened in Port Angeles."

"It must have been terrible for Flora, to have him torn away from her like that, especially if your father really was his child."

"Yes," Winnifred said, her voice somber. "I wish I'd learned all of this when she was still alive. I could have talked to her about it. I always knew she was a strong woman, but I didn't understand just how strong. Imagine having to keep your grief a secret from everyone."

I didn't want to imagine it. The mere thought made my heart ache for Flora. I realized how fortunate I was that there'd been nothing to keep Brett and me apart, to prevent us from living our lives together.

While Winnifred and I finished our tea, we spoke about the future rather than the past. She filled me in on the status of preparations for Wild West Days, and I told her how well the building façades had turned out. By the time I left the museum, it was the end of Brett's workday. We exchanged a few text messages, and he agreed to meet me in town so we could drive by Dean's house.

When Brett picked me up in his work van, I took pity on him and agreed that we could make a stop at Johnny's Juice Hut on Main Street before doing any sleuthing. After hours of working out in the sun, he needed a cold drink.

Once we both had slushy, cold bubble teas—mango for me and coconut for Brett—we continued on our way, following the directions Tommy had given me. I worried that we might have trouble finding the right house without an actual address, but it wasn't difficult at all. The giant stump in the front yard was as good as a signpost.

Brett didn't stop in front of the house, but he did slow down enough that I could get a good look. As Tommy had said, the white paint on the house had seen better days. It appeared more gray than white and had peeled away in places. Dean might get paid for refinishing floors, but he clearly didn't spend much time sprucing up his own home.

Even though the front grass was in need of cutting, I didn't bother suggesting that Brett knock on Dean's door and offer him a business card. I didn't want to risk Dean connecting Brett to me, and I doubted we'd learn anything with that strategy.

A mud-splattered, black pickup truck sat in the driveway, but I couldn't see any signs of movement in the front yard or through the windows. Just as the house was about to disappear, I spotted a plume of smoke rising up into the sky from behind it.

"Does it look like he's there?" Brett asked as he took a left at the next corner so we could circle around the block.

"I saw smoke coming from the backyard," I said. "Maybe he's burning yard waste."

"In which case, he's most likely home. Should we call it a day?"

"Not yet." I wasn't ready to give up. "Is there a way we can get a look into his backyard without approaching from the front?"

Brett pulled his van over to the curb and parked. We were one street north of Dean's house now.

"There's a trail that runs through the woods behind his place," Brett said. "The undergrowth might be thick off the path, but it's possible we could get a glimpse into his yard." He lifted his bubble tea out of the cupholder. "What exactly are you hoping to find?"

"I don't know," I admitted. "We probably won't find anything, but I want to know more about him. He's my strongest suspect at the moment."

Brett took a drink of his bubble tea. "Let's leave the van here. It'll only take a minute to reach the trailhead on foot."

I took a quick sip of my drink, drawing a couple of tapioca pearls up through my straw, and then returned it to the cupholder. We climbed out of the vehicle and followed the sidewalk down the road. Brett had estimated correctly; we reached the start of the trail within a couple of minutes.

Moments after we entered the woods, the road disappeared from sight, and the forest swallowed us up. It was like we'd entered a different world. Leafy green deciduous trees grew here and there between the evergreens, and birds sang in the trees above us. Sunlight filtered down through the canopy, but the trail we were following was shaded for the most part. Still, the air was warm and scented with the sweet smells of spring.

I found myself enjoying the walk, even though I couldn't completely erase the sense of urgency humming through my bloodstream. The beautiful weather and gorgeous surroundings tempted me to slow down and enjoy the moment, but I couldn't keep my pace at anything less than a brisk walk. My curiosity was too strong of a driving force.

After a few minutes of following the trail, Brett slowed his pace. "We should be getting close to the back of Dean's place."

I couldn't see any houses from our vantage point, but I knew they weren't far off. Treading carefully, we veered off the path, heading in the direction of what we hoped would be Dean's house. Fortunately, the underbrush wasn't too thick. It impeded our progress here and there, and we took care not to crush any ferns or huckleberry bushes, but we were able to keep moving steadily.

We both tried to keep our footfalls quiet, but it was impossible to avoid stepping on some twigs and broken branches. A few cracked here and there under our feet, but not too loudly.

Soon, I caught a glimpse of a house through the trees.

I moved a few more steps forward and gently pushed aside a branch of an evergreen. The house up ahead was green with gray trim.

"We're not quite there," I told Brett.

We turned around and retraced our steps to the trail. It would be easier to walk on the path than to keep crashing through the underbrush, especially since we wanted to make a quiet approach to Dean's property.

We knew from our drive down the street that the green and gray house stood two properties away from Dean's. When we thought we'd finally gone far enough to align ourselves with his property, we left the path and trekked through the underbrush again.

This time, when the house came into view, I knew right away that it was Dean's. I slowed my pace, taking extra care to move quietly as I drew closer to the tree line. Brett followed right on my heels.

I stopped once I was about fifteen feet from the edge of the woods. I stood behind the large trunk of a Douglas fir, using it to shield myself from sight, in case Dean happened to glance our way. Brett tucked himself in next to me, and we both peeked around the tree. Even though we weren't right at the edge of the forest, we had a good view of Dean's backyard.

The grass behind the house had been cut more recently than the front, and a fire pit sat right in the middle of the yard. A small fire crackled away within the circle of rocks. At first, I didn't spot Dean, but then he came out of the house through the back door, carrying a cardboard box.

I sucked in a breath and ducked behind the tree, Brett doing the same. I leaned against the rough bark of the trunk, silently counting to ten before risking another peek out from behind the tree.

Dean set the cardboard box next to the fire and was grabbing handfuls of paper from the box and dropping them into the flames. The fire danced higher, greedily licking at the new fuel.

"That's definitely not yard waste," I whispered.

"Maybe he burns all his waste paper instead of shredding or recycling it," Brett said, keeping his voice equally low.

"Maybe," I said.

"You're not convinced."

I bit down on my lower lip, still watching Dean. "I'd like to be able to confirm if that's what he's doing."

"If we get any closer, he'll see us," Brett cautioned.

"I know."

We continued to watch Dean from our hiding spot as he thrust more papers into the flames. After dropping another small pile into the fire, he fished a cellphone out of his pocket and held it to his ear. I couldn't hear what he was saying, but after a few seconds, he turned away from the fire and walked toward the house at a casual pace.

Instead of going indoors as I expected, he headed around the side of the house, disappearing a few seconds later.

I eased out from behind the tree. "This is my chance."

"Marley..."

I could tell Brett wasn't keen on what I was about to do next.

"If you see him coming back, hoot like an owl," I said.

"Marley, I don't think—" he started to say.

I was already creeping through the undergrowth.

As soon as I broke free of the tree line, I sprinted across the yard to the fire pit. My heart pounded in my chest, more from the fear of getting caught than the brief spurt of exertion.

I stared into the flames, and my heart almost stopped. Amid typed letters and what looked like financial statements, were smaller, older sheets of paper with handwriting on them.

I recognized them as the letters written by the Jack of Diamonds.

Chapter Twenty-Two

Several of the pages had already ignited. I used the toe of my shoe to nudge the closest sheets out of the fire. Then I dropped to my knees and blew out the flames. The fire had already completely engulfed at least two pages of the letters, and they disintegrated into ashes before my eyes. I'd managed to save three sheets. I had no idea how many had already burned before I reached the fire pit.

I took a quick look into the cardboard box. It was full of papers of various sizes. When I rifled through the contents, I didn't spot any more of the letters written by Jack O'Malley.

Every second was precious, so I quickly snapped photos of the pages I'd saved from the fire. As I took the last picture, Brett hooted like an owl. It was a decent impression, but I knew it was him.

I didn't waste time thinking. I sprinted back into the woods, trying to be quiet once I was in the forest, but still moving quickly until I reached Brett. I ducked behind the tree and leaned against him, gasping for breath.

"That was close," he whispered into my ear.

"The letters." I mentally kicked myself. "I left them there."

"*The* letters?" Brett asked with surprise. "Hold on."

He was watching whatever was happening in Dean's yard. I peeked around the trunk.

Dean stood a few feet away from the fire pit, facing his house. Brett's uncle Ray, wearing his sheriff's uniform, was striding across the lawn toward Dean, two deputies at his side. Ray held a folded paper in his hand.

"What's going on?" I asked, still whispering.

We watched as Ray spoke to Dean, holding up the paper for him to see. Dean grabbed it from Ray's hand. He appeared to be arguing with Ray.

Chloe's boyfriend, Deputy Rutowski, broke away from them and approached the fire pit. As he drew closer, I saw that he had a camera in one hand. He checked out the box and then noticed the rescued letters at the edge of the pit. He crouched down to examine the scorched pages and took some photos of them.

"I think they've got a warrant to search Dean's property," Brett said. I'd come to the same conclusion.

"What should we do?" I asked. "Should we let them know we're here?"

"I don't think that's a good idea," Brett said. "I think we'd better get going."

I had to agree. Kyle had already found the letters I'd saved. Announcing our presence wouldn't help in any way. It might even get us charged with trespassing.

We moved as stealthily as possible back to the trail. No one yelled out for us to stop, so I figured our presence had gone unnoticed. Back on the path, Brett and I jogged out of the forest and down the street to his van.

"Do you think they're searching Dean's place because he's a murder suspect?" I asked once we were driving away.

"Could be," Brett said. "But who knows how many shady things that guy is mixed up in."

"Good point. Other than the letters, it looked like he was burning financial statements. And I saw someone else's name on one of them."

Brett stopped the van before turning onto Wildwood Road. "Did you recognize the name?"

"The last name was Browning, but I didn't see the first. Do you know anyone by that name?"

"Sure, there's a Browning family that lives on Orchard Lane."

"The same street that Dolly and Winnifred live on." I wondered if that had any significance. I didn't see how it could.

"Were the letters the ones that went missing?" Brett asked. "The ones written by Jack O'Malley?"

"The very same." I checked out the first of the photos I'd managed to take of the partly burnt letters. A hum of energy zipped through me. "I took pictures of the pieces I managed to save. And I swear this is the same letter Jane showed me at the museum."

"So the letters really were stolen," Brett concluded.

"And," I added, "Ray may well have nabbed Jane's killer."

* * * *

When we'd returned home, and Bentley had been out for a walk, I studied the rest of the photos I'd taken of the singed letters. I was more certain than ever that the first photo depicted one of the pages Jane had held in her hands that day at the museum when she first discovered the letters. The other pages I'd managed to pull from the flames didn't appear to be in chronological order. I wasn't even sure if they were part of the same letter.

Some of the writing was illegible because parts of the page were burnt, and other parts were left charred and blackened with soot. The few lines I could read made me sit up straight on the couch.

"Holey buckets!"

"What is it?" Brett asked from the kitchen, where he was checking the curry we'd left simmering on the stove.

"This letter confirms what Winnifred suspected," I said. "On this page, Jack says, 'We'll start a new life together, you, me, and our baby.'"

Brett grabbed two plates from one of the kitchen cupboards. "So Flora Penrose really was pregnant with the Jack of Diamond's kid."

I'd already filled Brett in on my visit with Winnifred and what we'd talked about.

"She must have been."

The page I was examining wasn't the first or last of any letter, so it didn't have a date on it. Still, I figured there was a good chance it was written close in time to the 1907 letter that Jane and I had first looked at.

"I should call Winnifred and tell her what I found." I was already scrolling through the contacts on my phone.

"But then you'd have to admit that you were on Dean's property," Brett pointed out. "If that gets back to Ray somehow, he won't be happy."

"True."

I still wanted to tell Winnifred what I'd found. With this page as evidence, it was highly likely that her father was Jack O'Malley's son. I knew she'd want to know about this letter, but I also knew that Brett was right. I wasn't keen on having to explain my presence on Dean's property to Ray. I couldn't guarantee that one of these days, he wouldn't lose his patience and charge me with trespassing or some other crime. He wouldn't *want* to do that, but he might feel he had to. I didn't want to put him or myself in that position.

"The information will come to light another way," Brett said, as if he'd read my thoughts. He probably did know exactly what I was thinking. "I'm sure he'll notify Winnifred about the letters since she's currently in charge of the museum."

"That's true." Realizing that made me feel a bit better about not running straight to Winnifred with the new information. "Maybe I should call Ray and see if he's arrested Dean for Jane's murder."

"How about we hold off until morning?" Brett suggested. "You don't want to tell him how you found out about the search warrant, do you?"

"No," I conceded. I definitely didn't.

By morning, the news that Dean's place had been searched would probably be all over town. Then I might not have to ask Ray anything.

I wished that I could force time to move faster. Since I couldn't, I did my best to forget about Dean and the letters until the next day.

* * * *

The small-town grapevine didn't let me down. I didn't even have to wait for the first customers of the day to arrive at the pancake house. When Leigh showed up shortly before opening, she had news to share.

"Have you heard that the police were at Dean Vaccarino's place yesterday?" she asked me as she hung her purse in her locker.

"With a search warrant, right?" I said.

"That's what I heard from my neighbor this morning. And he was arrested. Dean, not my neighbor."

That was what I'd been waiting to hear.

"For murder?" I checked to be sure.

"I don't know, actually," Leigh said. "But I'm sure someone will know."

She was right about that.

"My cousin Nell lives next door to Dean," Ed informed me when he and Gary arrived for their favorite breakfast of blueberry pancakes, sausages, and bacon. "She overheard a lot of what was going on. She says the sheriff arrested Dean for possession of stolen property."

"Not murder?" I asked with disappointment.

"Not that she heard."

"But they could always add that charge later," Gary pointed out. "If they have enough evidence. Do you think Dean's the one who killed Jane Fassbender?"

"He's a suspect, at the very least," Ed said before I had a chance to respond. "Nell heard Dean saying that he didn't steal anything from the museum and that he had nothing to do with the murder."

"So they did question him about the missing letters," I concluded.

"He was probably lying when he said he had nothing to do with the murder," Gary said before digging into his breakfast.

"Most likely," Ed agreed as he poured maple syrup over his stack of pancakes. "I wouldn't believe anything that comes out of that guy's mouth."

"I certainly wouldn't bet on him telling the truth," I said.

I wondered if there was any evidence to tie Dean to the murder, since he apparently wasn't ready to confess. Ray hadn't arrested him for that crime yet, but that didn't mean the sheriff's department wasn't building a case so they could.

I desperately hoped that was exactly what they were doing.

Chapter Twenty-Three

Since the news was all over town about Dean's arrest and the search of his property, I decided to visit Winnifred on the way home to talk to her about the letters. I walked over to the museum first to see if she was there, but no one answered my knock on the front door. The same thing happened when I tried the back door.

I decided to try my luck at her house. Winnifred had pointed out her place on the night of Dolly's attack. She lived in a cute white Victorian four houses away from her cousin's. Like Dolly, she still lived in the house where she'd grown up.

When I turned onto her street, I noticed a red Ferrari parked at the curb, a few houses away from Winnifred's. I figured it had to be Evangeline and Richard's car. I didn't think anyone else in Wildwood Cove drove a Ferrari.

Sure enough, the front door of a dark red Victorian with black trim opened, and Evangeline stepped out onto the porch in a tight, hot pink dress and stilettos.

"Hurry up, Richard," she called over her shoulder before navigating the steps in her high heels.

A second or two later, Richard emerged from the house and locked up behind them. If they noticed me walking in their direction, they gave no sign of it. As I reached the pathway that led to Winnifred's house, the Ferrari's engine roared to life, and the car zoomed off down the street. It was already around the corner and out of sight by the time I reached the front door.

This time, when I knocked, I received a quick response.

"Marley, come on in," Winnifred said in greeting when she opened the door.

"I saw Evangeline and Richard leaving the red house up the street," I said as I stepped into the foyer. "Is that their place?"

"It is," Winnifred confirmed. "They only spend a few weeks a year in Wildwood Cove, but they like to keep a house here."

Krista appeared behind her great-aunt's shoulder. "I was about to come see you at the pancake house."

"Have you heard about Dean Vaccarino?" I asked.

"That's why I was coming to see you," Krista said. "He stole the letters that my grandma donated to the museum."

Winnifred invited me to take a seat in the living room. "Unfortunately, he was burning the letters along with a bunch of other papers when the sheriff and his deputies arrived on the scene."

"But they saved some of the pages from the flames," Krista added. "And several more were still among the papers that Dean hadn't tossed in the fire yet."

That was a relief. I hadn't thoroughly searched through all the documents in the box. I hoped most of the letters were still there, rather than in the pile of ashes in the fire pit.

"Do you know how many pages were destroyed?" I asked.

Krista frowned. "No, but hopefully not too many." Her face brightened. "But guess what?"

"Dean's been charged with Jane's murder?" I hoped that was the latest news.

"Not as far as we know," Winnifred said. "But if he's the one responsible, I hope Sheriff Georgeson throws the book at him."

"I'm sure he will." At least, I hoped he'd be able to find enough evidence to do so.

"The sheriff came by with photos of the letters they found at Dean's house," Krista said, getting back to her news. "He says we'll get the letters back eventually, but he wanted someone to confirm whether they were the same ones that went missing from the museum."

"He'd hoped I could do that for him," Winnifred said. "But since I never had a chance to see the letters, I told him to get in touch with you or Krista."

Her great-niece picked up the story. "Then I showed up as he was leaving, so he gave me the photos to look at. They were definitely the ones that my grandma donated. I didn't read all of them before the box went to the museum, but I remembered a few lines from one of the letters."

I was glad to hear that. Now I didn't have to admit that I'd been snooping around Dean's place.

"It's great to know what happened to them," I said. "And even better that some of them were saved from the fire. But if the letters went missing when Jane was murdered, why wasn't that enough to tie Dean to her death?"

"Perhaps it will be," Winnifred said. "Although maybe they can't prove that the letters were taken right when Jane was killed. At any rate, Dean is facing a charge of possession of stolen property, and Sheriff Georgeson mentioned that they're investigating him for possible identity theft."

"Apparently he had a bunch of other papers that he was burning too," Krista said. "Sheriff Georgeson thinks he stole them from people's recycling bins."

That explained the financial documents I'd seen in the box by the fire pit.

"Including recycling bins from this street," Krista added, "judging by the names and addresses on some of the papers. Luckily, Aunt Winnie shreds everything with any personal information on it before it goes out of the house, and I do the same for my grandma."

"Krista and her cousins bought me one of those cross-shredders," Winnifred said. "I'm more grateful than ever now that I know what Dean Vaccarino was up to." She shook her head and clicked her tongue. "Even if he's not guilty of killing Jane, that young man is certainly a crook."

"I can't disagree with you there," I said.

Krista sat up straighter. "But we're forgetting the most important part of all this. Do you want to tell her, Aunt Winnie?"

"You go ahead, dear," Winnifred said.

Krista's eyes shone with excitement. "One of the pages that the sheriff photographed was from a letter I barely looked at before donating the box to the museum. We were able to read some of it from the picture, and it confirms that Aunt Winnifred's grandmother, Flora Penrose, was carrying Jack O'Malley's child."

I did my best to act as though I hadn't already read that excerpt for myself. "Do you think that child was your father?" I asked Winnifred.

"The dates fit," she said. "I think it's more likely than not."

Krista beamed. "I think it's exciting. Aunt Winnie is the granddaughter of the legendary Jack of Diamonds!"

"Notorious might be a better word," Winnifred said. "We can't forget that the man was a criminal. However," she added, a smile forming, "it does make for an interesting family tale."

We chatted a while longer about the letters and what they'd revealed.

"I should probably get going," Krista said after glancing at her phone. "I really just came by to see Aunt Winnie for a few minutes, but when the sheriff stopped by, my plans got derailed. I was hoping to clean up my grandmother's attic this afternoon."

"Do you need any help?" I asked.

When I glanced Winnifred's way, she gave me a knowing smile, but didn't comment.

"I wouldn't say no," Krista said. "I took a look up there on the night my grandma was hurt. The whole attic looks like it was hit by a tornado."

"I don't need to be anywhere for the next while," I said. "I'm happy to lend a hand."

Krista readily accepted my offer, and we walked the short distance to Dolly's house, where Krista let us in with her key.

When we reached the attic, I saw that her description wasn't much of an exaggeration. Boxes were tipped over, and their contents spilled across the floor. Books, papers, knickknacks, and holiday decorations were scattered everywhere. There was barely a free spot on the floor to stand on.

"It's not too late to run away if you want to," Krista said when she saw the look on my face. "I know it's an overwhelming mess."

"There's no way I'm leaving you to deal with this all on your own," I said.

That was the truth. Even if I knew for sure that there was no hope of finding any helpful clues among the chaotic jumble, I couldn't leave Krista to clean it up alone.

So, without wasting any more time, the two of us got to work.

* * * *

Two hours later, Krista and I were hot, thirsty, and covered in dust. We'd made decent progress with cleaning up the attic, but there was still plenty left to be done. To my disappointment, we hadn't come across any other letters penned by the Jack of Diamonds, or anything else that might give me a clue as to why Jane was murdered.

Of course, it was possible that Dean stole the letters for some reason unconnected to Jane's death, even if he was the murderer. But killer or not, I couldn't think why Dean would want the papers, especially since he'd ended up burning them, or had at least planned to. I didn't see how he could have mistaken the old letters for anything that would have helped him with his identity theft scheme.

Krista declared that we were done for the day and insisted that she'd enlist the help of one or more of her cousins to finish the job with her at a later date. She offered to get me something cold to drink, but I declined. I'd texted back and forth with Brett earlier, letting him know what I was up to, and I'd told him I'd be home by six. He'd promised to have dinner ready for me when I arrived, and if I didn't leave now, I'd be late.

As thirsty as I was, I parted ways with Krista, my grumbling stomach and my parched throat sending me homeward at a brisk pace.

Chapter Twenty-Four

By the time the following Wednesday rolled around, the preparations for Wild West Days neared their completion. Brett had volunteered some more time in the evenings to set up the building façades, and the old west street in Wildwood Park needed only a few finishing touches. The event would open the next evening, and I didn't know of anyone in town who wasn't looking forward to it. Brett and I had already made plans to spend time at the park on Thursday evening so we could check out the festivities.

I had plenty to do before then. I needed to schedule more interviews, for starters. Three more people had responded to the ads for the jobs at The Flip Side. Hopefully, these candidates would be more promising than the first two; otherwise, my staffing shortage would continue indefinitely, and that wouldn't be anywhere near ideal.

Since it wasn't even seven in the morning, I wasn't about to call the job applicants yet. I decided to wait until mid-morning to do that. With luck, I'd have all of the interviews scheduled by the end of the day.

I was in the midst of going over the dining room one last time, making sure everything was ready for opening at seven when Leigh arrived.

"Morning," she called out as she came in the front door. "Looks like another beautiful day."

"It's gorgeous," I agreed.

I'd taken my time on my walk to work that morning. The beach was peaceful—no one out there but me and the birds—and the rising sun glinted off the waves.

"Do you have a minute to chat?" Leigh asked once she'd put her purse away in her locker.

"Of course." I set aside the stack of menus I'd just tidied on the cash counter.

"I've come to a decision about your offer," Leigh said. "And I'd like to accept."

A smile broke out across her face at the same time as one did on mine. "That's fantastic!" I gave her a hug. "I know you're the perfect person for the job."

"I think it'll be great," Leigh said. "And I'm grateful for the opportunity. With all three of my kids in school now, it feels like the right time to take this step."

"I'm thrilled. We'll have to set up a time when we can go over everything. To start, would you like to sit in on the interviews for the new server position? I'm going to call the applicants today to set them up."

"I'd like that."

"I'm hoping to schedule the interviews for next week, after Wild West Days."

"My kids are sure looking forward to that," Leigh said. "Greg and I are too, to be honest. It sounds like it's going to be a fun event."

We cut off our conversation there because the first customers of the day were already outside the door. I hurried over to flip the sign and let them into the restaurant.

Between the breakfast and lunch rushes, I managed to slip away to the office for a few minutes to phone the job applicants. I got in touch with two out of three and scheduled interviews for them the following week. I made a note to try the third applicant again later and then headed back out front to help Leigh with serving.

It took me by surprise to see Ray, in ordinary clothes, seated at a table with his wife, Gwen. She showed up at the pancake house every now and then, often with her sister-in-law, Brett and Chloe's mom, but Ray spent long hours working as the sheriff and didn't often have a chance to come by The Flip Side for a meal. Usually, his visits were short ones to talk to me about whatever investigation I might be mixed up in at the time.

Leigh had already provided Ray and Gwen with coffee and had taken their orders, but I stopped by their table. I really did want to say hello, but in all honesty, I had an ulterior motive as well.

"Have you charged Dean with murder?" I asked Ray once we'd exchanged greetings and small talk.

He didn't appear the least bit surprised that I'd turned the conversation in that direction. He'd probably known I would the moment I approached them.

"No," he replied. "He won't be charged with Jane Fassbender's murder."

"But he was lurking around the museum that night," I reminded him, no doubt unnecessarily. "And he had the letters that were inside the building with Jane."

"He claims he never went inside the museum that night."

"And you believe him?" I asked, unable to keep a hint of disbelief out of my voice. "He doesn't strike me as a very trustworthy guy."

Gwen smiled as she picked up her coffee mug. "Don't worry. Ray doesn't trust him."

Ray added cream to his coffee. "Dean says when you and Brett saw him at the museum, he was planning to break in. While he was refinishing the floors, he noticed several items that he thought were valuable."

"And he wanted to steal them," I concluded.

"Under the cover of darkness, when everyone had left the museum," Gwen said. She'd clearly talked this over with her husband before.

"Except the museum wasn't empty," Ray said.

"Because Jane was there after hours." I knew she had been, since she'd been murdered there either that evening or sometime during the night. Brett and I hadn't seen any lights on at the museum, but there could have been one on in a back room.

Ray nodded. "He was waiting for her to leave, but after you and Brett saw him there, he gave up on the plan and left." Ray held up a hand before I could ask why he'd accepted Dean's word on that. "Shortly after you and Brett saw him at the museum, Dean showed up at the Windward Pub. He was propping up the bar there until closing."

He paused, and I stepped back as Leigh arrived with their meals. She set a plate of raspberry orange pancakes and hash browns in front of Gwen and a stack of blueberry pancakes and crispy bacon before Ray.

After they thanked her, Leigh swept off to another table where an elderly couple was ready to order. I needed to get back to helping her, but I thought I could spare another moment or two.

"So, you know that Jane was killed after Brett and I walked past the museum and before the Windward Pub closed for the night?" I surmised.

"The post-mortem narrowed down the window of death," Ray confirmed as he doused his pancakes with maple syrup.

"Then he has an alibi." I could hear the disappointment in my own voice.

Gwen gave me a sympathetic smile. "We were all hoping the case would be wrapped up quickly."

"No one more than me," Ray said.

I knew that was the truth.

Something still bothered me, though. "But Dean had the letters. And the letters went missing from the museum."

"Dean claims he didn't know the letters were in that box of papers," Ray said. "He figures they must have been in one of the recycling bins he scavenged from."

"Do you believe that?" I asked, not sure how much stock to put in that claim.

"I'm not sure yet," he said. "It's possible that he broke into the museum before Jane showed up that evening, despite what he claims. We tracked Jane's movements for that day, and we know she left the museum around five o'clock before returning later on."

"Sometime after eight," Gwen added. "She made a phone call to Winnifred Woodcombe at that time."

That was definitely after Brett and I had seen Dean lurking about the museum. At the time, it didn't look like he had anything he could have stolen from the museum in his possession, but he could have easily hidden letters—or anything small and compact—in his pockets or under his T-shirt.

"Does that mean you found Jane's phone?" I asked.

Ray shook his head as he cut into his pancakes. "She called Mrs. Woodcombe from home. Jane didn't have a cell phone."

"But she did," I said, puzzled. "I saw her with it when we found the letters."

Ray set down the forkful of food he'd been about to eat. "Are you sure it was hers?"

"It seemed like it was. It even had Jane Austen cover art as the lock screen, and Jane was a big fan of Austen's books."

"Hm." Ray seemed as perplexed as I was. "The only phone number currently under her name is her landline at her house."

"Maybe she's been borrowing a cell phone from a family member?" I suggested.

"Her only remaining family member is her sister, who lives in Sweden," Ray said. "I'll get in touch with her again and see if she knows anything about it."

I circled back to the subject of Dean. "Even if Dean did break into the museum before Jane showed up on the night she died, why the heck would he steal the letters of all things? Surely there were other small items that would be easier for him to sell."

"So maybe he was telling the truth when he said he didn't take the letters on purpose," Gwen said. "Maybe they really were mixed in with someone's recycling."

"But why?" I asked. "How did they end up there?"

"That," Ray said as he cut into his stack of pancakes, "is a mystery that remains to be solved."

* * * *

Before Ray and Gwen left the pancake house, I asked about the progress of the investigation into the hit-and-run. Unfortunately, Ray didn't have anything he could tell me about the case. I hoped that meant he simply couldn't share any new information with me, and not that no progress had been made.

After closing the restaurant and saying goodbye to Leigh for the day, I returned to the office and phoned the third job applicant again. This time I had success and set up a time for the following week when the young woman would come in for her interview.

That was one more task off my plate. I hoped I'd find a suitable person for each position by the time the interviews were over next week. Then, once Leigh and the successful applicants settled into their new positions, I could focus on my future with Brett.

I was almost finished cleaning the dining room when Ivan emerged from the kitchen.

"Everything all right?" I asked when he hesitated by the cash register.

"I'd like to leave early today," he said. "I'll put in extra time tomorrow to make up for it."

"No worries," I assured him. "Is everything okay?"

Ivan rarely left early, and he was often the last to leave at the end of the day. Even so, it was more the hint of uncertainty in his eyes that prompted me to ask the question.

"Everything's fine," he said gruffly, the uncertainty disappearing so quickly I wondered if I'd imagined it. "I just need to go to Port Angeles before the end of the day."

"All right," I said. "I'll see you tomorrow morning then."

He gave me a curt nod before disappearing into the break room. A minute later, he left through the back door.

I remembered Lisa mentioning that Ivan had been acting a bit mysterious lately. I wouldn't have thought anything of him leaving early, if not for his unusual demeanor—as brief as it might have been—and the fact that Lisa was wondering what was up with him. I would have simply assumed he had an appointment to get to, medical or otherwise. When I considered everything together, however, I couldn't help but wonder what was going on.

He wasn't the only one who seemed slightly out of sorts lately. I hadn't forgotten my mysterious conversation with Tommy about Sienna. During her shifts on the weekend, there had been a couple of moments when it seemed like she wanted to say something to me, but then she'd changed her mind. Since she'd already confessed that she had some anxiety about leaving for college at the end of the summer, I figured it had to be something else entirely.

Was she planning to give up her job at The Flip Side earlier than I'd anticipated?

Maybe that was it. Maybe she was scared to tell me, because the pancake house was already short on staff.

If that was the case, I'd have to get it out of her sooner rather than later. I'd understand if she needed time to prepare for the new chapter in her life, but the more warning I had, the better.

I doubted I'd ever know what was behind Ivan's early departure. He was a reticent man at the best of times and rarely ever shared much about his personal life. I had no intention of prying into his business. With Sienna, on the other hand, I might have to pry to get to the bottom of whatever was going on with her. I hoped it wasn't anything serious, and I hoped she wouldn't be leaving The Flip Side earlier than expected, but whatever was happening, I was determined to support her in any way I could.

Chapter Twenty-Five

On Thursday, more than one customer showed up at The Flip Side in a cowboy hat. A couple of people even had boots to match. Ed and Gary outdid everyone, however. They both showed up for breakfast, fully decked out as wild west sheriffs. They wore gambler hats and rifle frock coats, which they removed before sitting down, but not before posing for photos with several other customers. Beneath their coats, they wore silk puff ties tucked into Galloway vests, dark trousers, and boots. The final touches were the pocket watches, leather holsters—with replica pistols—and the shiny sheriff's badges affixed to their vests.

Everyone was impressed that they'd gone to such lengths to look the part for the role they'd be sharing over the next few days. Leigh and I made sure to get our photos taken with them, but I hoped to get another later on, with the wild west town as a backdrop.

I was as excited as everyone else for the event to get underway. It didn't officially start until five o'clock, so I was able to finish up my workday without rushing. I enjoyed the stroll home along the beach, where children and dogs splashed in the shallows, apparently unfazed by the chilly water. I'd dipped my toes in the ocean the other day and had hopped back out immediately. It would be another couple of weeks before I'd dare to go for a swim.

While walking home, I texted Lisa, asking if she was planning to go to Wild West Days that evening. I didn't have to wait long for a reply. She said she and Ivan were hoping to check out the event, but it would depend on what time she finished work.

Her next message really grabbed my attention.

We need to talk ASAP!

What's wrong? I wrote back, wondering if I should be worried.

Nothing's wrong. It's something good. I'll tell you later!

I typed out another message.

Leaving me in suspense?!? No fair!

She sent back a winking emoji.

I responded with an emoji with its tongue sticking out, but then said I'd keep an eye out for her and Ivan. After that, I tucked my phone in my pocket and enjoyed the rest of my stroll, all the while trying to guess what Lisa wanted to talk about.

As soon as I'd arrived home and had given Flapjack a cuddle, I took Bentley down to the water so he could bound about and burn off some energy. By the time we returned to the house, Brett had arrived home from work. I hosed off Bentley's sandy paws while Brett took a quick shower. After that, the two of us walked over to Wildwood Park.

It looked like half the town had arrived before us. People young and old milled about in the park, taking photos and chatting with friends. Shortly after Brett and I reached the park, the mayor gave a short speech and declared the first-ever Wild West Days underway.

Brett and I strolled along the wild west street he helped build, walking hand-in-hand as we admired the finished project. Everything looked great, and the volunteers who'd dressed up in period costume to take on the role of colorful characters helped to bring the place to life.

Gary was playing the sheriff at the moment, and I got my photo with him in front of the old west jail before he had to get ready for the stagecoach robbery re-enactment, which would be repeated several times over the weekend. Brett and I cheered for Gary when he arrested the scoundrels and hauled them off to jail.

By the time the show was over, there was already a long line for the mechanical bull riding.

"Do you want to give it a try?" I asked Brett, secretly hoping he'd say no. I was getting hungry, and I figured the wait would be at least half an hour.

"I'd rather eat," he said, to my relief. "You?"

"Food is my choice too."

We were about to make our way over to the food trucks lining the northern side of the park when I spotted Tommy coming our way on his crutches. Keegan was there as well, but he stopped to talk to someone else as Tommy headed over to meet Brett and me.

"It's great to see you out and about," I said. "How are you feeling?"

"Pretty good." He grinned. "And I haven't scared any young children yet, so I'll call that a win."

"The bruises are hardly noticeable now," I said, glad to see that they'd almost faded, along with the abrasions on his face.

"How are the ribs?" Brett asked.

"Okay, as long as I don't try to do too much." Tommy winced as a young woman was flung from the mechanical bull into the inflatable ring that surrounded it. "I'm thinking I'll have to give the bull riding a pass."

"Probably a good idea," Brett said.

"Have you heard anything new about the hit-and-run investigation?" I asked Tommy.

"No." Some of the cheerfulness faded from his face. "I've kind of lost hope that the driver will be found. I guess there wasn't enough to go on."

"Don't give up on Ray yet," Brett said. "I know for sure he won't quit looking."

Tommy's mood brightened again. "You're right. He called me yesterday to assure me that he's still on the case, and I appreciate that."

Keegan came over to join us then. We chatted for a few more minutes and then parted ways with them and resumed our trek over to the food trucks. We decided to order from the grilled cheese truck, which had specialty melts on the menu, along with fries, salads, and milkshakes. The delicious smells wafting from the truck made my stomach rumble and my mouth water.

While Brett and I waited in line behind three other people, Sienna waved at me, catching my eye. She was in line at a funnel cake truck with her friend Ellie, whom I'd first met the previous spring when she took part in an amateur chef competition.

"I'll be back in a minute," I told Brett, leaving him to stay in line while I darted around a few people to get to Sienna.

She and Ellie had already paid for their orders, and the food truck owner handed them each a funnel cake, Sienna's drizzled with chocolate and Ellie's with strawberry sauce.

"How are you enjoying the event so far?" I asked the girls once we'd moved into the shade cast by a maple tree.

"It's really cool," Ellie said.

"And the food's delicious." Sienna took a bite of her funnel cake. "We're going to check out the stagecoach robbery later, but then we're heading down to the beach to meet up with some friends."

"I'd better tell my mom about that," Ellie said. "I'll be right back."

She set off towards another maple tree where her mother was chatting with two other women.

Sienna was about to say something, but she hesitated and apparently thought better of it, taking another bite of her funnel cake instead. I took her arm and gently tugged her farther away from the people lined up at the nearest food truck.

"Okay, spill," I said once we had more privacy.

Her eyes widened. "Spill what?"

"Whatever it is you've been wanting to say to me for the past couple of weeks. I know there's *something*. Can't you just tell me?"

Sienna stared down at her funnel cake but didn't take another bite. "I'm nervous."

"Why?" I asked. "Are you wanting to leave The Flip Side before August?"

"No!" Her gaze shot up to meet mine. "Is that what you thought?"

"I wondered."

She sighed. "I wouldn't leave The Flip Side at all if I didn't have to."

"I thought you might need some time to get ready to head off to college."

"I don't need to stop working to do that." She hesitated. "Unless you want me to?"

"No way," I said quickly. "I'm going to miss you like crazy when you go." She smiled briefly. "Same."

"So why are you nervous?" I asked, getting back on track.

She dropped her gaze to her food again. "I don't want you to think I'm stupid."

"Sienna, I would never think that," I assured her with complete sincerity. "You can tell me anything, and I promise I won't judge you. No matter what."

She bit down on her lower lip and glanced around as if making sure no one else could hear us. I wondered if I should be worried about what she was about to say.

"Okay," she said to start. "You love mysteries, right?"

"Understatement of the century."

She smiled at that. "And you like *reading* mysteries, right?"

"Of course. More than any other genre." I had no idea where she was going with this.

"Well…" She drew in a deep breath and then blurted out, "I wrote a mystery novel and was wondering if you'd read it and tell me what you think."

Her words came out so fast that it took a moment for my brain to register them. As soon as their meaning sank in, my face broke into a smile.

"Sienna, that's fantastic! I didn't know you were writing a book!"

"I didn't want anyone to know," she whispered. "My mom knows, and I told Tommy recently, but they're both sworn to secrecy."

"But that's such a great accomplishment," I said. "Why wouldn't you want anyone to know? And why were you nervous about asking me to read it? I'm thrilled that you want me to."

Cautious hope showed in her brown eyes. "Really?"

"Of course."

She kept her voice low. "I wanted it to be a secret because I didn't know how it would turn out. If no one knows about it, then I don't have to be embarrassed if it's total garbage."

"I can guarantee you right now that it's not total garbage," I said. "But I can also understand why you don't want to announce it to the world. Yet, anyway. No matter what anyone else might think, though, the fact that you wrote a book from start to finish is really amazing."

She smiled, and I thought I detected a slight shimmer of tears in her eyes. "Thanks, Marley. I had so much fun writing it, and…" She lowered her voice to a whisper again. "I've decided that I really want to become a published author."

I gave her a hug, being careful not to cause her funnel cake to tumble to the ground. "I think that's awesome. And I'm really honored that you want my feedback."

"Even though I'm nervous, I'm excited to know what you think since you're a mystery expert and all."

"I don't know about being an expert," I said, "but I do love mysteries, and I'll help you out any way I can."

Her smile grew brighter. "Thank you. But you'll be honest, right? If it sucks, don't pretend it doesn't."

"I already know it doesn't, but yes, I'll be honest."

She looked as though a weight had lifted off her shoulders. "You have no idea what this means to me, Marley."

"And you have no idea how much it means to me that you asked for my help."

Ellie was heading back in our direction, and Brett was paying for our food, so we prepared to go our separate ways. First, though, Sienna told me that she would email me her manuscript later that night, and I promised that I wouldn't share her secret with anyone other than Brett, who would also be sworn to secrecy.

Brett and I found a free picnic table at the quieter end of the park and sat down to enjoy our dinner. The cheese melts were so gooey and delicious that I wished the food truck was a permanent fixture in Wildwood Cove. The fries and chocolate milkshakes tasted equally good. The fries were crisp and salty, and the milkshakes were creamy, cold, and packed full of chocolate flavor.

"I'm not sure I can move now," I said, once we'd polished off our food. Brett treated me to the lopsided grin I loved. "I take it you're still not interested in mechanical bull riding then."

I put a hand to my full stomach. "No way." That would be a disaster. Despite over-indulging, I managed to get to my feet. We returned to the heart of the festivities, where we took part in a cowboy boot toss and gold panning. I found a few flecks of gold, and Brett turned up a tiny nugget.

By the time we'd finished panning, the daylight was starting to fade from the sky. I decided to take a few more photos before it got too dark, even though I'd likely be back on the weekend to take in more of the event. I used my phone to snap pictures of the old west street and some of the people in period costume.

Two costumed men hanging outside the saloon were pretending to argue, using plenty of old west insults.

"Yer so ugly you could scare a buzzard off a gut wagon," one yelled.

"If yer brains were dynamite, there wouldn't be enough to blow yer nose!" the other man threw back.

I laughed and filmed a short clip of them on my phone. Right after I'd stopped filming, I heard someone call my name. I turned around to see Lisa heading my way, her smile brighter than the sun had been earlier in the day.

"Hey," I said, "I'm glad you made it. Are you here alone, or is Ivan with you?"

"He's here. He's buying us some food." Her eyes sparkled as she took my arm and guided me off to the side of the old west street, away from the crowd gathering around the saloon.

"What is it you wanted to tell me?" I asked her. "You left me in suspense."

"I know. Sorry about that, but I really wanted to tell you in person." She looked like she was about to burst with excitement.

"No more suspense," I told her.

She held up her left hand and wiggled her fingers. The evening sun glinted off a diamond ring.

My eyes widened, and my jaw dropped. "Is that what I think it is?"

"If you're thinking it's an engagement ring, then yes."

"Oh my gosh!" I threw my arms around her and squeezed before letting go. "Since when?"

"Since last night at dinner. Well, right after dinner. We took a walk along the beach, and that's where he popped the question."

"That sounds romantic." Brett had proposed to me on the beach too, and I couldn't have picked a better spot. I hugged Lisa again. "I'm so happy for both of you."

She was still beaming when I released her. "Thank you. It's like I've been floating on a cloud ever since."

"I know what you mean." I remembered the feeling well. "Did you see it coming?"

"No. Although with hindsight, maybe I should have."

I looped my arm through hers as we half-watched Brett having another go at the cowboy boot toss while we continued our conversation.

I connected dots in my mind. "Ivan's mysterious trips to Port Angeles."

Lisa held up her left hand again. "He was buying the ring. He picked it out on the first trip to the jewelry store, but he didn't know my ring size. When he went back, he took one of my other rings with him, so it's a perfect fit." She admired the ring, looking the happiest I'd ever seen her.

"So when's the big day?" I asked. "Have you set a date?"

"Not yet. I'm still getting used to the fact that we're engaged. And I haven't even told my parents. After we eat, we're heading over to visit them so we can share the news."

"They'll be happy, right?" I asked.

"Definitely. It took them time to warm up to Ivan, but now they adore him."

"Good."

I could understand her parents being wary of Ivan at first. His muscles, tattoos, and habit of scowling belied the heart of gold within. He also wasn't the easiest man to get to know, but anyone who spent time with him soon found out what a good man he was.

"I'm so thrilled for you two," I said.

Ivan headed our way, carrying food and drinks on a cardboard tray. Before he had a chance to say anything, I launched myself at him and gave him a big hug.

When I looked up at his face, I could tell I'd taken him by surprise, but at least he'd managed not to drop the food.

"Lisa told me about the engagement," I said as I stepped back. "And it's the best news I've heard in a long time."

Brett came over to join us then, so Lisa showed him the ring too. As he gave Lisa a hug and shook Ivan's hand, I noticed a very rare sight—Ivan's usual scowl was nowhere to be seen.

Chapter Twenty-Six

After Ivan and Lisa left for her parents' place, Brett and I didn't hang around the park much longer. Brett took part in one more game of the cowboy boot toss, and this time managed to win a prize by landing three boots inside the hula hoop. He handed me his prize—an adorable stuffed donkey—and took my hand as we set off for home.

Once we were ready for bed, I placed the donkey on the top of our chest of drawers.

"First toy for our future baby?" I said as I climbed into bed.

"I like the sound of that." Brett got into bed next to me.

I settled against the pillows and grabbed my e-reader from the bedside table. I'd loaded Sienna's manuscript onto it as soon as we'd arrived home.

I was vaguely aware of Brett reading a paperback next to me, but mostly the world faded away as I delved into Sienna's opening chapters. I'd fallen so far into the story that I was momentarily disoriented when Brett nudged me.

"You planning to read all night?" he asked.

I glanced at the clock. "Whoa. It's that late?" A whole hour had disappeared since I'd started reading.

"Sienna's book must be good," Brett said as he switched off the lamp on his side of the bed.

I'd told him about Sienna's manuscript on our walk home from the park earlier.

"So good." I reluctantly shut off my e-reader and set it aside. I didn't want to put the book down, but I had to be up early in the morning.

I switched off my lamp as Brett shifted closer so he could put his arms around me.

I snuggled up against his chest as my thoughts drifted away from the engrossing story Sienna had written.

"What's wrong?" Brett asked after several seconds of silence.

"Nothing, really," I said. "I just remembered how Tommy said he'd given up hope that the hit-and-run case would get solved."

"You haven't given up hope too, have you?"

"Not yet." I got to the point of what was really on my mind. "But I wish I could do something to help."

Brett ran a hand down my hair. "You've already done lots."

"It doesn't feel like it. The driver still hasn't been found."

"You went looking for Tommy when he was missing," Brett pointed out. "Who knows how long he would have been lying in that ditch if you hadn't."

I suppressed a shudder. "I can't even bear to think about it." I fell quiet for a minute before speaking again. "Still, I wish I could help identify the driver."

"What are you planning?" Brett asked as he tucked my hair behind my ear.

"Nothing. Yet. I don't know what to do."

"Don't worry," he said, and I could hear the humor in his voice. "It'll come to you. Just be sure to let me know once *you* know."

I smiled into his chest. "Are you going to be my partner in crime-solving?"

"Partner in everything," he said.

I raised myself up on one elbow so I could kiss him. "Forever."

* * * *

By the next morning, I did have a plan. It wasn't much of one, but at least it gave me something to focus on. I couldn't put it into action until after work, so I tried to stay focused on other things in the meantime. As soon as I had The Flip Side ready to open, I sent a text message to Sienna, telling her how much I loved her book already and how I'd had trouble putting it down. I didn't want to leave her in suspense. Hopefully my text message would put her at ease.

Everything I told her was the absolute truth. I'd read the first several chapters the night before and another one over breakfast. I would have kept reading if Brett hadn't pointed out the time to me.

Sienna's book was a cozy mystery, my favorite kind. I already adored her spunky heroine, Caroline, and I enjoyed the seaside setting and the cast of quirky characters. I could tell that Sienna had drawn upon her experience of growing up in a small town, and her writing left me truly impressed. I didn't doubt that she could have a career as a writer if she set her mind to it.

Many of the customers who showed up at the pancake house for breakfast, brunch, and lunch had attended Wild West Days the night before. Most intended to go back again either this evening or over the next couple of days. I didn't hear a bad word about the event, and it seemed everyone was hoping this wouldn't be the only one of its kind. When I brought up the idea of Pirate Days, which had been mentioned at Brett's poker night, several customers voiced their enthusiasm for it. I decided it was worth making a suggestion to the committee that had organized Wild West Days.

I didn't have much time to pause for a rest while The Flip Side was open, but after closing for the day, I enjoyed a late lunch of frittata in the kitchen while Ivan prepared a few things for the next day and tidied up.

"How did things go with Lisa's family?" I asked.

I suspected I already knew the answer. It probably wouldn't have been obvious to anyone who didn't know Ivan well, but I'd noticed several times throughout the day that he didn't look as dour as usual. My guess was that meant that he was practically floating with happiness.

"It went well," he said as he washed his hands at the sink. "They seem happy for Lisa."

"I'm glad," I said with a smile. "I'm so excited for you guys."

He nodded his thanks as he dried his hands. "I'm a lucky man."

"And Lisa's a lucky woman."

I didn't stick around the pancake house much longer. I'd arranged to meet up with Brett in the late afternoon, so he could help me with my plan, such as it was. I killed time until he arrived home from work by taking Bentley for a walk on the beach. I even kicked off my shoes and dared to wade into the ocean up to my ankles. My feet didn't go numb immediately, which was a positive sign. Maybe the water would be warm enough for me to take a swim sooner than I thought.

After Brett arrived home, we hopped in his truck and drove along Wildwood Road in the direction of the highway.

"Whereabouts were Tommy's phone and wallet found?" Brett asked.

"Right around here, I think." We'd reached a gentle bend in the road.

I'd texted Tommy earlier in the day, asking if he could be more precise about where the items had been found. He asked Ray and got back to me, saying they were located in the bushes near the final bend in the road before the highway. The highway wasn't yet in sight, but I could hear cars zooming by now and then.

Brett pulled his truck onto the grassy verge and shut off the engine. I hopped out and jumped across the dry ditch. Ferns and bushes grew directly in front of me, with the forest starting within a few more feet.

"I should have brought a big stick," I said, eyeing the bushes I intended to search.

"I've got something that might work." Brett reached into the bed of his truck before joining me across the ditch. He passed me an old broom handle.

"Thanks. That'll help." I used the stick to nudge aside some ferns so I could get a look beneath them.

"What are you hoping to find?" Brett asked as we worked our way along the edge of the ditch, searching the bushes.

"Tommy's camera, ideally." I knew he'd love to have it back. "Other than that, I don't really know. I guess I just need to feel like I'm at least trying to help out."

"I'm sure Ray and his deputies came out and had a look after Tommy's wallet and phone were turned in," Brett said.

"I know." Which meant we were likely wasting our time.

That seemed to be the case as the minutes passed, with us turning up nothing other than a few pieces of trash. Brett collected those—while wearing work gloves—and put them into a garbage bag he'd retrieved from the truck.

After we'd searched all the way up to and around the bend, we moved a few feet into the woods and headed back toward the truck, checking among the trees and undergrowth. Again, all we turned up was some trash.

"At least we're cleaning up the environment," I said with a sigh of disappointment when we arrived back at our starting point. "I knew we weren't likely to find any clues, but it really would have made Tommy's week—maybe his entire month—if we'd turned up his camera."

"The driver probably kept the camera," Brett said, and I knew he was likely right about that. "Or maybe he or she forgot about it and ditched it somewhere else later on."

I considered that possibility. "That could have happened. If the driver tossed Tommy's things on the passenger seat, the camera could have fallen off. The driver was probably panicking or close to it. He or she might not have realized they'd forgotten to toss it out."

"But in that case, the camera could be miles away," Brett pointed out. "If the driver didn't hold onto it, that is."

"True." My shoulders slumped, but then another thought raised my hopes again. "But maybe they didn't drive very far before realizing they'd forgotten about the camera."

"We can't search all the way along the highway," Brett said. "Even if we had a whole search team, that wouldn't be practical. We don't even know if the driver turned left or right onto the highway. If they went out there at all."

I had to concede that he'd made good points. There weren't all that many places to stop between where we stood and the highway, but there were a few houses and a road that led off through the woods and curved around to the southern part of the town.

"Can we search a little longer?" I asked, not ready to give up quite yet. "Another twenty minutes, and then I promise we'll quit."

Brett agreed without complaint. I gave him a kiss, appreciating how he so willingly humored me time and time again.

We jogged along the road to the farthest point we'd reached during the first phase of our search and continued on beyond that point. As the twenty-minute mark ticked closer, my hopes faded. I had nothing more to go on in terms of identifying the driver who'd hit Tommy, and it didn't look like his camera was anywhere to be found.

I was within minutes of admitting defeat and giving up when something glinted in a small shaft of sunlight filtering through the trees. I ventured farther into the woods, using the broom handle to shift aside some vines and spindly branches that almost tripped me up. I crouched down and parted some ferns.

"Did you find something?" Brett asked, twigs snapping beneath his feet as he came over to join me.

"It's a cell phone." I reached out to pick it up, but pulled my hand back before making contact with the device. "We know it's not Tommy's phone, so it can't have anything to do with the hit-and-run, right?"

Brett knew what I was getting at. "You're worried about contaminating evidence? It's probably not an issue, but I guess there's always a chance the driver robbed other people that night."

I stood up, leaving the phone on the ground. "You're right. Better safe than sorry."

"Here." Brett took off his work gloves and handed them to me.

I slipped them on. They were too big for me, but they would still protect the phone from my fingerprints. I picked up the device.

"It doesn't look like it's in bad condition," Brett said. "It probably hasn't been here too long."

I tried to turn it on. Nothing happened.

"The battery is dead, but that's not surprising." I checked the back of the phone. It had a plain black case and no special identifying features. "No clues as to whom it belongs to, but it's the same model as mine. If I charge it and can get it to turn on, maybe we'll be able to figure out whose it is."

"Worth a try," Brett agreed.

"There's no point in telling Ray about it yet, is there?" I asked as we walked back toward the truck.

"Let's wait until we've at least tried to find out who the owner is. Someone probably just lost it."

I figured he was right about that.

When we arrived home, I hooked the phone up to my charger and plugged it in before we turned our attention to preparing dinner. I made some curried couscous while Brett chopped up vegetables and marinated some jumbo shrimp. He took the shrimp and veggies out to the barbecue while I kept an eye on the couscous.

As I fetched two plates from the cupboard, I heard Brett talking to someone out on the back porch.

"You've got a visitor, Marley," he called through the open French doors.

Sienna stepped into the house. "Do you really like it?" she asked before I had a chance to say hello.

She looked cautiously hopeful. I didn't have to ask to know what she was talking about.

"Like isn't a strong enough word," I said. "I love it. You're so talented, Sienna. For real."

She squealed with delight and threw her arms around me, squeezing all the air out of my lungs.

"Can't…breathe," I gasped.

She released me. "Sorry!" She bounced up and down. "You really think it's good?"

"Yes." I took her by the shoulders. "It's seriously amazing. I'm ten chapters in and can't wait to read the rest."

Brett poked his head in through the open door. "Do I get to read it next?"

Sienna's eyes widened. "I don't know if my nerves can handle that. I've been a wreck ever since I emailed it to Marley."

"I guess I'll have to wait till it's published, then," Brett said with a grin before disappearing from sight.

"I'm so happy." Sienna looked almost giddy. "Thank you so much for reading it."

"Believe me, it's my pleasure," I assured her.

Sienna hung around for a few more minutes before heading home for her own dinner, a bright smile lighting up her face.

By the time Brett and I had finished eating and had cleaned up the kitchen, I figured the phone would have enough of a charge to turn on if it wasn't damaged inside.

"Let's see if we can get this thing powered up." I unplugged it from the charger and hit the power button, using a tissue to protect the device from my fingerprints. I almost cheered when the phone turned on.

The smile dropped from my face a few seconds later.

I recognized the background of the lock screen.

It was one of the covers for *Pride and Prejudice*.

I was holding Jane Fassbender's missing cell phone.

Chapter Twenty-Seven

"We need to call Ray," Brett said as soon as I told him about recognizing the lock screen.

I set the phone down on the kitchen table, taking even more care now to ensure that I didn't leave any fingerprints on it. I hoped the tissue hadn't wiped away any that had already been there.

Brett had his phone out and was putting a call through to Ray. He had a short conversation with his uncle before hanging up.

"He'll be here in about ten minutes," Brett said.

I sat down at the kitchen table and stared at Jane's phone, which had gone to sleep. "So, Jane's killer stole her phone and then ditched it at the side of the road?"

"Seems like it," Brett said.

"But why steal it in the first place?"

"Maybe it had some incriminating evidence on it?" he suggested.

"In that case, it would have been smarter to destroy it rather than simply tossing it in the bushes."

"Someone who just committed a murder might not be thinking too clearly."

"True," I said. "But doesn't it seem strange that we found it so close to the spot where Tommy's wallet and phone were found?"

"Maybe." He didn't sound entirely sure.

I bit down on my lower lip as I continued to stare at the phone.

"What are you thinking?" Brett asked.

"Do you still have that pen with the stylus on the end?"

"Sure. I think it's in the office." He headed down the hall to the front of the house. He reappeared seconds later with the turquoise pen.

Keeping the tissue between my finger and the device, I woke up the phone again.

"How are you going to unlock it?" Brett asked. "And don't you think it would be best to leave this to Ray?"

"Probably," I conceded, but that didn't make me give up on what I was doing. I was glad the phone didn't require a thumbprint to unlock it, but I had to figure out the six-digit passcode if I wanted to access anything on the device. "I wonder what Jane's birthdate is."

Brett opened the fridge. "You might be able to find out on Facebook." He held up a jug. "Sweet tea?"

"Please. And that's a good idea." I grabbed my own phone and searched the social media site until I found Jane's profile. Fortunately, she had her birthdate there for everyone to see.

I used the year and month, but without success. I tried again, changing the order of the numbers.

"Darn." I slumped down in my chair, feeling defeated.

"Someone at the sheriff's department will be able to crack it." Brett poured two glasses of sweet tea. "We need to be careful. Sometimes a phone will automatically get erased after ten failed passcode attempts."

"Ugh. You're right. I can't risk that. Even if the information could be recovered, I'm pretty sure Ray would be furious." I sat up straight. "Hold on. Jane loved Jane Austen's books. She even has the *Pride and Prejudice* cover as her lock screen."

Brett set one of the glasses on the table for me. "So you're thinking her password could be Austen-related."

"I'm hoping so." I used my own phone to access the Internet again. This time I looked up Jane Austen's birthdate. December 16, 1775.

I entered the numbers 121775 with the stylus.

The phone unlocked.

I exhaled with relief. "It worked!"

Brett kissed the top of my head. "I married a smart woman."

"It was a lucky guess, really," I said. "Although I probably shouldn't argue with that statement."

"It's a truth universally acknowledged," Brett said with a grin.

I smiled at that, although my attention was already shifting back to Jane's phone. I used the stylus to take a look at the photos on the device, but they all seemed ordinary to me. She had a few pictures taken at the museum and others of flowers growing in someone's garden.

I checked her text messages next, but nothing jumped out at me as unusual or incriminating. She'd exchanged messages with Evangeline about the museum's reopening party, and she'd also sent a few texts to Dean about the refinishing of the museum's floors. Frankie was also in her contacts, but the messages they'd exchanged were unremarkable. The next conversation was between Jane and Adya Banerjee.

Have you seen my silver bracelet? Adya had asked a few days before Jane's death.

No. Did you lose it? Jane had responded.

Maybe, was Adya's reply.

No further messages followed.

So Adya probably had told me the truth when she'd said she was searching Jane's office at the museum for a lost bracelet. But why would she think it would be in Jane's desk? Maybe she assumed that if Jane had found it in the museum, she would have tucked it away for safe-keeping. Considering how much Adya disliked Jane, it surprised me that she would have spent any time at the museum, but if she'd lost something there, she must have been present at some point.

"Anything of interest?" Brett asked from across the room. He'd settled into an armchair with his glass of sweet tea.

Bentley stood beside the chair, his tail wagging as Brett stroked his curly fur.

"Not really," I replied.

"Ray should be here any minute."

I knew why he'd mentioned that. It probably wouldn't be good if Ray found me searching through the phone when he arrived. Although I'd likely have to admit to my snooping anyway, since I wanted him to have Jane's passcode.

Before giving up, I checked the call log on Jane's phone. I remembered that she'd phoned Winnifred from her home's landline shortly after eight on the night she died. I now knew that wasn't the last call Jane had made before she was killed.

At twenty-seven minutes after eight, Jane had phoned a number that had no contact information connected to it.

I wanted to jot down the number Jane had called, but footsteps sounded out on the back porch, and Bentley shot out the door. I pushed the phone aside with the stylus as Ray, in his sheriff's uniform, appeared with Bentley bouncing around him with excitement.

I got up from my seat at the table. "If we'd had any idea that it was Jane's phone, I never would have picked it up, and we would have called you right away."

Ray nodded, his serious gaze shifting from me to the phone sitting on the table. "I understand." He looked to Brett. "You said you found it near where Tommy Park's phone and wallet were located?"

"Tommy told us where his things were found," Brett said. "This phone was a little farther along the road."

"Closer to the highway," I added.

Ray produced a pen and a plastic evidence bag from his pocket. He nudged the phone with the pen until it slipped into the baggie.

"And how do you know it's the one Jane had in her possession?" Ray directed the question at me.

"It's the same model as mine, so I charged it and turned it on," I said.

"We were hoping to find a clue as to who it belonged to," Brett chipped in.

"I recognized the lock screen right away." I pressed the power button through the evidence bag, and the phone lit up in Ray's hand. "It's the same *Pride and Prejudice* cover art as I saw on the phone Jane had."

"I see it's passcode protected," Ray observed before the screen went dark again.

"Um. About that." I wasn't eager to confess the full extent of my snooping, even though I knew I had to.

Ray heaved out a sigh. "Let me guess. You cracked the code."

Behind Ray, Brett was fighting a grin, but his uncle didn't look amused. His serious expression hadn't changed one bit since he'd arrived.

"I did," I said, unable to help feeling sheepish in the face of Ray's steady gaze. "It's 121775. The month and year of Jane Austen's birth."

Ray stared me down until I was ready to squirm. "And I'm guessing your fingerprints are on it."

Brett came to my defense. "We tried not to leave any."

I pointed out the tissue and stylus lying on the table. "I picked it up with the tissue each time. I almost touched it when I first found it, but then we wondered if it could be related to the hit-and-run."

"We thought maybe the driver had robbed more people than just Tommy that night," Brett explained.

"So I made sure not to touch it directly. I used the stylus on the screen." I winced. "I hope I didn't wipe away any fingerprints that were already there."

"We'll find out soon enough." Ray didn't sound angry, but he also didn't sound impressed.

"I'm sorry," I said. "We really didn't suspect that it could belong to Jane until we turned it on."

"I understand that," he assured me. "But once you knew it was hers, you should have let it be."

"Fair enough," I conceded.

I wasn't about to bring up the fact that I'd snooped through Jane's photos, text messages, and call log. I didn't think there was much point. Ray and his deputies would check out all those things themselves. Telling him what I'd done would only make him more annoyed with me, something I wanted to avoid.

Ray glanced out the window, where the daylight was starting to fade. A few puffy clouds over the ocean were tinged with pink and orange.

Ray held up the bagged phone. "Any chance one of you can show me exactly where you found this?"

"I can," I offered, eager to make up for my transgressions.

"I'll take Bentley for a short walk while you're gone," Brett said.

I gave him a kiss and followed Ray out the back door. Brett held onto Bentley's collar, keeping him from bounding after us.

I caught a glimpse of the beautiful sunset in the western sky as we descended the porch steps, but then I jogged to catch up to Ray, whose brisk strides had already taken him around the corner of the house. We climbed into his cruiser and, within a couple of minutes, I pointed out the spot where I'd found Jane's phone.

"Did you ever find out why the phone wasn't under Jane's name?" I asked as Ray pulled over to the side of the road.

"It turns out Jane had a foster brother growing up, and they've remained close as adults. According to her sister, Jane probably got the phone from the foster brother. He's off backpacking in South America. We're in the process of tracking down any phone numbers in his name, so we should know soon if the one you found is a match for any of his."

We got out of the cruiser so I could show him the exact bush that had concealed the device.

"It's close to where Tommy's things were found, right?" I said as Ray surveyed the area.

"The person who found them picked them up just around the bend." He pointed back down the road toward the area Brett and I had searched first.

"Don't you think it's an awfully big coincidence that Jane's phone was found so close to Tommy's?"

"Sometimes coincidences are just coincidences..."

"And sometimes they're not?" I guessed at what he'd left unsaid.

The only acknowledgment he gave me was a slight tip of his head to one side.

As much as I wanted to interrogate him about his investigations, I decided not to push my luck. While we drove back down the road through the deepening darkness, I bit my tongue and forced myself to contain all the questions trying to bubble their way out of me.

Chapter Twenty-Eight

The Saturday morning breakfast rush left me run off my feet and extra glad that I had more interviews lined up for potential new staff members. At least Logan was in the kitchen today, helping to lighten Ivan's load. The first customers were waiting outside the door when I opened the pancake house at seven o'clock, and many more followed on their heels. I didn't even have a chance to tell Sienna about finding Jane's phone until midmorning, when the rush of hungry customers finally eased slightly.

"It must have been Jane's killer who tossed her phone in the bushes, right?" Sienna asked, after listening to my every word of the tale with bated breath.

"It does seem most likely," I said.

We had to pause our conversation so Sienna could take orders and I could clean up a table that a group of four had vacated moments before.

"And it's just a coincidence that Jane's phone was so close to where Tommy's was found?" Sienna asked a moment later as we both headed to the kitchen. Her tone of voice told me she found that hard to believe.

"I've been wrestling with that very question." I lowered my voice to a whisper as we entered the kitchen. "But I don't see how the two crimes could be connected."

Sienna dropped off the order slips she'd brought with her and then headed back out of the kitchen, but not before sending me a pointed look, silently telling me she wanted to continue our conversation.

Ivan watched my every move as I loaded a stack of dirty dishes into the dishwasher. I sent him an innocent smile on my way back out of the kitchen, but I doubted that I'd fooled him. He might not have been able to hear what Sienna and I had said, but I knew he suspected that we were talking about Jane's murder.

Sienna practically pounced on me when I emerged from the kitchen. "Maybe the killer was in a panic after murdering Jane and was driving too fast and hit Tommy." She said all that in a whisper so no customers would overhear.

"I considered that too." The possibility had run through my head the night before, along with a few others, until I'd put an end to all speculation by losing myself in Sienna's book. "But Tommy was hit west of the museum, and the driver was heading east."

She considered that. "And the driver would have been going the other way if they were fleeing the murder scene."

"Plus, the hit-and-run might have taken place later than the murder," I added.

"But we don't know that for sure?"

"No," I confirmed. "I suppose it's possible the driver who hit Tommy was in a rush to go kill Jane."

Sienna's eyes widened. "That must be it!"

We had to put an end to our conversation then as business had picked up again, and a steady stream of customers wanted to satisfy their hunger with some of Ivan's delicious cooking. I wasn't quite as convinced as Sienna that Jane's killer was also the driver who'd struck Tommy. Even though I felt deep down that it wasn't a coincidence that the two phones were found in the same area, I couldn't make all the puzzle pieces snap together in my mind.

What still troubled me was why the driver would have stopped and taken the time to steal Tommy's possessions. Tommy hadn't been able to identify the driver, but the culprit still put himself or herself at risk of being seen by stopping and getting out of the car rather than driving away immediately. If someone was on their way to commit a murder, why would they risk being seen heading in that direction? Of course, it was possible that the murderer didn't plan to kill Jane. It could have been a spur of the moment reaction during an argument or disagreement. In fact, the choice of murder weapon made that seem more likely.

I shook my head, trying to get all the questions and scenarios to settle in my mind so I could focus on work. I had some success with quieting my thoughts, thanks to the demands of the lunch rush, but the best distraction came a short while later when Richard Hobbs walked into The Flip Side.

He picked up a days-old newspaper from the stand by the door and took it with him to a vacant table in the restaurant's far corner. I wasn't quite as surprised to see him at The Flip Side as I had been to see Evangeline dining here, but I still hadn't expected him to show up for a meal. I figured he was much more used to fine dining, as was his wife.

"Hi, Mr. Hobbs," I greeted as I held up the coffee pot. "Coffee to start?" He nodded, so I filled his mug.

"Is this your first time at The Flip Side?" I asked as I poured.

"I thought I should try it out," he said by way of reply. "My wife was here the other day and was surprised to find that the food was good despite the...quaint atmosphere."

It didn't surprise me that Evangeline had said something like that. At least she'd admitted that the food was good.

I handed Richard a laminated menu. "I'm glad she enjoyed her meal enough to mention it to you."

He studied the menu as he spoke. "My wife mentions everything to me. I get a blow-by-blow account of every conversation and every hour of every day." He let out a weary sigh. "I came here for some peace and quiet as much as for some food."

I wasn't sure what to say to that, so I didn't comment. "Should I give you a few minutes with the menu?" I asked instead.

He assured me that he didn't need more time and ordered the bacon cheddar waffles with sausages and hash browns.

Not long after I delivered Richard's waffles to him, Adya Banerjee came into The Flip Side with two other women. Leigh served the group, so I didn't have any contact with Adya, but seeing her reminded me of her brief text exchange with Jane, and the time I found her in Jane's office, ostensibly searching for her missing bracelet.

As closing time drew nearer and the crowd of diners dwindled, I slipped into the office, where I'd left my phone. I sent a quick text message to Marjorie, asking if her friend's granddaughter knew anything about a missing bracelet belonging to Adya. I wasn't sure what kind of information I was fishing for, exactly, but I had some unanswered questions about Adya, and I was hoping to put at least one to rest.

I left my phone on the desk and returned to the dining room.

"I hung out with Tommy yesterday after school," Sienna said after the last diner had gone.

I flipped the sign on the door. "Did you beat him at Mario Kart again?"

"My kids love that game," Leigh said as she slipped past us on her way to deposit dirty dishes in the kitchen.

"Me too," Sienna said. "But we played other games this time. He beat me, but that's only because the games were new to me. With a little practice, I can take him."

I smiled as I wiped down a table. "I have no doubt. I saw him at Wild West Days on Thursday night. I'm glad he was able to get out and about."

Sienna stacked dirty plates on one of the tables. "Except, he kind of overdid it."

I paused in my cleaning. "Is he okay?"

"His ribs were bothering him. He figures he shouldn't have spent so much time out at the park."

That wasn't good.

I decided I should check on him. "I'll stop by his place after I finish up here. I'm sure I can find some food to take him."

"He'll like that." Sienna fetched her belongings from the breakroom. "Don't forget to keep me up to date on your investigation."

"I might be too busy reading your book to investigate," I said with a smile.

"Somehow, I don't think you could ever be too busy for sleuthing." She flashed me a cheeky smile and disappeared out the front door.

Leigh left a minute or two later, and I soon finished cleaning the dining area. I checked my phone and found a couple of responses from Marjorie. Her first message told me she would check with Desiree, her friend's granddaughter, about the bracelet. About half an hour later, she'd messaged me again.

Desiree says Adya kicked up a fuss about losing a silver bracelet a few weeks ago. She told some of her colleagues that she thought Jane might have stolen it. Is this significant?

Maybe, I wrote back. *I'll let you know. Thanks for the info!*

No wonder Adya had been searching Jane's desk. If Jane really had stolen the bracelet, as Adya believed, that was one logical place to look for it, and the museum was easier to access and search than Jane's house. I realized I didn't know where Jane lived. I hadn't heard any rumors about her house being broken into. That didn't mean Adya hadn't been there, but if the police had responded to a break-in, the news probably would have spread through town.

I wondered if Adya had an alibi for the time of Jane's death. If Adya truly believed that Jane had stolen her bracelet—whether or not she was right—that strengthened Adya's motive for murder. That perceived injustice combined with Jane's promotion and her behavior at the staff meeting might have pushed Adya over the edge.

I wasn't sure how to go about finding out if Adya had an alibi. I didn't know anyone close to her, so I figured I might have to strike up a conversation with her myself. Exactly how I'd go about getting the information I wanted, I didn't yet know. That was something I'd have to think over. In the meantime, I wanted to check on Tommy.

I stopped by the kitchen, where Ivan insisted on using some leftover batter to cook crêpes for Tommy. He made s'mores crêpes, one of Tommy's favorite dishes. I also popped an apple cinnamon scone and a chocolate chip muffin into a paper bag for him. The last two remaining chocolate chip muffins went into another bag for me and Brett to enjoy later.

On my way out of the pancake house, I returned to the office to fetch my tote bag. My gaze landed on my phone, where it sat on the desk. I thought about the phone call Jane had made before her death. I'd wanted to copy down the number while I was looking at Jane's phone, but Ray's arrival had cut short my chance to do that. When I'd returned home from showing Ray where I'd found Jane's phone, I'd scribbled the number down on a scrap of paper. At least, I hoped I'd written it down correctly. By that time, I wasn't positive that I hadn't muddled up the last couple of digits.

I wanted to try calling the number to see who would answer, but I'd left the scrap piece of paper at home, and I couldn't remember more than the first three digits off the top of my head. I'd have to try the number later, I decided as I pushed aside my disappointment. Tommy was first on my priority list. After I'd visited him, hopefully I'd have a chance to follow that line of investigation before I had to be at the museum for another round of volunteering.

Chapter Twenty-Nine

As I walked up the cement pathway to Tommy's house, the door opened. At first, I thought that Tommy had seen me approaching and was coming to greet me, but then Evangeline emerged from the house. I stopped in my tracks, surprised. She paused on the porch to say something to Tommy, who was propped up on his crutches in the foyer, and then she turned and managed to descend the steps gracefully, despite her stiletto heels. If I'd worn shoes like hers, I'd have broken my ankle on flat ground. I could never have safely navigated a set of stairs. She made it look deceptively easy.

"Hello," she said in an airy voice as she passed by me.

I returned the greeting and watched her go. She climbed into a black BMW parked by the curb and sped away a moment later.

"She's about the last person I would have expected to see here," I said as I climbed the steps to the porch.

"I know, right? But it was about the gala." Tommy shoved the door shut and led the way to the living room. "She said she wanted to give me a bonus because of what happened on my way home. I told her it wasn't necessary, but she insisted." He used one of his crutches to point out a white envelope sitting on the coffee table. "Two hundred and fifty bucks!"

"That was generous of her." Maybe I needed to revise my opinion of Evangeline. Clearly, she wasn't entirely wrapped up in herself.

I set the takeout container and paper bags next to the envelope.

"I'll say." Tommy sank into an armchair and set his crutches aside. "She'd already paid me well for the photos."

I smacked a hand to my forehead. "Of course! The photos! I can't believe I never asked you about that before. Were you still able to deliver them, even though your camera was stolen?"

Tommy eased his broken leg onto a footstool. "Fortunately. I uploaded all the photos to my cloud before I left the gala."

A thought began to take shape in my mind. "You don't think…"

"What?" Tommy asked. Before I had a chance to respond, he added another question. "Is that food you've got there?"

I'd almost forgotten about the crêpes and other treats I'd brought for him. "S'mores crêpes, a muffin, and a scone."

"You know, you're welcome to visit me any time."

I laughed. "I'm guessing you want the crêpes right away."

"Please."

I fetched him a plate and some cutlery from the kitchen.

"So, what were you thinking?" he asked after he'd enjoyed his first bite of the crêpes.

"It's probably a long shot, but what if your camera was stolen because of the photos on it?"

Tommy paused before digging into his crêpes again. "Then the driver probably would have been someone who was at the gala. And they might have hit me on purpose." After I nodded in agreement, he continued. "And they took my phone and wallet to make it look like a general robbery?"

"That's what I was thinking," I said.

Tommy didn't appear convinced by the theory. "What would anyone want with my pictures from the gala? They aren't very exciting, to be honest. Just a bunch of people in formalwear mingling, eating, and drinking."

I sank back on the couch. "You're right. It doesn't sound likely that anyone would be worried about the photos." I sat up straight again. "Could we take a look at them, just in case?" I wasn't quite ready to give up on the theory, even if it was full of holes.

"Sure," Tommy said. "Could you grab my tablet? It's in the room across the hall."

I jumped up and fetched the tablet, which I found on the bedside table in Tommy's temporary main floor bedroom. I handed the device to him, and he woke it up and accessed the photos.

"Here you go." He handed the tablet back to me. "There's a whole bunch of them."

I pulled a chair over so I could sit next to Tommy while I scrolled through the photos. I soon saw that his assessment was accurate; the photos weren't very exciting. They showed various gala attendees, all dressed in tuxedos and gowns, mingling and enjoying the food and drinks. Two waiters dressed in black and white were visible in the background of some of the pictures. Frankie Zhou was one of them. I didn't know the other.

I kept my eye out for anyone else I recognized. A few people had familiar faces, but I didn't know their names. In between two batches of photos of mingling guests were pictures of Evangeline up on a raised platform, apparently giving a speech. Some of the photos were close-ups, and others provided a wider view, showing a few people standing to the side of the stage, applauding.

"What exactly are you looking for?" Tommy asked once I'd scrolled through dozens of pictures.

"I really don't know." I sighed as I reached the end of the photos. "I was hoping for a clue of some sort, but I'm not surprised there isn't one." I set the tablet on the coffee table.

"The hit-and-run probably didn't have anything to do with the gala," Tommy said. "It might have been one of the guests who ran me down, but I doubt there's any deeper connection than that."

He was most likely right.

We spent the rest of our visit talking about other things. After his trip out to Wild West Days, he'd spoken on the phone with his mom, and she'd convinced him to go and stay with his parents in Seattle for a week or two. I'd miss him while he was gone, but I was glad he'd have someone to help him out on a daily basis.

"My sister's coming to pick me up on Monday," he said. "So I can still make it to the museum's reopening party tomorrow."

"Remember not to overdo it this time," I cautioned him.

"I'll be careful," he assured me. "But I didn't want to pass up an opportunity for free food."

That brought a smile to my face. "Why doesn't that surprise me?"

I gave him a gentle hug and then set off for home, wishing I'd been able to do more to bring the hit-and-run driver to justice.

* * * *

I stayed at home long enough to let Bentley out in the yard for a few minutes and give him and Flapjack fresh water. With that done, I grabbed the scrap of paper I'd jotted the mystery phone number on and dashed out the door again. The museum's reopening party was scheduled for the next evening, and I'd promised Winnifred that I'd help set up for the event.

For the most part, the party would take place in the front and back yards of the museum, although people would be able to stroll through the main floor of the building to get a look at how the renovations had turned out. Thankfully, the weather forecast was promising blue skies and sunshine yet again. If a storm were to roll in, the party would likely have to be postponed.

Frankie was supposed to be helping out with the preparations, but when I arrived at the museum, Winnifred informed me that he'd come down with a bad case of the stomach flu and wouldn't be able to help out after all. Fortunately, Sienna's mom, Patricia, had promised to lend a hand, and she arrived soon after I did. We started with mowing the lawn, which had grown quite tall since Brett had last cut it, and sweeping the porches.

Then we strung twinkle lights and colored lanterns in the yard, with the help of a stepladder we'd found in the museum's basement. I knew the lights and lanterns would make the yard look magical once the sun set on the night of the party. While we worked, I could hear the occasional strain of country music drifting over from Wildwood Park, where Wild West Days was still in full swing. The organizers had booked a couple of country music bands to provide entertainment on the weekend. I'd heard there would also be square dancing and line dancing in the evenings.

"I'm afraid I have to run home now," Patricia said once we'd finished with the lights and lanterns. "I've got guests checking in this evening."

Patricia ran a bed-and-breakfast out of her family's beachfront Victorian.

"No worries," I said. "I think we got all the hardest jobs done."

After a few parting words, Patricia hopped in her car and drove off.

"How's Dolly doing?" I asked Winnifred when I found her in the museum's kitchen.

"Much better, I'm relieved to say. She's out of the hospital now, and she'll be coming to the party tomorrow, at least for a little while."

"That's great." I was glad to hear she was on the mend. It was bad enough that someone had attacked her. If she'd suffered permanent injuries as a result, it would have been even worse.

"Speaking of which," Winnifred said, "I promised to cook her dinner tonight." She glanced at her watch. "I'll have to head over to her place now."

"Is there anything else you want me to do here?" I asked.

"You've already done so much. The volunteers coming tomorrow can handle everything else."

I checked the time on my phone. "My husband won't be done at work for another hour, so I really don't mind sticking around."

"In that case, I did want to give the kitchen and washroom a good cleaning."

"I can take care of that," I assured her.

"Thank you so much, Marley. I really appreciate your help."

She directed me to some cleaning supplies located in a cupboard in the main floor powder room. She left me a key to the museum so I could lock up later, and I promised to put the key through the mail slot of her house on my way home.

As soon as Winnifred was gone, I got busy with cleaning. I finished the washroom and was about to start on the kitchen when a knock on the back door startled me. I peeled off my rubber gloves, spotting Krista through the window.

"Winnifred's gone over to Dolly's place," I said once I'd let her in and said hello.

"Darn. I probably left just before she arrived," Krista said. "I went to the grocery store on my way here. I would have come right away, but I really needed to grab a few things before the store closed."

"She's probably still at Dolly's house," I said. "She was going to cook dinner for her."

"Right. I forgot about that in all my excitement. I guess grandma did too."

"Excitement?"

Krista pulled a sheaf of papers out of her purse.

I noticed right away that they looked familiar. "Are those…?"

"More letters from Jack to Flora?" Krista finished for me. She smiled, her eyes bright with excitement. "Yes, that's exactly what they are."

Chapter Thirty

"For real?" I hardly dared believe what Krista had said.

"A hundred percent." She handed me the papers.

The handwriting matched that of the other letters. "Where did you find them?"

"In my grandma's attic, tucked away in one of the few boxes the intruder didn't touch."

"Thank goodness for that." I sifted through the papers Krista had given me. There appeared to be at least three multi-page letters. "This is so exciting!"

"Even more exciting than you think."

"How do you mean?" I asked, curious. "Do they reveal more family secrets?"

"You could say so, but not my family's secrets."

"Who's then?"

Krista almost answered but then snapped her mouth shut and shook her head. "You should read them. Jack tells the story better than I can."

I glanced with reluctance at the counter I'd yet to wash down. "I promised Winnifred I'd clean the kitchen."

Krista grabbed the rubber gloves I'd left by the sink. "I'll work on that while you read."

"I can't leave you to do all the work," I protested.

"Please do. I really want you to read what's in the letters."

She had me so intrigued by then that I couldn't argue any further. I took a seat at the small kitchen table and lost myself in the first letter, barely aware of Krista washing the counters and mopping the floor.

Although I got caught up anew in Jack and Flora's love story, I didn't notice anything in the first letter that would have made Krista so excited. She looked over my shoulder as I started in on the next one.

"This is where it gets interesting," she said, before going back to mopping the floor.

Eager to know what she knew, I continued to read.

My darling, you asked how I came to know the Oldershaw family's secret, so I will share the story with you now. These events took place more than a year ago, before that fateful day when we met. I'm sure you remember when Charles Becker's widow, Elizabeth, passed away. I recall you saying that she and your mother were fast friends. Shortly after she passed, I was out after nightfall, on my way to pay a clandestine visit to the home of a gentleman with far more money than he needed. He was, as luck would have it, out of town for the week.

This gentleman's home was next door to Elizabeth Becker's vacant one. As I slipped from shadow to shadow, I noticed Millicent Oldershaw approach the late Mrs. Becker's house. She moved with an attempt at stealth, as if trying to remain unseen. She was not particularly skilled in that regard, though I suppose that is to be expected of a proper lady. Most definitely not proper myself, I was able to follow her unobserved. She uncovered a key from beneath a stone in the back garden and entered the Becker house through the kitchen door.

If she'd done that during the day, unconcerned about being seen, I would have thought nothing of it. However, her suspicious behavior piqued my curiosity, and I waited in the garden until she emerged several minutes later. She hid the key back under the rock and hurried off home. I didn't fail to notice that she was gripping a book which was not in her possession when she entered the house.

I tried to put the matter out of my mind, but I have always been an inquisitive fellow. The following night I paid a visit to the Oldershaw residence while the family was out at a party. When I searched the Oldershaws' bedroom, I found, secreted beneath the mattress, a book of the same size as the one I'd seen Millicent carrying the night before.

When I studied the first few pages of the book by moonlight, I saw that it contained handwritten recipes. A note on the first page declared that the recipes were Mrs. Elizabeth Becker's creations. At the time, I assumed that Millicent Oldershaw had wanted the recipes as a keepsake to remember her friend by, though I did find it odd that she had retrieved the book under the cover of darkness and hid it away. I returned the book to its spot beneath the mattress, helped myself to a few jewels, and made a quick exit.

I didn't think of the matter again until recently, with the establishment of Oldershaw Confections. As I perused the candy company's offerings, it took me by great surprise to find that the names of the candies matched those of the recipes I'd seen in Mrs. Becker's book. I've always had a very sharp memory, and I remain convinced that the confections sold by the Oldershaws' new company were made from Mrs. Becker's recipes.

Yet I have not found any indication that Mrs. Becker has been acknowledged as the author of the recipes, nor that her heirs have been in any way compensated. On the contrary, I understand that the company claims that all its recipes are Oldershaw family recipes.

Of course, I am not one to cast stones, considering my less than honorable profession, but I thought you would find it most interesting to note that Millicent Oldershaw, whom you have described as imperious and haughty, is not quite so respectable as she would like you and the rest of society to believe.

The rest of the letter talked about how eager Jack was to see Flora again, but the last couple of paragraphs barely registered in my mind.

I set the letters on the table, my thoughts spinning.

Krista tugged off the rubber gloves and dropped them in the sink. "See what I mean?" she asked, her eyes bright with excitement again.

"Oh my gosh!" I was still furiously connecting dots in my head. "If Jack was right about the Oldershaws stealing Elizabeth Becker's recipes, that's…"

"Scandalous?" Krista offered. "Unscrupulous? Damaging?"

"All of the above," I said.

Krista dropped into the chair across from me. "Right? It happened more than a hundred years ago, but if this got out it could still damage the company today."

"Do the Beckers have any descendants?" I asked.

"I did a quick online search before I came over here. They didn't have any children, but they have indirect descendants through Mrs. Becker's niece, Georgina."

"Who might not have known about the recipes," I said.

That would explain why, as far as I knew, no fuss about the recipes' source had ever been kicked up before.

"The niece's descendants are scattered around the country now," Krista said. "But I'm sure they'd be interested to know that they might have a claim to some of the Oldershaw family's wealth."

"I think Sheriff Georgeson would be interested too."

Even if it turned out that Mrs. Becker's descendants had no legal leg to stand on after all this time, the resulting scandal could damage the company's reputation if the information were to go public.

There was something I wanted to do before getting in touch with Ray. Maybe I had a way of testing the theory taking shape in my head. As I told Krista about the last phone call Jane had made before her death, I dug the scrap of paper out of the pocket of my jeans and smoothed it out so I could read the number. I entered the digits on my phone.

I thought I was about to satisfy my curiosity and get some proof for my new theory, but instead of reaching a person or voice mail, a recorded message told me the number I'd dialed was not in service.

Disconnecting, I frowned at my phone.

"What's wrong?" Krista asked.

"The number's not in service."

I studied the scrap of paper again. Maybe I'd mixed up the last two digits. I hadn't been completely sure about them when I'd jotted down the number the other night.

I tried the call again, this time switching the last two numbers.

I heard three rings before someone picked up. A woman's voice sounded in my ear.

"Hello, you've reached Oldershaw Confections. How may I help you?"

"Sorry, wrong number," I said and hung up.

Krista leaned forward. "What is it?"

She hadn't failed to notice my wide eyes.

I was going to tell her about the call and my theory when a sharp knock on the back door nearly sent me falling out of my chair.

Before either of us could get to the door, it burst open, and Evangeline Oldershaw walked into the museum like she owned the place.

Chapter Thirty-One

I plunked my phone on top of the letters and jumped out of my chair, turning to face Evangeline while trying to hide the letters from view with my body. My heart pounded in my chest.

"Winnifred!" Evangeline hollered, scarcely even glancing at Krista and me.

"She's not here," I said, relieved to hear that my voice sounded steady even as my legs shook beneath me.

Evangeline directed her attention our way for the first time. "The party is tomorrow. She should be here getting ready."

"She has been," I said in Winnifred's defense. "And Krista and I have been helping."

"Winnifred's at my grandmother's place." Krista's voice quivered with fear, but so slightly that I hoped Evangeline wouldn't notice. "My grandma just got out of the hospital, and Aunt Winnie's cooking dinner for her."

Evangeline let out an exasperated huff, as if Winnifred had somehow greatly inconvenienced her. She took a few steps farther into the kitchen. I shifted to the side, but it was pointless. I could no longer hide the letters from her view.

Her gaze landed on the old papers, but to my relief, she didn't seem to take much notice of them.

She rested her hands on her hips. "I hope everything is in order for tomorrow. I generously donated money to cover all the expenses. I don't want the party to be a flop."

"I'm sure it won't be." My heart rate slowed as I realized that Evangeline didn't seem to have any suspicions about what Krista and I had been discussing when she arrived.

"Did you see the decorations?" Krista asked, sounding like she was desperate to make polite conversation. "They look great."

"They'll do, I suppose." Evangeline said without a shred of enthusiasm. She turned for the back door. "I guess I'll have to phone Winnifred to make sure everything is in order."

She strolled out of the museum without glancing back.

It took great restraint to keep myself from slamming the door behind her. I locked it as soon as I had it shut, and I watched out the window until I saw Evangeline drive off down the alley in her black BMW.

Krista collapsed into a kitchen chair. "That was frightening. I was so afraid she might have overheard us somehow. She probably would have had a fit if she found out that we knew about her family's secret."

I sank into a chair too. "I think we would have had to worry about more than just a fit." I tapped the letters. "Jack said that Flora asked him how he knew the Oldershaws' secret. He might have originally mentioned the secret to her in person, but I'm guessing he told her in a previous letter."

Three seconds ticked by loudly on the kitchen's wall clock.

"Hold on." Krista caught on to what I was getting at. "You mean, he probably told her in the letters I donated to the museum? The ones that were stolen the night Jane Fassbender was killed?"

I nodded. "When I made that phone call a few minutes ago, it was picked up by someone at Oldershaw Confections. It's a local number, so it probably connects to the company's office here in Wildwood Cove."

"And that was the last number Jane dialed before she died." Krista put two and two together. "Jane told someone at Oldershaw Confections about what was in the letters."

"And shortly after, she was murdered."

Krista's face paled. "We're lucky to be alive! If Evangeline had noticed the letters here on the table, she might have wanted to kill us too!"

"That's what I was afraid of," I said. "My legs turned to jelly when I saw her."

Krista pressed a hand over her heart. "I'm so glad I didn't know that she was a killer when she was here. I would have passed out."

"We don't know for sure that she's the killer," I pointed out. "But she's now one of the two likeliest culprits, in my mind."

"The other being her husband?"

"That's what I'm thinking." When I picked up my phone, I realized that my hands were trembling slightly. "I'm going to call the sheriff."

While I did that, Krista put the kettle on, declaring that she needed a cup of peppermint tea to settle her nerves.

I counted my lucky stars when Ray answered the phone. I didn't want to have to leave a message about something so important.

I tried my best to sound coherent as I told him about the newly discovered letters, what Jack revealed in them, and what I thought had happened on the night Jane was killed. I probably wasn't as clear as I'd hoped to be, because Ray asked me to repeat a couple of things.

"I'll be there in twenty minutes," he told me after asking where I was. "I'll need to get those letters from you."

"See you soon," I said before hanging up.

Krista had found mugs and tea bags in one of the kitchen cupboards. She offered to make me a cup, and I accepted. My nerves needed settling too.

"I'm going to tell Aunt Winnie what we found." Krista pulled out her phone and started composing a series of text messages.

I followed her lead and sent Brett a message, telling him what Krista and I had discovered. Then I got to my feet and paced across the kitchen, unable to sit still. I glanced nervously out the window, glad to see that the backyard was empty. At least it was still light out. It would be dusk soon, but for the moment, we'd be able to see anyone approaching the house from the back, as long as we kept an eye on the window.

I couldn't help but worry that Evangeline might come back. What if she realized that the papers we had on the table resembled the stolen letters?

The kettle boiled, and Krista grabbed it after setting her phone aside. She brewed two cups of tea and set them on the table, but I didn't touch mine right away. Even after the tea had a chance to cool, I couldn't bring myself to take more than a sip or two. My stomach was too wound up in knots.

I was about to check my phone to see if Brett had replied to my text when another loud knock sent my heart into overdrive again. This time, someone was at the front door.

"That must be the sheriff," Krista said, already hurrying toward the front of the museum.

"Hold on." I scurried after her. "Ask who it is before you—"

Too late.

She'd already unlocked and opened the door.

Richard Hobbs pushed his way into the foyer, an antique pistol aimed right at us.

Chapter Thirty-Two

"Evening, ladies."

Richard's voice sent a shiver of fear along the back of my neck.

He took a step toward us. Krista moved back and bumped into me. She clung to my arm as Richard shoved the door shut with his foot.

"Isn't she a beauty?" he asked with a nod at the antique pistol in his hand. "I bought her especially for Wild West Days. Good thing I got some ammunition for it too. Turns out it's good for more than just a prop." He let out a brief chuckle that only heightened my fear.

"What's this about?" I wondered if there was any chance that we could bluff our way out of this.

Richard's cold smile dashed any hopes of that. "Let's not play stupid. I know you found more letters from that thief, Jack O'Malley. My wife called me, wanting me to run an errand for her. She mentioned that she saw you with some letters right here in the museum. It drives me crazy when she tells me every detail of her day, but this time it actually came in handy. As soon as she told me about the two of you, I decided to hotfoot it right on over here."

I knew we had to keep Richard talking. Ray might not arrive for another ten minutes. Somehow Krista and I needed to delay what was coming until he could get here.

I fought to keep myself from panicking. "Why do you care about the letters?" I asked, my voice steadier than I'd thought it would be.

Richard frowned. "That's none of your business."

"If you're going to kill us, why not tell us?" Krista said, with only a slight tremble to her voice.

I gave her arm a grateful squeeze. I was glad for the help with keeping Richard occupied.

Instead of answering Krista's question, he waved the gun toward the corridor. "Go down the hall. To the office."

We had no choice but to obey. I wasn't keen on taking my eyes off the gun, but we turned around slowly and made our way toward Jane's office. I couldn't help but feel we were walking to our final stop. Somehow, we had to make sure that didn't turn out to be the case.

"When Jane called Oldershaw Confections on the night of her death, you answered, didn't you?" I guessed.

"You know even more than I thought," Richard said from behind us as we entered the office.

I wondered if I'd made a mistake, but I was pretty sure he'd already decided to silence us permanently before I'd mentioned the phone call.

"And it's a good thing I answered," he went on. "I almost missed the call. It came as I was getting ready to leave the office for the gala. If Jane hadn't reached me that night, who knows who else she would have blabbed to."

"Why did she call you?" Krista asked as she and I slowly turned around to face Richard and his pistol again.

"She was hoping to get Evangeline, but my wife was already waiting for me out in her car. Jane said she wanted to give Evangeline a heads-up before some damaging information got out. Like she was doing us a favor." He practically spat out the last word.

"So you decided to silence her and get rid of the letters," I said. "And Jane's phone, so no one would know she'd contacted you."

"I met her at the museum and tried to buy her silence. When that didn't work, I did what I had to do."

Krista and I stood with our backs to Jane's desk. Richard had stopped one step inside the room, blocking the route to the door. Not that we could have made a run for it with the gun pointed right at us.

"And then you broke into Dolly Maxwell's house the other night to look for more letters." I knew I was right about that.

"If you hadn't interrupted me, maybe I would have found them," Richard said. "Then we could have avoided this whole mess. Unless," he added as an afterthought, "you found them somewhere else."

"You attacked my grandmother!" Anger had replaced some of Krista's fear. "She's a frail old lady!"

"And it pained me to do it." Despite his words, Richard didn't sound the least bit sorry. "But she stood in my way, and I had interests to protect."

"You mean your wife's wealth and the reputation of her family's company," I said.

He glared at me. "You see, that's exactly what I was afraid of. I figured that scoundrel O'Malley might have spilled the secret in more than one letter. I was right to get over here on the double."

"But you're still too late," I said. "We're not the only ones who know what's in the letters."

Richard smirked. "A likely story. But I highly doubt it."

"It's true," Krista said. "And the cops are on their way here as we speak."

"Plus," I added, "the police have the records for Jane's cell phone now. They'll know Jane called Oldershaw Confections shortly before she died."

The first crack in Richard's confidence showed, but only for the briefest moment. His expression hardened. "No more chitchat."

My heart broke into a gallop, but I fought to stay calm. "If you shoot us, the neighbors will hear the gunshots."

"Maybe." Richard didn't appear concerned. "But maybe not. Haven't you heard the racket from the park? They're even firing off blanks every time they do that stagecoach robbery performance. If the neighbors are home, I doubt they'd think twice about a couple more shots, even if they do sound a bit closer than the others."

There could be some truth to that. The realization tightened the knots in my stomach.

Richard took a step closer to us. Krista and I tried to back up, but there was nowhere for us to go with the desk right behind us. I searched my memory, trying to recall if there was anything on Jane's desk that I could use as a weapon. I didn't think there was the last time I'd looked, and if I so much as glanced over my shoulder now, that might prompt Richard to shoot us sooner.

"I really am sorry to have to do this," he said, "but there's no other way around it. I tried to tie up all the loose ends earlier. I even managed to keep my alibi sealed tight. If you two had minded your own business, we wouldn't be in this situation."

The comment about his alibi brought me a new understanding.

"You're the driver who hit Tommy Park." I felt certain I had that right. I'd previously discounted the idea, but Richard had just told us that he and his wife had driven to the charity event in her car, the black BMW, rather than his red Ferrari.

Richard narrowed his eyes at me. "What makes you think I was involved in that?"

"You had to leave the gala to kill Jane, right? And there was a risk that someone could have noted your absence."

"But they didn't." He sneered. "They were all so focused on my wife making her ridiculously long speech. She never knows when to stop."

"But you were worried about the photos," I guessed.

"All right. So I was. That pesky photographer kid snapped a photo of me as I came back into the banquet room. I didn't want anyone seeing that picture or noticing that I was missing from most of the other photos. They might have started poking holes in my alibi. So I took steps to make sure that wouldn't happen."

"You intentionally ran Tommy down and stole his camera. Taking his phone and wallet made it look like a regular robbery and prevented him from calling for help."

Richard glared at me. "You're a smart woman." It didn't sound like a compliment.

"But *you* weren't smart enough," I said. "Tommy uploaded the photos to his cloud before leaving the gala."

"So my wife told me. I was worried at first, but luckily a couple of women mostly blocked the view of me returning to the gala. And Evangeline never even noticed that I was absent in all but a handful of the photos. She's always so focused on herself. She didn't notice that I left right after the gala either. She was too busy chatting with the caterer and the last guests to leave. I got the kid's camera and went back to the banquet hall without her realizing I wasn't there all along. Sometimes I think she forgets I even exist."

He sounded sorry for himself, but I didn't have an ounce of pity for him.

He squared his shoulders. "Enough chatter. I need to get back to Wild West Days. I don't want to miss out on my chance to ride the mechanical bull."

He pointed the gun directly at my heart.

A shadow shifted out in the hallway.

There was a blur of movement followed by a sharp crack.

Richard's eyes widened for the briefest of moments. Then he crumpled to the ground, unconscious.

I stared at him, trying to register what had happened.

"Aunt Winnie!" Krista practically threw herself across the room and into her great-aunt's arms.

"You're unharmed?" Winnifred asked as she hugged Krista.

"Yes." Krista pulled back, wiping tears from her cheeks.

"Marley?" Winnifred checked with me.

I managed to find my voice. "Yes. Thank you."

"My mother always thought it was frivolous of my father to have this silver-handled cane commissioned," Winnifred said, as calm as could be. "I think she'd take that back now, if she could."

She smiled at the cane she held by the shaft. For the first time, I noticed a smear of blood on the silver handle.

Richard still lay unmoving on the floor. Blood seeped from a wound on the back of his head.

"Thank you, Mrs. Woodcombe," I said with heartfelt gratitude. "You stopped a murderer and saved our lives."

Her blue eyes were bright as she smiled at me. "It's Winnifred, remember?"

Chapter Thirty-Three

"How did you know we were in trouble?" I asked Winnifred the next evening.

The museum's reopening party was in full swing. Twilight had descended over Wildwood Cove, but the lights and lanterns Patricia and I had hung the day before lit up the backyard. People mingled, chatting with friends and neighbors while enjoying the delicious finger foods that Diana the caterer had provided for the event.

"I didn't until I opened the back door of the museum and heard Richard's voice," Winnifred replied.

She held a flute of champagne in one hand while her other hand rested on the handle of her cane. It was a plain mahogany cane rather than the silver-handled one—the sheriff's office still had possession of that one.

Ray had arrived on the scene moments after Winnifred did, and the three of us hadn't had a chance to chat since.

"I'd just set Dolly's dinner on the table when I received Krista's text message," Winnifred said. "I was so eager to get a look at the letters myself that I decided to head over to the museum right away. When I realized Richard was there...After reading Krista's text, I knew there was a good chance that Jane's killer was either him or Evangeline. And what innocent reason would Richard have to visit the museum that evening? None that I could think of. So, I decided a bit of stealth was in order."

"Thank goodness you did," I said.

Krista put an arm around her great-aunt and gave her an affectionate squeeze. "You're our hero."

I smiled. "I second that."

"I'm just glad I showed up when I did," Winnifred said.

I thought back over everything that had happened. "There's one thing that still doesn't quite make sense to me. I overheard Jane and Evangeline arguing about the plans for this party. When Evangeline suggested she might go over Jane's head to get what she wanted, Jane threatened her. She said she knew something about Evangeline, something to do with the Sea Spray Cottage Resort in Port Angeles last fall."

"Ah," Winnifred said. "I have an idea what that might have been about."

"Don't leave us in the dark, Auntie," Krista urged.

"There was a rumor going about town a few months ago that Evangeline was having an affair," Winnifred explained. "More than one person saw her in Port Angeles looking very cozy with a man who definitely wasn't Richard."

No wonder Evangeline had gone so pale when Jane had made the threat.

"Why do you suppose Flora never revealed the Oldershaw family's secret?" I asked.

"Knowing my grandmother," Winnifred said, "she wouldn't have wanted to cause a fuss. Perhaps she thought it was best to let sleeping dogs lie. Or maybe she didn't want to have to explain how she found out about the secret." Winnifred took a sip of champagne. "I have to say, Evangeline can be a real pain in the neck, but she and Jane organized a great party. The food is delicious, and the champagne is too."

"Speaking of food, I think I'll go try some of it," I said, my stomach giving a rumble of hunger.

I excused myself from Winnifred and Krista and headed over to the food tables at the other end of the yard. On my way there, I smiled and waved at Lisa, who was surrounded by several women who were admiring her engagement ring. I was glad to see my friend beaming with happiness.

Before reaching the food, I made a short detour. I'd spotted Tommy arriving through the back gate, along with Keegan and another of his roommates. His friends headed straight for the food, but Tommy saw me coming and paused, leaning on his crutches.

"I'm so glad you're here." I gave him a hug, careful not to knock him off balance.

"So am I." He took in the sight of the crowd. "Looks like a great turnout."

"I think half the town showed up, but you got here in time because there's still plenty of food."

"That's definitely a good thing," he said. "I'm starving."

"Do you want me to fill a plate for you?" I offered.

"Keegan said he'd do that, but thanks."

I told him I'd grab him a chair and quickly fetched one from the porch. When he was settled, I resumed my path toward the spread of food. Several other people were wandering around the tables, selecting food, so I took one of the paper plates stacked at the end of the nearest table and waited for my turn. I nearly toppled over when Sienna tackle hugged me from the side.

"Thank you so much, Marley!" She squeezed me tight before letting go. "The notes you emailed me are super helpful."

"I'm so glad," I said once I had my breath back.

After the events of the previous evening, I'd needed a relaxing morning. I'd spent the first several hours of the day finishing Sienna's book and typing up some feedback. Her writing really impressed me, and the story had kept me riveted all the way to the end. In my notes, I pointed out a few plot threads that she'd left dangling, and a couple of other small issues, but I hadn't found any major problems. I was no expert, but I thought she had a really strong manuscript, and I knew for sure that she had an amazing writing talent.

"I'm super excited to get to work on the next draft." Sienna's gaze drifted to all the food laid out before us. "But I'm going to need some brain fuel for that."

"Good thinking," I said as she grabbed a plate.

The crowd at the food tables had thinned, so we worked our way around, adding finger sandwiches and hors d'oeuvres to our plates. I munched on the delicious food while chatting with Sienna and Patricia.

I'd almost emptied my plate when I spotted Ray across the yard, dressed in jeans and a T-shirt. When he headed over to the food tables, I approached him.

"I'm glad to see you made it," I told him as I snagged another couple of sandwiches.

"It's been a long day," Ray said as he loaded up his plate, "but I needed to eat, and I thought it would be nice to relax for a few minutes."

"Did you work all night?" I asked.

It had been quite late when I'd finished giving my statement the night before, and at the time, it seemed as though Ray's work had only begun.

"Just about," he said. "And then all day again."

"Did you get a confession out of Richard?"

Ray poured himself a cup of coffee from the urn at the end of the table. "No such luck. He lawyered up right away. I'm not expecting him to confess anytime soon."

"But the statements Krista and I gave will help, right?" I didn't even want to think about the case against Richard falling apart.

"Definitely, and we have a fair amount of other evidence against him. Dean Vaccarino has admitted that he stole recycling from Richard and Evangeline's house while he was looking for documents to help him with his identity fraud scheme. He didn't realize that there were letters mixed in with the other papers until he got home."

"It would have been smarter for Richard to burn the letters instead of putting them out with the recycling," I said.

"It's a good thing for us that he's not smarter."

I agreed with that wholeheartedly. "Do you think Evangeline knew what he'd done?"

"I'm pretty sure she didn't. She was horrified when she found out. I don't think she wants anything more to do with Richard. He was so concerned about preserving the Oldershaw family's reputation and wealth—and by connection his own—but now he's gone and dragged the family name through the mud. I'm betting Oldershaw Confections will do their best to distance the company from him in the weeks to come."

I took a bite of a delicious cheese puff. "Has he been charged with the hit-and-run too?"

"We added that charge this morning," Ray said. "We found Tommy's camera when we executed a search warrant at Richard and Evangeline's house, and there are some scratches and a small dent on the front bumper of Evangeline's BMW."

Relief eased the remaining tension in my shoulders. It sounded as though both Jane and Tommy would now have justice.

Several other people swooped in to speak with Ray, so I tossed my empty plate in the bin beneath one of the tables and wandered off. When strong arms snaked around my waist from behind me, I smiled.

"Were you giving Ray the third-degree?" Brett asked, his tone teasing.

"Maybe a little." I leaned back against his chest and closed my eyes, soaking in the comfort of having him close.

We lapsed into silence, muted conversations and laughter surrounding us. Brett kissed the top of my head. "Everything okay?" he asked quietly.

I opened my eyes and looked around at all the familiar faces gathered beneath the fairy lights and colorful lanterns. Many of my friends, neighbors, and in-laws were present, all safe and happy.

"Better than okay." I smiled and tipped my head back so I could look into Brett's eyes. "Everything's perfect."

Recipes

Raspberry Orange Pancakes

2 tablespoons melted butter
1 cup milk
2 teaspoons lemon juice
1 1/2 cups flour
1/4 cup sugar
3 teaspoons baking powder
1/4 teaspoon baking soda
2 teaspoons orange zest
1 large egg
1/2 cup orange juice
2 teaspoons vanilla
1 cup raspberries, fresh or frozen
Vegetable oil for greasing

Melt the butter and set aside to cool. Combine the milk and lemon juice and set aside to thicken.

Mix together flour, sugar, baking powder, baking soda, and orange zest. In a separate bowl, beat together egg, milk/lemon juice, orange juice, vanilla, and butter. Make a well in the dry ingredients and add the liquid ingredients. Mix until just combined. Fold in raspberries.

Ladle batter onto a greased skillet and cook on medium heat until bubbles form on the top and don't disappear. Flip and cook second side until golden brown.

Thyme for Breakfast Frittata

1 tbsp olive oil
1/2 cup chopped onion
1 tsp minced garlic
1 small zucchini, thinly sliced
1/2 cup red bell pepper, chopped
1/2 cup sliced mushrooms
1 tbsp chopped fresh parsley
1/2 tsp dried dill (or 1 tbsp fresh)
1/4 tsp dried thyme (or 1 tsp fresh)
Pinch chipotle chili powder
1/4 tsp ground black pepper
Dash Worcestershire sauce
8 eggs, lightly beaten
1/4 cup milk
1/2 cup crumbled feta cheese

In a bowl, whisk together the eggs, milk, black pepper, chili powder, and Worcestershire sauce. Set aside.

In a 10-inch, non-stick skillet, heat the olive oil over medium heat. Add the onion and garlic. Cook, while stirring, for approximately 2 minutes, or until the onions begin to soften. Add the zucchini, bell pepper, and mushrooms. Cook until the vegetables have just softened, approximately 5 minutes. Stir in the parsley, dill, and thyme. Cook for another 30 to 60 seconds.

Reduce heat to low. Evenly distribute the vegetables in the skillet. Pour the egg mixture over the vegetables. Sprinkle the feta cheese on top. Cover with a tight-fitting lid and leave to cook until the eggs are completely set, approximately 18 minutes. Remove from heat. Slice and serve while hot.
Serves 4.

Strawberry Rhubarb Crêpes

Crêpes:

2 cups all-purpose flour
3 cups milk
4 eggs
2 tbsp. sugar
1 tsp. vanilla
Butter or oil for greasing pan

Sift flour and sugar into a mixing bowl. In a separate bowl, whisk together the eggs, milk, and vanilla. Make a well in the dry ingredients. Pour in half the liquid ingredients. Whisk until smooth. Add the remaining liquid ingredients. Whisk until smooth again.

Optional: Refrigerate batter for up to six hours.

Heat crêpe pan or small skillet over low heat for several minutes. Grease lightly. Increase heat to medium and leave for 1–2 minutes. Pour 1/4 cup batter into the pan. Tilt and swirl to coat the pan. Cook until lightly browned. Remove from pan.

Filling:

2 cups chopped rhubarb
1 cup water
3/4 cup sugar
1/4 cup cornstarch
1/2 tsp cinnamon
1 tsp lemon juice
2 cups sliced strawberries
1 tsp vanilla extract

In a large saucepan, combine the rhubarb, water, sugar, cornstarch, and cinnamon. Bring to a boil. Add the lemon juice and strawberries. Reduce heat and simmer, stirring occasionally, until rhubarb is tender, approximately 15 minutes. Stir in vanilla extract and remove from heat.

Spoon filling onto crêpe, roll, and top with whipped cream.

Acknowledgments

I'd like to extend my sincere thanks to several people whose hard work and input made this book what it is today. I'm forever grateful to my agent, Jessica Faust, for helping me bring this series to life, and to my editor at Kensington Books, Elizabeth May, for helping me shape this manuscript into a better book. The art department has created gorgeous covers for the series, and I appreciate all the work the entire Kensington team has put into this book. Thank you to Marguerite Gavin for doing such a great job of narrating the audiobooks, and thanks also to my review crew and all the readers who have returned for another of Marley's adventures in Wildwood Cove.

Keep reading for a special early excerpt!

USA Today Bestselling Author
SARAH FOX

CLARET AND PRESENT DANGER
A Literary Pub Mystery

In this thrilling mystery by USA Today bestselling author Sarah Fox, deadly happenings stick around like red wine stains on white tunics when the Renaissance Faire visits Shady Creek, Vermont.

The Trueheart Renaissance Faire and Circus has rolled into town, attracting locals who can't wait to spend a few summer days lost in a whimsical world of all-knowing fortunetellers and daring acrobats. Well-read pub owner Sadie Coleman is swept up in the magic herself when she serves drinks to the faire's resident wizard, the shamelessly brazen illusionist Ozzie Stone, and scores two tickets to his dazzling performance.

Sadie has no complaints about indulging in a free show with her new beau, craft brewery owner Grayson Blake. But while Ozzie is an instant crowd-pleaser, the real surprise comes when he collapses in the middle of his set. It's not part of the act—Ozzie is dead, seemingly poisoned by someone who wasn't clowning around about silencing the outspoken showman.

The terrifying situation intensifies when police eye one of Sadie's employees, last seen caught in a suspicious fistfight at the fairground. With so much at stake, Sadie must strain through a suspect list longer than her cocktail menu to find the real killer. But when another performer is murdered, it becomes clear that bringing the mixed-up murderer to justice will be about as dangerous as walking the high wire after happy hour...

Look for *Claret and Present Danger*, on sale now!

Claret and Present Danger
Chapter One

The sword blades glinted in the sunlight. The crowd watched with anticipation as the weapons clanged together again and again. The duelers managed to make it look like their fight wasn't choreographed, and now and then, they hurled renaissance insults at each other. Both men wore a combination of leather and plate armor but still managed to lunge and dodge with relative agility. I wasn't sure how they could stand the heat in their costumes. Summer was in full swing in Shady Creek, Vermont, and the sun was beating down from a gorgeous blue sky.

The taller of the two fighters parried a blow and then moved in for the kill. His opponent gasped as the sword blade slid between his arm and side, appearing from my vantage point as though it had pierced his abdomen. The wounded man staggered before dramatically falling to the ground.

The other man raised his sword in victory.

"Huzzah!" the crowd cheered, and I joined in.

"He killed him!" nine-year-old Kiandra Williams exclaimed as the crowd slowly dispersed, everyone moving on to check out other parts of the Trueheart Renaissance Faire and Circus.

"It was just pretend," my best friend, Shontelle, reminded her daughter.

"I know," Kiandra said. "I like the sound the swords make when they hit each other." She bounced up onto the balls of her feet. "Can we go watch the acrobats now?"

I checked the time on my phone. "It would probably be a good idea to go find seats."

The three of us made our way toward the red and white striped tent that stood near the far end of the park, which had been transformed into a renaissance village for the duration of the two-week event. This was my first time attending a renaissance faire, and although I'd been at the park for less than an hour, I was already thoroughly impressed.

There were various stalls and huts where people in period costumes demonstrated skills such as glass blowing, metalworking, basket weaving, leatherworking, and candle making. Many of the goods the craftsmen and craftswomen were making were available for sale, and I was considering doing some early Christmas shopping before the faire was over.

Musicians had gathered on a small stage, playing various instruments, including lutes, violins, and others that I couldn't name. Food vendors sold snacks from huts, and a tavern was set up in one of the larger structures, where adult fairgoers could sit down for a meal and enjoy a tankard of ale. Here and there, costumed actors interacted with each other and with the spectators. Kiandra, like many other children at the faire, had already had her face painted. She now sported a unicorn on one cheek and a butterfly on the other.

At the tent entrance, we handed over our tickets to a woman in a tightfitting bodice and full skirt, with a crown of flowers in her dark hair. Bleachers provided the unassigned seating in the tent. We'd arrived early, so we had our choice of spots. We decided on the third row back in the middle section.

"Sit next to me, Sadie," Kiandra requested as she plopped herself down on the bench.

I did as asked, and Shontelle sat on Kiandra's other side.

"We've got a good view from here," I said.

Kiandra's gaze traveled up and up. Her eyes widened. "Look how high that is!"

I followed the finger she was pointing up toward the ceiling of the tent. Way up high was a tightrope as well as two trapezes. I wouldn't have had the nerve to climb the ladder to get up that high, let alone swing out on a trapeze or balance along a wire.

I also noticed some silks hanging from the metal framework up near the tent's ceiling. I'd never watched a live performance with aerial silks, but I'd seen one on TV and thought we could be in for a spectacular show.

When I'd first heard that the renaissance faire was coming to my adopted home of Shady Creek, Vermont, the fact that it included circus elements had surprised me. Apparently, the faire used to be more traditional, but had recently added new attractions. Most people I knew were excited to take in both aspects of the faire, and so was I, starting with the acrobat show that was about to begin.

The bleachers quickly filled with spectators, and soon the lights dimmed. As the tent grew darker, I caught sight of a thin girl with wavy blond hair slipping into the tent while the ticket lady had her back turned. The girl appeared to be about eight or nine years old and didn't look familiar, but I didn't have a chance to notice anything more about her. She disappeared behind the bleachers, and music began to play, signaling the start of the show.

For the next hour, we were wowed by the high-flying feats of half a dozen acrobats. They walked the high wire, swung on the trapezes, flew through the air, and performed with the aerial silks. Kiandra was riveted the entire time.

"I want to do that," she whispered as a young woman let go of one trapeze and soared through the air before another acrobat on the second trapeze caught her.

"I don't think so," Shontelle said with alarm.

"Please!" Kiandra turned her beseeching eyes on her mother.

Shontelle put a finger to her lips. "We'll talk about it later."

She shot me a look of dismay over Kiandra's head. I didn't blame her for her concern. The thought of Kiandra flying through the air way up high terrified me, and she wasn't even my daughter.

At one point, I caught another glimpse of the blond-haired girl who'd sneaked into the tent. She watched the show from between two sets of bleachers, her eyes as wide as Kiandra's. When the show finished, I looked for her again, but she was nowhere to be seen.

As we headed out of the tent, Kiandra bounced up and down between Shontelle and me, chattering nonstop about the acrobats' amazing feats. She eventually wound down and asked for a snack. Shontelle and I were hungry too, so we wandered away from the tent in search of something to eat. We paused to study a poster affixed to the wall of one of the thatched huts. The poster advertised the most talked-about and anticipated attraction of the entire faire. Illusionist Ozzie Stone would be performing in the main tent each night.

I'd heard of Ozzie Stone before the faire arrived in Shady Creek. He'd appeared on a televised, nation-wide talent show a year or so ago, and his star had been on the rise ever since. I'd hoped to catch one of his shows, but when I inquired at the gate that morning, I was informed that the tickets for all his performances were already sold out. That had disappointed me, but I was still determined to enjoy the faire as much as possible.

We moved on from the poster and spotted a hut with a sign that read ROSIE'S FARE. Another sign indicated that the vendor sold burgers, fries, cheese melts, and milkshakes. Before we reached Rosie's Fare, we paused to watch a juggler performing for passersby. He looked to be in his mid-twenties and had curly brown hair. At the moment, he had four beanbags in the air. He wrapped up the juggling act by catching all of the beanbags. The crowd applauded, and he bowed.

"Now for some magic," he told everyone who was watching.

He had three upside-down cups on a roughly hewn wooden table. He picked up one of the cups and placed a ball beneath it.

As he opened his mouth to speak to the crowd again, another man strutted over to his side, a self-assured smile on his face. I knew who he was right away—illusionist Ozzie Stone. He wore a white shirt beneath a blue velvet cape with a black silk lining, just like his photo on his poster. He had piercing blue eyes, and his jet-black hair was a little on the long side. Despite the beautiful summer weather we'd been having in Vermont, I suspected his deep tan had been sprayed on.

There was a collective intake of breath from the crowd. I clearly wasn't the only one to recognize the illusionist.

"Lords and ladies," Ozzie said to the crowd. "If it's magic you desire, it's magic you shall get."

He whipped a blue mug out from beneath his cape and snapped his fingers. "Water, please, Tobias."

The juggler frowned but handed over a small pitcher of water that had been sitting on the table.

"Observe," Ozzie commanded, "as I instantly turn this water into a block of ice."

A hush fell over the crowd as he poured the water into the blue mug. As soon as the pitcher was empty, he turned the mug upside down. No water flowed out, but a small block of ice fell into Ozzie's waiting hand.

The crowd cheered, me included.

"That's so cool!" Kiandra exclaimed with delight.

It seemed Ozzie had captivated her almost as much as the acrobats had.

Out of the corner of my eye, I noticed the curly-haired juggler slink away, looking disgruntled. I couldn't blame him. Ozzie really had stolen his thunder, and he wasn't finished yet. For his next trick, Ozzie produced a small piece of paper and had a woman from the audience sign her name on it. He rolled up the paper and held it up for all of us to see. Then, with a flick of his hand, he made it disappear.

He fished a lemon out of his pocket, showed it to us, and then cut around the middle of it with a knife. When he pulled the two lemon halves apart, a rolled-up paper protruded from one half. Ozzie removed the paper, unrolled it, and had the woman from the audience confirm that it was the same paper she'd signed. We all burst into applause as Ozzie bowed.

While the illusionist posed for selfies with fairgoers, we headed over to Rosie's Fare and purchased our snack, which turned out to be more of an early lunch. Shontelle bought some fries and a cheese melt to share with Kiandra, and I bought a cheese melt for myself. All three of us ordered chocolate milkshakes. We needed something cold to drink to keep us from getting too hot in the summer sunshine.

I gave myself a brain freeze with the first sip, but after that, I drank more slowly and was able to enjoy the delicious creaminess of the chocolate shake. The cheese melt was heavenly too, and it calmed the growling of my hungry stomach. We ate at a rustic picnic table, watching the goings-on around us.

At one point a stout, costumed man came stumbling out of the tavern, another actor following on his heels.

"Away, you varlot! You rampallian!" shouted the taller man in the tavern's doorway. "I'll tickle your catastrophe!"

The stout man staggered about as if drunk. "You sodden, contumelious louse!" he yelled before weaving and lurching his way down the grassy walkway that stretched between the two rows of vendors.

I was pretty sure Kiandra had no idea what the insults meant, but she laughed along with Shontelle and me.

As I was finishing up my cheese melt, I caught sight of a dark-haired, attractive man dressed in a costume that included black boots, dark trousers, a leather doublet, leather arm bracers, and a gray cape. He carried a sword at his side, and his hair reached nearly to his shoulders.

"He looks like Aragorn from the *Lord of the Rings*," I said to Shontelle, with a nod in the man's direction.

"He really does," Shontelle agreed. "He's almost Viggo Mortensen's doppelgänger." She watched him walk by. "Very easy on the eyes."

"Don't let him hear you say that," a man's voice cautioned. "It'll go to his head."

I turned to find local man Matt Yanders standing next to our picnic table. Matt owned the Harvest Grill, one of Shady Creek's restaurants. He was also a member of the science fiction and fantasy book club I hosted at my literary pub, the Inkwell.

"You know him?" Shontelle asked Matt, her gaze returning to Aragorn's look-alike.

"As much as it pains me to admit it, he's my brother." Matt's grin softened his words. "Flint, you scobberlotcher, get over here!" he bellowed.

Flint's face broke into a grin when he spotted Matt. "It's my knave of a brother!"

Matt pounded Flint on the back when he reached his side. "Flint, allow me to introduce these three fine ladies, Shontelle and Kiandra Williams, and Sadie Coleman."

Flint bowed. "Ladies, I'm honored to make your acquaintance."

"Is that a real sword?" Kiandra asked him.

"But of course." Flint pulled the blade from its scabbard. "It's a weapon of the finest craftsmanship."

"Cool!" Kiandra said before taking a long sip of her milkshake.

"How are you enjoying your day, ladies?" Flint asked Shontelle and me.

"It's great," I said.

"We're having a blast so far," Shontelle added.

"Excellent! I'm glad to hear it."

A woman wearing several gauzy scarves and many bracelets breezed past him.

"Minerva!" Flint called out.

The woman stopped in her tracks and turned to Flint. She smiled when she saw him.

Flint gestured at her with a flourish. "Have you ladies met our most esteemed soothsayer, Minerva the Mysterious?"

Minerva came closer and addressed us. "If you wish to have your fortune told, I am most happy to oblige."

"For a price." Flint chuckled.

Minerva gave him a side-long glance. "Worth every penny."

"Undoubtably," Flint said.

"I wouldn't mind having my fortune told," Shontelle spoke up. "It sounds fun," she added to Kiandra and me.

"Then please," Minerva said, "come this way."

"I'll stay with Kiandra," I told Shontelle.

Her daughter waved at her, but most of her focus was on her milkshake.

Shontelle followed Minerva the Mysterious into a small tent across the grassy walkway from our picnic table.

Flint bowed again. "My ladies," he said to Kiandra and me, "I'm afraid I must depart. And you, you useless knave," he said to Matt, "we shall meet again, unfortunately."

Flint headed off, with several female fairgoers flitting along behind him, snapping photos with their phones.

Matt laughed before turning his attention to me. "I'll see you at the Inkwell sometime soon, Sadie."

I said goodbye, and he took his leave.

Kiandra finished off her milkshake with a loud slurp.

"All done?" I asked her.

She nodded and jumped up from the table. "Can we go look at the costumes?"

Next door to Minerva the Mysterious's tent was a costume rental shop. While we were eating, I'd seen two women go into the store dressed in regular clothing. Now they emerged, fully decked out in renaissance wear.

"Sure," I said in response to Kiandra's question. "Let's go take a look."

I gathered up all our garbage and tossed it in a nearby bin. Kiandra skipped off ahead of me and disappeared into the shop. I followed after her, pausing one step inside the door so my eyes could adjust to the dim interior.

We browsed the store for a few minutes until Kiandra lost interest.

"Let's go look at the hats," she said, when we emerged from the costume rental shop.

She dashed over to a shop called The Mad Hatter and tried on a pirate's tricorn hat.

"How about this one?" I suggested, holding out a blue velvet hat with a fake peacock sitting on top, the tail feathers cascading down over the back rim.

Kiandra removed the hat she was wearing, and I plunked the peacock one on her head. She checked her reflection in a small mirror set out for that purpose.

She giggled, and I snapped a picture of her with my phone, so we could show Shontelle later.

"You try this one," Kiandra said, handing me a gray cavalier hat with a single feather.

As we tried on several other hats, I noticed the curly-haired juggler we'd seen earlier standing nearby, speaking with a raven-haired woman who was texting on her smartphone. The device looked out of place, considering that she was wearing a renaissance costume.

"I deserve my own show, Rachael," the juggler was saying. "I could draw in as much of a crowd as Ozzie."

Rachael continued to tap away at her phone, not even glancing up. "It's not happening, Toby. How many times do I have to tell you? Ozzie is our biggest draw. And your strength is street busking."

"But—"

Rachael cut him off. "But nothing. That's all I've got to say on the matter."

Toby looked as though he was about to protest again when Rachael squirmed in her costume.

"This bodice is too tight," she complained. "You'd think Patty was trying to suffocate me when she laced me up."

For the second time in the past hour, Ozzie Stone appeared on the scene. He dipped down in a theatrical bow. "Allow me to assist you, milady."

While talking with Toby, Rachael's expression had been stern, a crease traversing her forehead. Now the crease smoothed out, and she smiled.

"Thank you, Ozzie." She turned her back to him.

Ozzie loosened the laces on the back of her corset and began retying them. As he worked, he spoke quietly into Rachael's ear. She giggled, her dark eyelashes fluttering.

Toby, the juggler, scowled at them, but they took no notice. He muttered something under his breath that I couldn't quite hear. Ozzie rested his hands on Rachael's shoulders, and she giggled again. Toby's nostrils flared, and he stormed away, disappearing into the crowd of fairgoers.

Look for *Claret and Present Danger*, on sale now!

Printed in the United States
by Baker & Taylor Publisher Services